A Land Fit for Heroes

Book 4
THE BURNING FOREST

A Land Fit for Heroes

Book 4

THE BURNING FOREST

PHILLIP MANN

VICTOR GOLLANCZ

LONDON

First published in Great Britain 1996
by Victor Gollancz
An imprint of the Cassell Group
Wellington House, 125 Strand, London WC2R OBB

A catalogue record for this book is
available from the British Library.

ISBN 0 575 06152 9

Typeset by Rowland Phototypesetting Ltd,
Bury St Edmunds, Suffolk
Printed in Great Britain by
St Edmundsbury Press Ltd, Bury St Edmunds, Suffolk

For
Jane Stafford
who gave me glimpses of the Wild Wood

. . . not forgetting
Matthew,
Ursula,
Anna,
Huw,
David,
Leo,
Pippy,
Octavia,
and Laura.

Twelve Seconds Distant

Welcome to the Earth.

But it is not quite the Earth which you and I know, though viewed from the moon you could not tell the difference. This world belongs in one of those parallel universes which exist, infinite in quantity, yet each in its own discrete time-shell, just slightly out of temporal phase with our own world and with each other.

This world, which we are now approaching, is displaced from our own by a mere twelve seconds. But that short time is sufficient to make this world wholly different from our own while yet remaining, in some ways, quite familiar. For instance, the hills and rivers and plains are largely the same, but the men and women who inhabit them are different. Their history and customs too are different, but in subtle and strange ways.

In this world the Roman legions never quit Britannia. Far from it. The Roman legions marched on and, after stamping their mark on Britannia, conquered the rest of the world. Wherever they trod they established their social systems, their laws and their military organization.

Though for a while Roma tottered before the northern tribes, it nevertheless survived to become the capital city of a vast eclectic civilization. Roma became renowned as a great seat of learning; as a cultural melting-pot and place in the sun for all races; as a home of good food, rare spices and fine red wine; as the place for hot gossip, love, philosophy and lust; as the centre of fabulous, profligate wealth and awesome world-rattling power.

Which is all well and good, but this book is not much concerned with Roma, or with the rest of the world come to that, but with just one small corner in the distant north-east of the moist and wooded province of Britannia.

*

When military resistance in Britannia ended with the defeat of the Celtic tribes, the province prospered. The Romans built their roads throughout the length and breadth of the country and ruled in the neat cities, small towns and military camps. Gradually they created an organized society based on urban living.

In the early days after the conquest, the political leader of this society, the Praefectus Comitum as he was called, was appointed from Roma. But soon this position was filled by members of the great aristocratic, military families that settled in Britannia and began to call that province home. These families controlled vast estates and enjoyed almost unlimited power. Their privilege was supported by two classes in the population: the Citizens and the Soldiers. These two classes were mainly drawn from native families who, in the early days, forsook the tribal life and accepted the *pax Romana* with relish. They became 'civilized'. As the decades stretched into centuries and the centuries ticked past, Roman rule began to seem like a law of nature. Given material comforts, security and a guaranteed place in society, the Citizens were hardly aware of the strict rules and regulations and limits under which they lived. Thus the clerks and sewermen, the cooks, cleaners, nurses, gardeners and candlestick-makers who made civilized life possible for the Roman military aristocracy hardly ever questioned their condition. As for the Soldiers, they were not encouraged to think about anything other than a pride in service and a delight in efficiency. They controlled the roads and the city gates.

But where the city walls ended, the wild wood began. Still, in the forests and moors and swamps which surrounded the Roman towns, life continued pretty much as it had for centuries: as it had since before the coming of the Celts and the earlier generations of men who built Stonehenge, yea back even unto the time of giants. In the different regions of what the Romans called Britannia, the old, green and ever-youthful spirits of tree, glade and river maintained their dignity and held sway among the people who lived close to the soil. To those who lived in the vast forests, their ancestors, almost as old as the hills, could be heard whispering in the trees and among the bubbling streams. At nightfall they murmured together in the shadows of the long barrows. Even so, golden lads and lasses made love in the meadows and on the hilltops and in the quiet places behind the barrows, and never thought about grave-dust.

To the ancient Roman families and the Citizens and Soldiers who served them, these woodlanders were primitive savages who could be tolerated because they posed no threat.

Christianity sprang up in some quarters but nowhere did it become as great a political force as in our world. Indeed, where it did survive, Christianity took its place as one sect among many, each of which celebrated in its own special way the sacrifice of a man or woman who chose death in order that humankind might be saved. These various creeds rubbed shoulders with older religions of earth and sky and of the Great Mother.

And all races and creeds walked the Roman roads.

We come to the present.

A pestilence, which began by ravaging the flocks of sheep in the continental provinces, has now shown greater virulence attacking other animals and even humans. Apart from shortages in meat, wool, skins and fertilizer, the disease has caused panic and economic disruption. Strangely, the pestilence has not appeared in Britannia, but only in the provinces of Gallia, Hispania, Germania and Italia, and this has led to speculation that it is a manifestation of the gods' displeasure.

In response, the new Emperor of the World, Lucius Prometheus Petronius, has decided to establish state sheep farms in Britannia and these will necessitate a burning of the land – at least, that is his overt intention, though in this, as in everything else, Prometheus has darker motives.

To accomplish his plan, the Emperor has appointed Marcus Augustus Ulysses, the senior member of one of the wealthiest and most powerful military families of Britannia, as his deputy. The plan is no sooner conceived than it is put into action. Nothing can withstand it . . . or so the Roman leaders believe.

But, even while the tubs of chemicals which will be used for the fires are being shipped to Britannia, movements are afoot in that country to resist the burning. Nature is beginning to rebel. Those humans who will lead the battle against the great destruction are by and large ignorant of the role they will play.

But they are learning. They are Miranda, Angus and Coll. They have experienced many changes in their being and are each, in their different ways, awaiting the next developments.

Miranda has become the guardian of a house of healing in the small community on the Wolds called Stand Alone Stan. Her position does not require medical knowledge but rather spiritual strength. Gradually, as she enters into her new role, strange powers have started to reveal themselves. She can visit the astral plane and see spirits of the dead; sometimes she enters other dimensions of Nature and flies with dangerous Faery creatures.

Miranda cannot control her evolution, she is like a leaf on a stream being swept along, but she is discovering her deeper powers, both savage and kind. Soon it will be time for her to assume her full power and act.

Angus the mechanic, the man hungry for knowledge, the man who works things out for himself, has studied history at Roscius' secret academy in the hills near Stand Alone Stan. But his knowledge, far from bringing him peace, has ignited fires of rebellion in him. After killing a man in a dispute, Angus was expelled from the college and escaped to the wild wood with his companions Sean and Perol. There they have met up with an ancient creature of the woodland called Drummer.

Now Angus, using all his skills as a mechanic, has brought the old mechanical fighting-dragon back to life. With Sean, Perol and Drummer he has set out to establish a terrorist band called the Dragon Warriors.

Their first serious act of rebellion was to attack the notorious prison camp called the Caligula. They have liberated prisoners in the hope that they will join the conspiracy to overthrow the Roman state.

Coll is the last surviving son of that same Marcus Ulysses who now serves as the Emperor's deputy. He was once called Viti but he has abandoned that name in favour of a tree-name – for Coll is the name of the hazel tree, the tree of intuition.

Coll is a sad young man. He feels blighted by guilt for, in his days as a smart Roman officer, he raped Miranda. While living in a lonely tree-house close to Stand Alone Stan, Coll attempted to kill himself by filling his pockets with stones and jumping into a swiftly flowing river. But he was rescued by Gwydion, a rogue of the forest, who has now brought him back to health. Coll's discovery that Miranda has forgiven him releases a new sense of purpose in him. Without realizing quite what is happening, Coll has begun to tread the path of the Shaman . . .

We enter this world at the house of Cormac, the Singer, deep in the roots of an oak tree, far in the forest. Cormac is speaking . . .

1   Coll and Cormac

'At the portal of death,' said Cormac. 'The only gateway for a singer.' He was looking down at the white face of Coll. The young man lay on his back, his limbs tangled. The only sign that he was alive was his shivering.

Gwydion, who had carried Coll up the slope to Cormac's house, groaned and tried to rise but Cormac stopped him. 'Don't worry, lad. You've done well. I'll take over now. Rest now.' Gwydion's eyes closed and he sank back down on to the ground. 'But you made it just in time,' added Cormac to himself. 'Another hour and . . .' He said no more but breathed deeply like a fighter bracing himself. Then he threw back his sleeves.

Though he was old, Cormac was strong: the result of a lifetime spent walking under the trees, climbing slippery banks and fending for himself in all weathers. He gripped the shivering Coll under the arms and dragged him down the stone steps set in the earth slope and into the cavern under the oak tree. At the bottom he hoisted him over a rough-cut log which served as a threshold.

The doorway into Cormac's home was formed between two dark roots. Over the years since the house was first established, the constant coming and going of visitors had polished the twin roots to a dull sheen. Between the roots hung a simple screen of woven rushes. It was attached at the top, and the entire screen lifted and slipped over Cormac's shoulders as he dragged the unconscious Coll within. The rush door flapped back down, creating a draught which disturbed the flame of an oil lamp set just within the door, making it dip and bob.

They were in a small vestibule. Fur-lined coats hung against the walls, boots stood beneath them and notched walking sticks leaned in a corner. Cormac did not delay but dragged Coll through a low door closed with strips of overlapping cloth.

The room they entered was simple and comfortable and smelled of lavender and herbs. The twisting roots of the oak tree gave shape to the walls, and the soil between them had been pressed flat. Shelves containing plates and cups were inset into the walls. A tall cupboard of dark wood stood against one wall and beside it were carved wooden clothes boxes. A small stove and hotplate of the kind found in most of the woodland houses occupied one corner and was backed with slabs of slate. Above it hung dried flowers and herbs. The floor was of rammed earth and a carpet of animal skins was cast across it. A table with two chairs and a stool stood in the centre while an oil lamp hung down from the ceiling, casting a warm and friendly glow through the entire room. The only other piece of furniture was a large wooden chair which stood close to the hotplate, its severe lines softened by a thick-piled bear-skin.

Leading off the room were two tunnels, each just tall and wide enough for a small man such as Cormac to walk through without having to duck. These were formed between boulders of grey rock, and the dark roots of the oak tree snaked across them and plunged on into the earth.

Cormac hurried. Once inside he dragged the body down one of the small corridors. He passed several openings which led off to other parts of the warren and finally came to a small round room in which stood a low cot covered with a bright yellow woven quilt. Two oil lamps, each set in a niche in the wall on either side of the bed, cast a warm light through the room. Opposite the bed was a hotplate with a small flue which disappeared into the ceiling at an angle. Sitting on the hotplate, a billy-can piped steam which coiled and vanished up the flue.

Cormac sat Coll down on the floor and removed the heavy damp cloak and the leggings which were stiff with mud. Coll groaned as Cormac eased the shirt up and over his shoulders. 'Soon have you right,' the old man murmured.

Coll tried to speak but Cormac hushed him. He manoeuvred Coll into the bed and under the covers. Then he helped him sit up while he fed him a drink from the potion on the hotplate. Coll coughed and gagged, but enough of the liquid went down to satisfy Cormac. He let the young man lie back. 'Now rest a while. But don't recover too quick,' said Cormac, talking to himself.

He gathered up the damp clothes and hurried from the room.

Behind him a mouse jumped up on to the ledge beside one of the oil lamps. There it squatted down and began to clean its face with its paws, stopping occasionally to look at Coll with its bead-black eyes.

Night had fallen when Cormac again climbed out of the oak tree. He found Gwydion hard asleep, flat on his back, his head resting on one of Aristotle's blankets. Cormac chivied him awake and sent him stumbling down into the house. Before following him Cormac sniffed the air. He could smell rain coming again. He busied himself making sure the donkey had fresh water. 'We're going to be here for a while, Aristotle,' he whispered. 'And even so, I don't know whether we've time enough.' The donkey nodded. 'Bah. What do you know, you daft old donkey?' said Cormac fondly, stroking its ears. ''appen you're no wiser than me.'

Inside the house Gwydion had made himself at home as was the custom and was busy rummaging in a wooden chest, looking for clean clothes.

'There's nothing'll fit you in there,' said Cormac. 'There's a village not far. We can get you kitted out in the morning. For now, wear one of the winter coats.' He nodded towards the hall. 'And if you want a wash there's a spring just five minutes down the hill.'

Gwydion grinned. 'If it's all the same to you, Cormac, I'll sleep in my muck for the night. Reckon I'll sleep the clock round.'

'No matter if you do,' said Cormac. 'We'll not be going any-where for a while. Yon'un's in no fit state to move.' He nodded to the corridor which led to Coll's room. 'There's bread and cheese on the shelf and stew in the pot. Help yourself.'

Gwydion set to with a will. He didn't speak again until he was mopping up the gravy with a chunk of bread. 'So were you expecting us?' he asked.

'I was hoping. I'd sent out a call. But there's no certainty . . . There never is.' He spread his hands expressively. 'And if no one had come, well, I suppose I'd've just kept my bag of bones together for a few more years – but I'm a tired man, Gwydion. Tired.'

'I know what you mean.'

'Aye. Maybe you do,' said Cormac. 'We're all tired. We all need to sleep.'

Gwydion looked at Cormac steadily. He was not quite certain what the old man was saying. 'You're talking about death, aren't you, old man?'

'That. And more than that. The breaking of chains. The handing on. We've struggled for years and now . . .'

'I'm too tired tonight for riddles . . .'

'Aye. Get away and rest. I'm just an old man wondering . . . Gathering strength . . .'

'And I'll die when the time comes. If I'm lucky I'll be ready for it. If not . . . well there's bugger all I can do about it anyway. So sing your songs, old man. Make us laugh and cry. Bring young Coll back to health, and we'll see where we go from there.' So saying, Gwydion stretched and yawned, bunching the hard muscles on his battle-scarred shoulders and arms. 'I'll just have a pee up top. Then I'll turn in.'

Cormac sat in the roots of the tree in his comfortable wooden chair. He heard the bed creak as Gwydion climbed in and moments later he heard a deep snore which might have been a lion's growl. Then that sound ended as Gwydion turned, easing his hurt back and tired muscles.

Silence. Cormac heard the wind stir the branches of the oak tree. Even here, deep underground, the movement of the branches was transmitted to the roots. The rain came with a steady rustle of leaves and a sombre dripping. A mouse scurried into the room, its fur wet. It jumped on to Cormac's cloak and scampered up until it found a comfortable place in a folded pleat at his shoulder. There it squeaked in his ear.

Cormac sat for an hour or so, listening to the storm outside. He heard a wolf howl in the distance, and a bear growl in the thickets. Aristotle stamped and brayed softly. Cormac understood the messages and he reached for the black canvas bag which contained his cithara. 'Time to begin. The animals are telling me so,' he murmured.

He undid the buckles and removed the dark shiny cithara. It boomed to itself softly as he handled it. Then, muttering words

15

in the language of the people who had first visited this land, Cormac untuned the instrument and then re-tuned it. The bottom string was quite slack and made a deep rasping note. The top string was very tight and made a bright sharp sound. The middle two strings were tuned close together.

Cormac held the instrument close, tucking it into his shoulder, and then he let his fingers idly run over the strings, plucking out a melody. He began to sing softly. His eyes closed as he eased himself into a trance, using the song to carry him out and away and to summon the spirits of the long dead. Cormac was calling up all his powers as a singer, all the powers vested in him as protector of the sacred.

Cormac was alone in a wild place where a black wind bent the heather. This was not a place on Earth though it resembled the Earth. This was a land of no-being, a place of trysting, malleable as thought, a shifting landscape where gods and spirits could meet and universes collide without collision. Here stood Cormac, a hunched figure, dwarfed between the land and the sky, and he played his music into the teeth of the wind and dulled it. He sang to the earth. A stone stood up and became a man with wild hair, and eyes that were red. He sang to the air. The wind curled in the grass and became a tree which became a woman with bold face and red lips. Other figures gathered, shapes of fire and water, leaving whatever was their natural state and transforming to the image of the human, for that was the only shape that Cormac could understand. One by one the figures gathered close to Cormac and stepped into him, and as each entered him so the music changed.

Birds fell from the sky and nested in his skull.

Cormac cried aloud in agony when a bull charged through the heather, scratching the sky with its horns, and buried its head in his chest. It ate his heart and as it ate, the bull entered him and Cormac remained whole and strong. Only once did the music falter and that was when the earth opened and a swarm of black wasps surrounded Cormac, crawling on his face, in his lips and ears. But then they too fell away and the land became still. The music settled to a single rasping note as the darkness gathered and the temporary refuge established between time and space and consciousness dissolved.

Cormac lay stiff and still in his chair. The cithara was held in a grip of iron and his chest heaved with gasps as though the old man had been running. There was froth at his lips and a trickle of blood from his nose. He had shat himself too: the fearsome encounter to which he had exposed his spirit had racked his body and this was one of the consequences.

He stirred, opened his eyes and slowly eased himself upright. He set his cithara down on the ground by his chair. All his movements were slow and deliberate, like a man who is handling fragile ornaments aware of his own strength. He sniffed and grinned to himself. 'Disgusting eh? No bloody shame this physical realm, no respecter of the niceties.' He stood up uncomfortably and then made for the door. 'Round two, beginning.'

Cormac walked outside, picked up a bucket and climbed up the slab-topped steps. Rain was still falling and a blustery wind was shaking the bushes near the oak tree, but Cormac hardly felt it. He stood in the rain in the small clearing and looked about.

Everything was lit by a pale glow. Standing in a ring round the tree and facing in towards him were animals. Deer and bear, wolf and wild cat, fox and badger, snake and frog. A tiger with long teeth, rarely seen, stood beside the common rat and both ignored the peacock which stood with raised plumage. Here a wild horse from the uplands, its coat still flecked with sweat from its running, and a cow that had kicked its way out of the byre some miles distant and come lumbering through the woods. All had come, driven by what? By a music that they could not resist even if they had wanted to. They had come to offer themselves. They stood still, unconscious of why they were there, but present because they had to be. And there were more, Cormac knew, creatures standing in the shadows, humble spirits of trees and waters.

Cormac moved, edging round the clearing, under the baleful yellow eyes of the tiger. At the other side of the tree he came to a path which led down to a small spring where he could wash. The spring spilled over a ledge forming a waterfall. Fed

17

by the rain, the spring was a torrent. It sparkled with energy.

As he walked Cormac tugged at his old clothes, shrugging them over his shoulders and throwing them into the bushes. He took off his pants too and abandoned them. He stood in the rain and rubbed his body clean with leaves and clumps of moss. Then he filled the bucket and began a methodical washing of himself, starting with his hair and working downwards. He did not want to enter the spring in a dirty state. The spirit of the spring was an old friend. For Cormac she materialized as an old woman with a stern plain face and hair drawn back – and she greeted him without a smile.

'Come then finally, have you?'

'I have.'

' 'bout time too. And no putting that mucky bum in my clean water. Give yourself a bit more of a washing first.' Cormac did as he was bid. 'Heard you playing a while back. Something serious, is it? I haven't heard you play like that for what – a thousand years?'

'That was one of my ancestors you heard.'

'Ah well. You're all the same to me. Right, you'll do. Come on in, old man.'

Cormac stepped into the waterfall and crouched down. He felt the clean water sluice over him, not cold but fresh and invigorating. It touched him, teasing him and pummelling. 'Will we see much more of you?' asked the woman crouching beside him and with her arms round his shoulders.

'Aye, you will. I've a lot to teach. And he's not so promising.'

'Well bring him down to me when he's ready and I'll teach him a thing or two. But not till he's ready, mark you. Too much knowledge too soon can kill, you know that. It's only tough old buggers like you that survive.' She ran her fingers through his grey hair and pressed her hand to his forehead. For a few minutes they sat together, head to head. Then the woman rallied. 'Now out you go, old man. You've had enough.'

She planted a solid kiss on Cormac's lips and then he felt himself gently urged from the water. But before he left he drank deep, opening his mouth and letting the water tumble in.

'Cheeky old goat,' he heard her say, and for a few moments she took on the form he had known when he was a young man, newly come into his power and the randiest mortal walking.

Then he was out of the water and on his way back to the oak tree. The rain had stopped but the wind still blew. The animals were waiting, staring down towards the small waterfall.

'Away now,' called Cormac, waving his arm. 'You'll make an old man embarrassed. Get away back to your homes. I'll call you when I need you. Away now.' He waved again and the animals began to scatter. Moments later the clearing was deserted.

Cormac climbed down under the tree and dried himself carefully. Then he selected clean clothes – a simple white shirt, baggy comfortable trews and long stockings. Last he opened an old black wooden chest and removed a green cloak. The fabric was heavy, and while it was clean it was stained and patched and had seen better days. This cloak had been given to Cormac by his master on the day that he had made his first singing. How old it was Cormac did not know. Now he only used the cloak for special occasions.

So, clothed and feeling comfortable and at ease, Cormac picked up his cithara and made his way through to the room where Coll lay.

Coll was in a high fever, banging his head back and forth and trying to talk, calling out names. Cormac threw some herbs on to the small hotplate and soon the smoke of their burning filled the room. He took a clean cloth and wiped Coll's brow.

Cormac could see Coll's fever like a corona of smoke that threatened to choke him. But within the smoke, at its very heart, there blazed a strong and constant light – and that gave Cormac hope. He settled himself comfortably at the foot of the bed and began to stroke the cithara, pulling chords and brief lines of melody from the ancient instrument, trying to feel what harmonies would best help the troubled man.

While he seemed confident, Cormac was not. He was in uncharted territory. His wisdom told him that every situation had its own rules, and if he had any skill at all it was that he could recognize the signs for what they were, separating the seeds from the sand. Cormac moved close to the fever, willing it to reveal itself in a shape that he could comprehend, sending out his music like a web to entrap.

19

And he succeeded. The fever was a creature with many tentacles and many mouths. It was feeding on Coll, its mouths stuck deep into his body. Cormac played with more energy and though the fever writhed and hung on, it gradually began to diminish until finally it was no bigger than a starfish. It dropped away and was gone. The music touched the mind of Coll as he whimpered and cried. But gradually he settled and became still. His eyes fluttered and his lips moved as new dreams took hold of him.

Coll found himself walking in a grey world.

Far in front of him was a line of stone pillars carved like the columns of a Corinthian temple. These marked some kind of frontier for beyond them the landscape became bright, with green hills and blue skies and high silver clouds. Tethered just beyond the standing stones and shining in the sunlight was a pure white horse with golden hooves and a silver mane and tail. It stroked the ground with one of its front feet and then reared and whinnied when it saw Coll approach.

That horse can run like the wind, thought Coll and he hurried towards it. *That horse will carry me to places unknown. To rare adventures.*

But the distance was greater than he had expected, and somewhere Coll could hear music that distracted him, reminding him of the byre at Bella's Inn. Coll, who in those days was still called Viti, had tended the animals at the inn. All the horses there were dappled work horses, with great tufted hooves and big behinds and when they farted the flies fell dead. Coll laughed at the memory.

And when he laughed the white columns seemed to fade and the landscape dimmed. But Coll paid no attention. He hurried on, eager to see the horse.

'Viti. Hey, Viti.' Coll glanced about to see who was calling and saw his eldest brother Quintus. This man, the image of his handsome father, was leaning against one of the upright marble pillars and holding a flagon of wine. 'You've grown into a tough little runt. Come over here and let me look at you. Have a drink. Then we'll ride over the hill to the city. Everyone's waiting for you.'

Coll could hardly remember Quintus for he had died in a flying accident while Coll was still a child. Even so, Quintus had remained a presence in the great house at Farland Head long after his death. He was famous for his exploits: for his cruelty and his drunkenness. Coll approached him warily for somewhere, distant and almost hidden, was a memory of Quintus making him drink something which burned his throat. And Viti had cried until finally a nurse arrived and carried him away.

'See this hoss,' called Quintus. 'She's yours if you come on over.' Again the horse reared and whinnied.

'You don't have to listen to him, you know.' A new voice joined. Coll stopped in his tracks. This was a voice he remembered well. Felix, his second brother, one of the few male adults who had ever shown any kindness towards him when he was a boy. Felix had been killed in the Western Empire. He'd been a brilliant young man, by all accounts, skilled in language and diplomacy. Coll looked round and discovered Felix sitting on the ground with his back against one of the pillars. He was seated on a rug and rolled out beside him was a scroll on which he had been writing, for among his other accomplishments Felix was a poet, playwright and composer. 'You can make up your own mind. No one is called before their time. Some come early but none come late.'

Coll looked at Felix and was horrified to see that his body was covered with cuts that bled. The grass about him was stained with red. 'Sorry about this,' said Felix. 'But there are worse things than blood. Like betraying yourself. No man was ever true, but who was first true to himself.'

Quintus brayed with laughter and clapped derisively. 'Sententious shite. Call yourself a poet,' he shouted. 'It doesn't even bloody scan.'

Coll found his voice. 'Hey, hey, hey, you two. No squabbling. This is a serious time for me.' And even as he spoke the music behind him intensified and he remembered the calm face of Miranda as she stared at him a lifetime ago at the hospital in Stand Alone Stan.

'Clever woman that,' said Felix. 'Shame you ruined everything, eh?'

'Yes,' said Coll.

'So what are you going to become? A shade like us – full of piss and full of wind, the drunkard and the poet?'

'No,' said Coll and he turned round and faced the darkness which seemed to have crept up behind him. It seemed that he stared down a long dark tunnel and at the far end was an old man with a whiskered face hunched over an instrument which he played with fervour.

And at that moment Coll heard a roaring. It came from all about him. And there was a voice like iron cymbals crashing together. 'Turn again, Viti. Turn.'

Coll did turn and found himself staring into the insolent face of Alexander, the blond Roman youth he had killed at the Battle Dome. The man was taller than Viti and in top fighting condition. 'Come and join us, Viti. The fighting is marvellous,' and so saying the young Alexander hit Coll's brother Quintus in the stomach so that he sat down belching out wine, and then he kicked Felix who fell over like a body made of straw. 'Come and save your brothers. Come and fight me. You know who I am, don't you?'

'You are what is left of Alexander, just the spite and the lies and the jealousy – the rubbish. And those are not my brothers. They're just toys made to frighten children.'

The being that looked like Alexander howled. 'Fight me,' he roared and he charged towards Coll, covering the distance in a couple of bounds.

Coll felt hands like bands of iron grip him. 'You will fight me now as you never fought in the past.' Coll felt teeth against his throat and all the fighting reflexes, dinned into him through hours of practice at the Eburacum Military Academy, came to him. He twisted, hunched and butted and felt the strong arms weaken. But Alexander was not to be fooled. He went with Viti, causing him to lose balance, and then began to slam him with punches to the face and stomach. Wherever Viti turned Alexander was in front of him, dancing, slightly hunched, fists raised, ducking and weaving. 'Come and eat the worms you made me eat, Viti,' called Alexander, and he moved closer, his fists like darting snakes.

It's not fair, thought Viti and somewhere a small blubbering

22

child found voice inside him. He wanted to cry and run away. But a stronger presence, a being not yet fully born in him, made him stay. 'If you run now, there'll be no end to running. And the longer you run the harder it will be to stop running.' Coll heard the voice, which was his own voice, and he covered up, head down and weathered the punches.

Moments later he tried a punch of his own which missed its target but made Alexander dance back. That told Coll something: that his adversary was assailable. Coll yet had choice. He had a moment to take stock of things. The landscape had changed. The Corinthian columns were gone as had the white horse and the figures of Felix and Quintus. He fought in a grey place while all about him were shapes of music.

Coll lowered his guard slowly and stared at Alexander. 'I don't have to fight you. You are nothing, and I have a job to do. But when I do come here, I'll kick your arse so hard you won't sit down for a week.'

Alexander looked dumbfounded, and then he started to shrivel. Before Coll's eyes, the figure began to change. Soon he was no longer the insolent handsome youth modelled on Apollo. His face became black and blue and misshapen – a travesty of beauty. Ginger bristle sprouted from his cheeks and sides, and his feet were cloven lumps of flesh. On his head, tangled in his hair, he wore a crown of cow's horns and his eyes became closed and small until they stared out of his face like spear wounds. Coll wondered what mischief this change represented. It was very theatrical and left him unmoved, like a charade performed by a bad actor. Cautiously Coll moved round, looking for an opening.

It came quickly. Alexander, or whatever he had now become, ran at him clumsily and it was an easy matter for Coll to trip him and send him sprawling at his feet. The advantage lay with Coll. It would have been simple for him to move in with forearm and heel, but somehow the manoeuvre didn't seem worth the effort. Coll had been here before, in this situation on a killing field – too often – and always he got it wrong. The killing never really solved anything.

He began to turn away, sickened, and the thing at his feet transformed slowly into a blue snake with black markings like diamonds on its supple back. Coll was caught off-guard by its sudden beauty. The snake coiled round his feet and then it lifted its black-lipped face until it was level with Coll's eyes and its forked tongue flicked out. The snake laughed, snake laughter, and for a moment darkness fell ...

... for a moment Coll was aware of an old man who shone with green light and a tall man who shone with golden light and they were bending towards him.

'Are you Death?' whispered Coll lifting his arms to the old man and then he was assailed by music which battered him back into the dream-time, into the world where symbolic forms have life, and guide a man's destiny towards ...

... the snake was waiting. It was now a man with a snake's head and it stood in a desert where the wind lifted the sand and made it flow like small rivers. 'You must keep pace with me now,' said the snake and so saying it turned and began to run up the side of a rippled sand dune. Coll followed, lumbering and slipping in the soft sand while the snake figure danced ahead.

They ran down the far side of the dune and out on to a plain of boulders where there were bones bleached white. The snake figure never paused though Coll bruised his feet and began to tire quickly.

Once Coll stumbled and fell to his knees. The snake didn't stop. 'Lose me now and you'll never find me,' it called.

Coll heaved himself up and forced himself to run on. He seemed so slow. And the snake never slacked in its running.

The day passed. Night came.

Night passed and the day came.

And on. And on.

Coll lost all reckoning, but it seemed that he became lighter.

Late one afternoon when the shadows were long, they came to the ruins of a town. There Coll saw, sticking up out of the sand, the stiff, curled shape of a cithara similar to the one which Cormac played.

Coll paused in his running.

'Come on or you'll lose me,' called the snake man. But to Coll the find was too important and he stopped and stood looking at the old instrument lodged in the sand. He took hold of the cithara and pulled. It lifted easily, so easily indeed that he fell back and ended up sitting on the sand clutching the instrument to his chest. It boomed in his hands and rustled as the sand poured from it.

'Play us a tune?' It was the snake-headed man speaking. He had run in a large circle and now stood close to Coll. He was not even breathing deeply.

'I can't play.'

'Everyone can play.'

Coll tightened the strings which squeaked and groaned. Then he strummed them and was astonished when a rich chord filled the air.

'Now what?' said the snake man.

'Now I must carry this cithara with us,' said Coll.

'You can't,' replied the snake man. And before Coll could argue, he lifted the instrument from Coll's hands and danced away. He slung it into a satchel he carried on his back. 'Now you have an even greater reason to follow me,' he called, and began running. Coll followed.

Sun. Dark. Sun. Moon. Sun. Moon. Sun. Dark.

Finally Coll began to fail and to fade. Try as he would, he could not catch the snake man who scampered over the sand leaving scarcely a footprint.

Coll felt himself become yet lighter.

When he looked at his hands he saw that the skin was thin and dry and falling in flakes. He touched his face and there was no skin, no cheeks, no hair. There was hard dry bone only. He could place his thin bony fingers in the place where his eyes should have been. Coll was filled with the wonder of this. How could it be that he could run and think and see, but yet was no more than a pile of shambling bones?

Then finally the bones too fell away, dropping one by one – a digit here, a vertebra there, the skull rolling like a broken ball – until there was nothing left and Coll was a point of thought moving over the pale brown desert following a snake man who never tired and who carried the cithara at his back.

At last they came to a wide river. The water was black and

opaque like flowing pitch. The distant bank was shrouded in mist. Ominous and beautiful.

'Now you have a real choice,' said the snake man. 'You can either swim over or you can run back. The swimming is easy and the rewards are great.'

'I don't know,' said Coll. 'I don't know. Tell me what to do. I don't know anything. I don't . . .'

. . . abruptly the darkness fell. Dropping like a curtain.

Grey light of dawn. Lying on the grass. Again the old man bending over, holding a beaker: the golden man, lifting Coll bodily. The tree. Miranda watching.

Was she pleased?

Strange lights in a dark room – a smell of perfume, balm for the dead.

Then the darkness rose like smoke . . .

. . . and Coll found himself in darkness. This was a darkness like no other. It pressed in close. Slowly a great despondency settled on him. Why move? Why not move? Though the hopelessness dominated him, he could not stay still. He started to walk with his hands thrust out in front of him, and his hands touched damp moss which writhed and pulled at his fingers.

Buried. That was his single thought.

And then, *All ended.*

And finally, *Failed. I failed whatever it was I was trying to do.*

He moved on, because he could not help doing so, feeling his way, and slowly a faint light gathered round him. It did not bring hope – it was what was. Not better, not worse. Just what was.

Gradually Coll became aware that he was not alone – that as he walked there was one walking beside him. But when he turned he could not see his companion who always seemed to move just that bit more quickly. They never touched. Was it the snake-headed man? Coll wondered.

'Let me see you,' said Coll finally, but his companion never answered.

Slowly they entered a place of dark trees and bird-song greeted

26

them. A bird which repeated a simple melody sang enthusiastically from high in a tree. A grey light filtered down through the trees and when Coll held up his arm he could see his skin pale and slightly luminous. When he touched his face he could feel his flesh.

At some point his companion left him and Coll walked on alone while the bird sang lustily. But then he came to his name-tree, Coll, the hazel tree, the tree of intuition which sees straight to the heart of mystery. And there standing under the tree with his back to him was a dark figure whom Coll half recognized but yet could not place. He knew it was the companion that had walked close to him out of the darkness. It was not the snake man, though he carried a cithara at his back.

Coll now knew he had reached the end of his journey. This was the place to which all the paths of his life led. He looked at the back of the figure and he knew that whatever face the figure had, it would be more terrible than anything he might conceive and that seeing it might destroy him. But Coll had no choice. He had not come so far or walked so deep in despair, to give up now. Though this be the end, and darkness the reward, still he had no choice. 'Turn round,' he commanded.

Every fear that he could ever know possessed Coll. He clenched his fists. He bit his lips. He wanted to cry and turn away. He felt his bowels turn to water.

Unstoppable now, the figure slowly turned in the green twilight.

Coll cried out in surprise. He was staring at his own face: stiff, still, utterly composed and lifeless. The figure was himself – unsmiling and naked.

'Who are you?' breathed Coll.

'I am your Death,' said the figure. 'I have never left you. I will never leave you. I am the companion always at your side. I was with you on the bridge at Stand Alone Stan and I was with with you when Gwydion pulled you from the water. Now you see me without illusion. Now you know there is no need to fear me. I am your servant and I am your friend and I will be with you at the end when . . .'

'Sh . . . Will I always see you?'

'Not always.'

27

'Will I always be aware of you?'

'Sometimes you will forget.'

Pause.

Then Coll said, 'Can I touch you?'

Death replied, 'One day. You have made your decision. You chose Life. You have made that decision several times. Now you must move on. Now that you have faced me, there can be no more fear.' Then strangely Death smiled. 'What are you, Viti and Coll?'

'I am . . . I am whatever I become.'

And when Coll said these words Death suddenly unslung the cithara from his back, struck it once so that a mighty sound shook the tree, and then he handed the instrument to Coll.

Moments later Death began to fade. The air about Coll brightened. He found himself lying in a bed in a low-ceilinged room, smelly with the smoke of burnt herbs and sour with sweat.

Coll turned and found himself looking into the face of Gwydion who was holding a candle and staring at him intently. 'Are you all right?' asked Gwydion.

'I think I am,' murmured Coll. 'But where's the thingummy, the instrument? And where the hell am I? Eh?'

Gwydion shook his head. 'Don't know what instrument you're talking about. And as for where you are, you're a guest in the house of Cormac the Singer. And bloody lucky you are too.'

'Cormac? How did I get here?'

'That's another story,' said Gwydion. 'And that story can wait. I'm going to get Cormac.'

So saying Gwydion withdrew after placing the candle down on a small table beside Coll's head. Coll was alone. He stared into the flame and for a moment it seemed to carry him away. 'Are you there?' he whispered softly.

And equally softly came the whispered reply, 'Ever and always. I never sleep. Nor am I ever jealous. Make your way.'

Coll heard a shout and moments later Cormac shuffled into the room. The man seemed smaller than Coll remembered, shrunken. In his hands he carried his cithara.

'So, lad. You're back. We thought we'd lost you for a while there.'

'Cormac,' said Coll for the second time, making no attempt to disguise his pleasure. 'Of all people . . . But how come I am here? The last thing I remember was Gwydion and me stuck in a bloody great swamp and the rain coming down.'

'Don't excite yourself.'

'Where've I been?'

'You tell us.'

Coll thought back and was astonished to discover that he could remember everything that had happened to him – almost as though it were all still happening – but distanced, too. 'I've been on a journey,' he said. 'And I met . . .' He stopped. He could not bring himself to say the words. 'You'll think I'm mad.'

'Try us.'

'I met my Death.'

Gwydion's eyes gleamed. Cormac's eyes, deep sunken under his eyebrows, were inscrutable. 'And?' asked Cormac. 'Were you given anything?'

'I found a . . . I was given a . . .' Coll looked about on the small bed. 'I thought I had it with me. A cithara, a bit like yours only smaller, not so grand.'

Cormac let out a sigh. 'Where did you find the cithara?'

'I pulled it out of the sand near a ruined town. I made a tune of sorts and then the snake man took it from me . . .'

'Ah, that's for wisdom and the knowing of life. Go on. Who gave it back to to you?'

'Death did.'

'So now you know where your life goes.'

'Do I?' Coll was confused. So much was happening.

Cormac regarded him sternly. 'Well you've always got choice, of course. But we'll talk about that in the morning. Rest now.'

Coll nodded. His mind had begun to wander. Tiredness of an ordinary kind was taking him over and he did not feel able to respond to what Cormac was saying, still less understand him. At the same time he felt warm, and safe and secure in a way that he had rarely experienced in his life before. And for the time being that was sufficient. He lay back. 'How long have we been here?' he asked.

'Fourteen days come tomorrow. A full half cycle of the moon.

You arrived when she was just past the full and now she's just past the new. So you will start to learn with her.'

'That's a long time to be unconscious.'

Gwydion spoke for the first time. 'You weren't unconscious all the time. You raved a bit. Talked about what it was like when you were a boy with your brothers and some kid called Alexander. But we wiped you down and fed you, and cleaned you up like a right baby.'

Coll was embarrassed. He felt like someone caught doing something indecent in public. 'I suppose I should say thank y—'

'Don't say thank you,' shouted Gwydion and Cormac in unison.

Coll grinned. And the grin stiffened, for he was asleep. For a moment, before he relaxed, he looked like his invisible companion.

Cormac and Gwydion retreated to the next room. It was late in the evening but the hangings which closed the doors were tied back allowing the soft warm summer air to flow into the underground house. The ubiquitous stew of the woodlanders was steaming on the hotplate while the vapour disappeared up the flue. Cormac filled two bowls and carried them outside. Gwydion fetched some ale. The two men settled down in the clearing under the oak, making themselves comfortable on wooden chairs which Gwydion had built, shaping the wood with an axe. From this vantage point they could see down the hill to the place where Gwydion had climbed, carrying Coll. They could see over the trees to where the marsh was hazy with fog and insects. Beyond, just visible above the mist, was the shape of hills still golden in the setting sun.

'I feel like I've been through the ringer too,' said Gwydion, slurping his stew.

Cormac nodded. 'But now we must proceed with caution, but boldly too. There isn't much time.' Overhead the swallows dived catching insects. 'Tomorrow young Coll's got a big decision to make.'

'What's that then?'

'He's got to decide whether he wants to become a singer or not.'

'What, him?' Gwydion was genuinely astonished. While he liked Coll and was prepared to let bygones be bygones and help Coll to adapt to the world of the forest, he could not conceive of Coll becoming a singer. 'He's a bloody Roman.'

'I don't make the choice.'

'Even so.'

'It took me seven years before I started singing – mark you I was a lazy sod. I'll teach him what I can. That's if he wants to learn. If not, I'll turf him out on his ear tomorrow.'

Gwydion sat silent, absorbing the news. During the two weeks while Coll was in the otherworld, Gwydion and Cormac had spent their spare moments talking, exploring the changes taking place in their world. Gwydion had told Cormac about the things that he and Coll had seen at Castra Skusa and their strange journey through the flood. These conversations had rarely been resolved and had usually ended when Coll needed their attention. Now, with the danger passed, they relaxed properly for almost the first time.

'Why is everything so rushed?' asked Gwydion. 'I'm not talking about now as opposed to a hundred years ago when you were a kid. I'm talking about Coll. Why is everything so rushed with him?'

'Well,' said Cormac, easing round in his seat, 'as well as I can explain it . . . Have you seen waves coming in to the shore? They come in steadily and then whoosh, they hit the shore and all the energy gets released in a few seconds and the spray shoots up and the lather comes rolling up the sand faster than a horse can run. Well, we are at that moment just before the wave breaks. Don't ask me why. Ages change. The wheel turns. And the greatest savagery of any age is always saved to the end, like a wave breaking. You told me about those drums of fire-liquid you saw over yonder, you told me about the ships unloading at Cliff Town and that soldier who said the Romans were going to burn a bit of the forest?' Gwydion nodded. 'Well that's all part of it. But there's more. There's what causes those things to happen. Ideas that get out of hand when people forget they are human and part of Nature and begin to believe in abstractions. That's what is worst, and that's what is going to take all our strength. Well perhaps not mine directly but yours, and Coll's and that bonny lass Miranda and . . . well everyone finally. Not just us people either. I've listened to the birds and the animals. I've heard the talk in the groves at midnight when the trees share. Everything knows that we've come to a time of testing, but nobody knows the outcome. The fight is on, that's all.' He paused and refreshed himself with ale. Then he wiped the froth from his whiskers. 'Have I ever told you about my Master Gilli – the singer who taught me to sing? Well he had a phrase that keeps coming back to me. He used to end all his singings with the same words. "If it be now, 'tis not to come. If it be not to come, it will be now. If it be not now, yet it will come. The readiness is all." No one knew what the hell he was talking about, but those words used to send a shiver down my spine. I asked him to explain and he said, "You'll know when the time comes." Well I do. And the time is now.'

Gwydion drank deeply. 'My mam, old Bella, she once told me she thought I was special in some way and that was why she kicked me out of the house so young – so that I could get experience. I'm only twenty-five, or thereabouts, but sometimes I feel as though I'm a thousand years old. I've got more scars than I can count. It seems like I've spent all my life fighting, and thieving, and in betweens getting drunk and making love to as many women as I could. I live as though time's running out. So I know what you mean. Sometimes, I feel angry in a way that I know makes me dangerous. I know how the old ones felt – the ones that ran naked into battle and could terrorize the enemy with a look and a shout. I can do that. Sometimes, I feel this anger burning up inside me and I want to fight . . . it's like a lust I can't control. I bloody near brained young Coll on our way here just 'cos he got up my nose.' Gwydion laughed at the memory. 'And what I feel now is a savageness waiting – like I felt that time I was captured in a brothel by a Roman platoon. Did I ever tell you about that?' Cormac shook his head. 'Hell of a laugh. I was working as a bouncer at this brothel in Hispania – I even got paid for it – and this squad arrived one afternoon rounding up girls for an orgy. Well, I had to dress up in one of the courtesan's skirts and the soldiers were so pissed and eager with it that they never noticed – till it was too late. Anyway, there I was, dressed up in silks and bundled out for this orgy

... and where do you think it was? At the villa of the Praefectus Comitum of Hispania himself, no less. So anyway . . .'

The two men fell to yarning as the shadows lengthened.

They sat till the new moon swung up over the distant hills like a small silver ship and shone on the still marsh-water.

The ale was almost finished when Gwydion stretched. 'So what happens now, Cormac? What happens next to young Coll?'

'I put the word on him tomorrow. And if he accepts I begin to teach him, to in-ishiate him . . . in the arts of being a singer. And we'll be away a lot of the time.'

'Away? Where?'

'In the woods. In the dream-world too. He's a lot of journeys to make. And that's where your work comes in, old warrior. You are the guardian. You protect us wherever we are from eyes that spy and from anything else that comes nosing.'

Gwydion grinned in the darkness. 'I knew I'd come in useful.' He yawned. 'And what happens if he chooses not to be a singer?'

'He will die.' The words were said so simply. Gwydion stopped in mid-stretch. 'He has come so far and there is no middle way. He now knows so much and so little and there is no moving forwards except by beginning again. Besides, he knows just enough to be dangerous. So I will sing him one of the death songs and send him back to the darkness or you will take him down to the woods and come back alone.' There was a long pause. 'That would be sad and I hope it will not come to that – but he has a sad streak to his nature which might make him turn away from his best hope of fulfilment. But we'll find out tomorrow. He'll begin to recover quickly now that his mind is clear. The past has fallen away like baggage that he no longer needs. He's hungry to learn.'

Gwydion stood up and stretched again. 'Well I think I'll turn in, if it's all the same to you,' he said quietly. 'What about you? Do you want a hand down the steps? You're none too steady.'

'No,' said Cormac, standing up stiffly. 'I think I'll take a wander down to the stream. I fancy a bit of a natter.'

'Well don't fall in.'

'I should be so lucky.'

And thus ended the night of Coll's awakening.

*

33

The next day Cormac got Coll up shortly after dawn. When they had eaten a small meal they sat outside in the clearing and Cormac made Coll describe everything that had happened to him during the two weeks of his dreaming. As the tale unfolded Cormac explained the significance of every detail.

At the end Cormac looked at him closely and Coll was aware of the power of the old man's gaze. It was as though he was looking completely through him. It was not a hostile gaze but a look such as statues can have. 'So now, young Coll, you have a decision to make.'

'Have I?'

'Something guided you here? Do you agree?'

'I thought *you* did.'

'I provided the light, but you had to find your way.'

'Then I suppose . . . yes, I was guided. But what guided me?'

'You did. Don't look for mysterious structures. Concentrate on yourself. Let the good sense inside you have sway. When you comprehend your own strength, you begin to comprehend everything. I know, you've had a hell of a time and you are tired and weak. Nothing's prepared you for this – at least when I began I'd heard the singers since I was a child – even in my mother's womb I'd heard them – but you . . . ?' He shook his head. 'Strange who gets the call and who doesn't, eh? And the timing is always right, even when it seems all wrong. You can deny the call for many lifetimes . . . but still it will be there.'

'Speak simply.'

'All right. I have one question for you. "What do you want to become?"' And then before Coll could reply Cormac pushed him head-first off his chair and sent him rolling down the bank. 'Come back in an hour and give me your answer,' called Cormac, 'and take this with you, you might need it.' So saying he threw the cithara down the bank and Coll leaped to one side and caught the instrument before it could hit the ground and rolled with it, clutching it to him, protecting it with his body. When Coll finally came to a stop and looked back up the hill he found that Cormac had gone.

'Silly old man,' shouted Coll. 'You could've bust the bloody thing. Then where would we have been?' But there was no reply.

Coll was at a loss. He wandered round the side of the hill and he heard the birds singing above him, protecting their territory. That seemed important. Was there a message in all of that for him? Gwydion found messages in everything. He stopped and wondered what the other birds heard when all he heard was their song.

He wandered on and came to the tree called Coll. 'Hello, friend,' said Coll. 'Can you tell me what to do?' There was, of course, no reply. "Course, I've got to make my own mind up, haven't I?' Above him the birds hammered out their melodies. He moved on round the hill and eventually heard water tumbling. *A spring. Ha! Cormac's got it all laid on*, he thought, remembering, his own tree-house and the stream he'd had to walk to. He came to the waterfall and the sunlight was touching the water, lighting it up and catching the fine spray so that it created a flickering rainbow.

The tumbling water reminded Coll how thirsty he was and at the same time how badly he wanted to pee. He put the cithara down carefully, relieved himself in the bushes and then came back for a drink. On an impulse he put his head partly into the water and let it tumble into his mouth. As he did this he was blinded for a moment by the sun and the water poured over his face, into his ears and down into the space between his open shirt and his bare skin. He jumped back. It was as though the waterfall had played a trick on him.

He stripped off his shirt and hung it on a branch to dry. *How long have I got left?* he wondered. *And what am I going to say to old Cormac?*

He sat down above the waterfall and idly began to strum the strings of the cithara. He did not know how to play but he could see where the body of the instrument was worn with holding and where the singers who had used it had placed their fingers. He plucked the strings and was delighted at the rich sound that came from the instrument. A bird fluttered down and perched on a stone on the lip of the waterfall and watched him, its head on one side. Coll strummed more notes and the bird hopped closer. In the silence between the notes Coll heard the waterfall sing in its roaring manner, he heard the trees shift and their leaves rustle, he saw the sun on the water and then,

35

magically it seemed – though he knew it was not magic – the bird opened its beak and chirped to him. And in that moment Coll knew what he wanted. He strummed the cithara and its notes were appropriate. He wanted to belong, to this world, to this moment for there was no other moment. Beside him, Coll's invisible companion hummed along while Coll bent to his music. Music was the way to belong. Music united all worlds. Coll wanted to be a singer – like Cormac – able to heal and bring joy and ease sadness.

The thought was preposterous! Mad! Insane! He was dreaming! But the thought once born would not go away. It had snagged in him. And so, for better or worse, that was what he would tell Cormac and if Cormac told him to clear off, well so be it. At the same time, the thought seemed right – like pulling on your own shoes in the dark when there is a whole pile of shoes to choose from – and it made sense of everything.

He finished his playing and stood up. The bird flew away.

He climbed quickly up the bank towards the oak tree. Waiting there was Cormac and a few steps behind him stood Gwydion. Gwydion looked strangely ill at ease, angry almost, ready.

'So what is your answer, young Coll?' called Cormac.

'I want to become a singer, like you. I want to be your apprentice.'

'Well that's all right then,' said Cormac. 'You had me worried for a minute. So let's begin.'

2 Problems for Angus

All was not well with the Dragon Warriors.

The fighting force envisaged by Angus, forged by anger and tempered by outrage, had not eventuated. Indeed, most of the people who had been liberated from the Caligula camp appeared to have scant interest in the aims of the Dragon Warriors. They were glad to be released, of course, but in Angus' eyes they lacked a certain political awareness. Most seemed to prefer loafing about in the sun and drinking wine to studying strategy and unarmed combat. Moreover, the desertion rate was high and each day the number of former inmates remaining at the camp declined. People slipped quietly away under the trees. Eventually, some three weeks after the liberation, there were only twenty-four of the former prisoners left. And these, for the most, were not very promising as recruits.

None of the woodlanders remained. When the Caligula camp was liberated, they had provided the majority of the prisoners. Most had been picked up by the military authorities for small technical offences such as brawling at the city gates or walking over the roads in the forest rather than using the culverts under them and, since woodlanders had no rights, any offence could lead to their being despatched to the Caligula. The Battle Dome was always hungry. But as soon as they recovered, most of them just headed off to make their way back to their villages. They offered hospitality in abundance should Angus or Perol or Sean or Drummer ever visit their village, but they would not stay to join the Dragon Warriors. And this drove Angus wild.

'They lack discipline,' he shouted to Sean and Drummer one morning after they had said farewell to the last of the woodlanders. 'And they lack imagination. They don't seem able to grasp the big picture.'

Sean shrugged non-committally. He hadn't told Angus, but he too was finding it hard to hold on to what Angus called the 'big picture'. Sean and Drummer were now close friends and, strange to relate, Sean had become something of Drummer's disciple. He wanted to learn as much as Drummer would teach him about the wild wood, about survival and about the old ways. The pair of them spent days away from the camp living in the forest. Sean was discovering an inner peace and this undermined the anger he felt towards the Roman authorities. At the same time, Sean was starting to feel homesick for Hibernia; another fact which he had not disclosed to Angus.

Particularly disappointing were the members of the Citizen class who, in Angus' view, should have known better and upon whom he had pinned his hopes. Most had been sent to the Caligula for crimes such as robbery, arson, graffiti writing, drunkenness, general insubordination, vandalism and persistent laziness. While they lacked respect for the Roman authorities, they also lacked any sense of altruism and seemed to delight in frustrating Angus. Far from seeing the big red-headed man as their natural leader, most regarded him as the representative of Authority, and hence someone to be avoided. At best they gave him a resentful obedience, and at worst ridicule – when his back was turned. One by one the able-bodied decided to take their chance under the trees. Most hoped to find a village where they could settle down. A few intended to make for Eburacum where they hoped to mingle with the crowds and become, as it were, invisible. A vain hope, in which they did indeed show their ignorance. Most would not survive the wild wood and those that did stumble into Eburacum, dazed and hungry, would soon be reported to the city militia who would pick them up one by one. While the Roman state was inefficient in many ways, it was ruthlessly efficient when it came to managing its Citizens: and this efficiency was nowhere more evident than in the fact that most of the Citizens were unaware of being managed.

Angus was baffled by the desertions. At night he lay awake trying to understand. 'Don't they understand that unity is strength?' he asked Perol. 'They're just wandering back to servitude. Don't they want to stand up and oppose their oppressors?'

'Seems not,' said Perol. Then she added tactfully, 'Perhaps most of them have been so badly damaged by the State that they can no longer think for themselves.'

'Suppose so,' said Angus with a sigh. 'You know I tried to

read them a bit of Sara Mill's essay on liberty, but no one was interested. By gum, I never thought it would be so hard to get people moving. Then last week I found one of them had used the mechanics' workshop to make a duplicate key to the wine cellar. Would you credit that? We risk life and limb to rescue the buggers from the Caligula and all they can do is devise ways of nicking our wine.'

'So what did you do?'

'Took the key. Banged a few heads together and told them to clear off if they didn't like it here.'

'And . . . ?'

'And they did. That kind of thing's been going on for weeks. Now there's only three of them left I can really trust! Three. I ask you. One of them is old Wallace and he's half gaga, one is Deric the Lame who's a good gardener but who wouldn't know the business end of a spear if he sat on it, and the other is Peter the Scribe who left his glasses behind when we escaped from the Caligula and is so short-sighted he can hardly see to pick up a cup. And we'd hoped for a tough fighting force! Some hope!' Perol put her arms round him and held him tight. Angus when he was upset and vulnerable brought out all her deepest maternal feelings.

One truth that Perol kept to herself was that she was having more success than he in organizing her team of Dark Sisters. There had been fewer women than men among the released prisoners, but what the women lacked in numbers they made up for in intensity. They had a very focused sense of outrage. Some had been forced to witness the killing of husbands and brothers, others had been raped or molested and then thrown into the Caligula for complaining. Now there remained just seven women in all. They were aged from fifteen to thirty-five and they had formed a close and supportive group. In general this group was more interested in healing their wounds than in bringing the State to its knees, though one or two had an anger that gnawed at them. They accepted Perol as their mentor and this meant that Perol was discovering new things for herself. She was discovering companionship.

That was the total complement of the Dragon Warriors! The roll-call was not impressive. Angus and Perol, Sean and

Drummer. Wallace Duff, Deric the Lame, Peter the Scribe and Edna, Betsy, Ruth, Estelle, Ada, June and Gargamelle.

The rest of the people who lived at the camp were either children or belonged to a small group of men and women who had lost their wits as a result of their treatment in the Caligula and who had retreated into a variety of private spaces. Angus did not know what to do about them: they had never been foreseen in his calculations.

Last but not least there was Garlyck who seemed at home in all company and whose grinning face always managed to pop up just where he was least wanted or expected.

'Him I could do without,' growled Angus. 'He's bad for morale. Just keep him out of my sight, that's all.'

Eventually Angus called a council of war to explore the situation, and everyone assembled in the dining-room where Angus addressed them.

'We need new blood,' he said looking round, 'if we are to become an effective instrument of social change. I do not need to remind you that even as we sit here, the oppression of the Roman state continues unabated. Still the innocent are being rounded up and taken to places such as the Caligula camp. Still power resides in the hands of the few who manipulate it to serve their own ends. Now, I have called this meeting in a spirit of openness and trust so that we can decide what action to take. Several alternatives suggest themselves. We could take the Dragon down towards Petuaria. There's a prison there and we could liberate a few colleagues. However, our last experiment, apart from the destruction of the camp, was not a resounding success in the personnel department, present company excepted.' Here Angus' eyes fell on Garlyck who smiled at him serenely. 'Or we could enter one of the small woodland communities and try to convince them to join us. Again that course doesn't look very hopeful. In fact I don't think most of the woodland communities could organize their way out of a bucket with a hole in the bottom let alone plan political strategy. Thirdly, we could commit another outrage, try to embarrass the Romans, perhaps knock a few of them off in the process and at least begin to show that they are vulnerable.' He paused. One of the children who had climbed through the window into the room to see what was going on had clambered up on to Gargamelle's vast lap and fallen asleep. Wallace Duff was smiling to himself at some fond memory and was clearly not paying much attention. 'So, what do you think? Anyone got any better ideas? Anyone got any questions?'

Silence. And then Garlyck raised his hand and Angus groaned inwardly. He'd told Drummer not to let Garlyck in but the young man had wangled his way round Drummer somehow.

'Yes?' said Angus heavily.

'Why do you want to kill?' asked Garlyck, his voice clear and penetrating.

The question caught everyone off-guard. It had the obvious ring of a challenge.

'What do you mean?' asked Angus, though he had heard the question plainly enough.

'You seem to like the killing, to believe in it, and I don't understand why. I want you to explain and since this is an open forum as you said, and since we are all Dragon Warriors, for better or worse, I thought you wouldn't mind explaining a bit of the basic philosophy. Why do you want to kill?'

There was silence and Angus found that everyone, including those who had been dozing off, were now looking at him with interest. 'Well,' he began. 'If everyone is happy for us to have a brief digression from the main topic, I have no objection.' There was a general rumble of agreement and people shifted round in their seats, making themselves comfortable, as though getting ready for a story.

Angus began. 'I want it to be clearly understood from the outset that I do not advocate killing for the sake of killing . . .' Angus was not quite sure what he was going to say next, but as he spoke he remembered the style of his former teacher Marcus, at Roscius' Academy, and he tried to emulate somewhat that man's manner. 'Far from it, for were I to do so I would place myself at little remove from the rat which devours its own species and the rogue dog which kills sheep with a bite, not for food, but for pleasure. I regard killing as a necessary, albeit regrettable, means to an end. The simple fact is that we have no choice.' He pronounced these last few words very distinctly, staring down at the frowning faces which looked up at him. 'We have no choice. For the Roman state to which we are opposed itself depends on a ruthless slaughter of whoever or whatever stands in its way. From the earliest days of its founding, it has depended on Might deciding what is Right.'

Angus was beginning to warm to his theme. He was rather enjoying the absolute silence of attention too. Even the children stared at him with large serious eyes from their position in the sun at the window sill. Only one of the deeply disturbed boys sat muttering to himself as he pulled the head of a dandelion to bits.

'If we wish to change things, if we wish to stop injustice, we must speak to the State in the only language which it understands. And that language is violence.' Angus here banged his fist down on the table to bring emphasis to his words. 'Only when the State is threatened will it begin to change. Ultimately, every state depends on the willing cooperation of the people. Without that cooperation we have stagnation, lethargy and passivity – but those qualities conceal a deep anger, like water that becomes still just before it boils, and the anger of a people, when unleashed, will know no bounds.'

Wallace Duff raised his hand. 'How do you know all this, Angus?'

'I figured it out for myself. I studied history. I opened my eyes to what was happening all about me. Some time after we escaped from the Battle Dome the village we were in was attacked. I saw things there that I had never witnessed before, not even in the Battle Dome where we were used to blood and guts. I saw terror used with a cold calculation. Women raped and butchered. Children carved. Men humiliated with torture. I saw soldiers behave worse than . . . worse than anything I could have conceived. That was a turning point for me. I could not understand what was happening, I felt such pain in here . . .' he pointed to his head, 'and in here.' He pointed to his heart. 'It was as though my blood was on fire. And the only way I could stop the hurting was by finding out what had caused these things. And so I decided to learn. And what I learned was that the morality of the leaders of a state always filters down. If the leaders are cruel in mind, they will appoint cruel men and women to serve them. And what is perhaps worse, they set up their beliefs and call them tradition, so that nothing can change. And they can't be dislodged.' Angus paused and drew breath. He could feel himself becoming angry even as he spoke. 'And after I had learned all this, I decided to do something about it. Because a man or a woman who sees an injustice and knows it to be an injustice and turns away, is condoning that injustice. It may sound a bit precious when I put it like that, but that is the truth. I cannot turn away from injustice and nor can Perol or Sean. So we started the Dragon Warriors. So we attacked the Caligula. So we freed you and all the others. So we will attack other targets. So we will inevitably end up killing more Romans. I don't especially like it but I see it as an inevitable outcome of the course of action we have chosen because we are fighting the State with its own weapons.' He paused and looked round. 'There, I hope I have explained everything?'

Angus sat down. He glanced across at Garlyck and was surprised to see that that man was smiling in his quiet serene way and nodding. Angus did not know what that meant. Then Garlyck rubbed his fingers through his stiff white hair and finally raised his hand. 'May I speak?' he asked.

Angus nodded.

'Well. First I want to say thank you for explaining things so clearly. I didn't expect anything so well thought out or so compassionate. I salute you, Angus. Your instincts are admirable. But as regards your means . . . well, there I am afraid we must differ. I want to begin by asking you a few questions, if I may.'

'Fire away.'

'This violence you speak of . . . this killing of a few Romans so that the State feels discredited . . . when will it end?'

'When the State changes.'

'Ah. And when will that be? When there are no Romans left to kill? Or do you believe that those human beings who constitute the Roman state will one day discover charity and compassion and transform places like the Caligula into holiday camps?'

'We will assess the situation at regular intervals to determine what changes have taken place and what future action is necessary. We have the radio link. We tune in to what the Romans are up to. We keep ourselves informed. But beyond that, and at a deeper level, we evolve. We are not static. We discover new tactics. It may take longer than my lifetime to change the State. It may take six hundred years. But it will happen.'

'I see. Essentially then *you*, or your descendants, decide. And you make your decision based on whatever information manages to filter down to this woodland retreat. That's a big burden of responsibility, Angus. You have appointed yourself both judge and executioner – an unholy alliance as I am sure your study of history has taught you.'

'It's early days yet,' said Angus evenly. 'And we don't have a final programme worked out. We are learning as we go. We don't have much history yet. So don't try to make me say things that I haven't.'

'Well you haven't really answered my question then. When will the killing end? You must have an answer to that. You must have thought about it. You can't just chop someone's head off and then five minutes later say, "Oh sorry. We've rethought our position in the light of new information. That killing was a regrettable mistake. Sew the head back on and give him a drink of brandy."'

A few people laughed but Angus silenced them with a look. Garlyck continued as though nothing had happened. 'Such a position is daft and dishonest. Are you telling me you started a process of killing and you don't know when to stop?' Angus reddened. But Garlyck pushed on. 'That's the trouble with you theoreticians of violence. You get hold of an idea and you forget about people. You talk about re-assessing the situation, about ideas evolving, about concepts developing. You forget that killing is final. That it is ultimate and for ever. Once it is done it cannot be undone. Though intellectually you might turn somersaults and push yourself round a hundred and eighty degrees so that white becomes black and what was up is now down, there is nothing you can do about the body that lies face-down in the street. 'Course if you've got a conscience, you might feel guilt for what you've done. But you can feel guilt till the cows come home: still there's not a sodding thing you can do to make a

44

dead woman or man sit up and take notice. But there is something even worse . . .' He paused.

'Go on,' said Angus.

'I mean, finally who cares about a vicious little intellectual drowning in his own guilt. What is worse is that violence begets violence. You push the first stone over the headland and soon you have an avalanche. You set an example and others follow. I mean look at you. You are following the Roman state. You say you are opposed to the Romans, but the truth is you have learned from them. You are following them like a sheep following a sheep, and all your bleating about justice and cruelty and terror is not much different from the Romans' bleating about security, civilization and the rest of it. Baa, baa, baa.'

Angus jumped to his feet. 'Don't you bloody say that to me,' he shouted.

Sean put his hand on Angus' arm. 'Away, Captain. It's just a word.'

'Touched a nerve have I?' said Garlyck. 'Has someone else called you a sheep? Are you afraid that people'll think you a coward? No, I know you are not a coward. But is that why you like the killing? Because it makes you feel powerful?'

'No,' said Angus. 'I just don't like being insulted, that's why.'

'Well, I'm not trying to insult you. I like sheep – they do tend to follow one another a bit mindlessly, but that's not their fault. Anyway, my intention is not to insult but to argue with you. I'm sorry.'

Angus sat down. A vein was throbbing in his temple. When Garlyck had uttered those few words 'Baa, baa, baa', all Angus' memories of his fight with Pozzo had come flooding back.

'Continue,' said Angus.

'Right,' said Garlyck. 'So there's the first reason for rejecting your notion of killing – it is just more of the same. You and the policies you advocate are just another aspect of the thing you pretend to oppose. A bit silly, finally, isn't it? Anyway, enough said, moving on.' Garlyck looked out of the window for a few moments gathering his thoughts. 'There's something very seductive about violence, isn't there. Believe me I know. You can get hooked on it like on a drug. Of course you deny it – we'll deny anything if we don't want to believe it. To my mind, violence is just another face of power, and power is the most corrosive force on the face of this earth. If you want to know what a man or woman is like, put power in their hands and watch what they do. And that is why I am watching you, Angus. You are a great man and in so many ways a good man, but you are a very dangerous man too – and that is why I am here.'

'What do you mean?'

'I'm not dangerous – well, not in the same way as you are – except to people like you, to powerful people who always want to tell other people what to do. I'm here to hobble you.'

'What?'

'You heard. I'm here to tell you that your whole notion of the Dragon Warriors is rubbish, that it'll end in disaster and misery. It is based on faulty reasoning, and though it may make you feel good for a while, it will achieve nothing. Do you really think the Roman state will totter because you ride out on your Dragon? Of course it won't. All you'll do is get the Romans riled up and then they'll come hunting more prisoners. No, if you want to defeat them you've got to be more radical and far more imaginative.'

'I suppose you've got a better idea?' said Angus.

'A better idea? Yes. But it's not the kind of idea that'll please you.'

'So try me. Come on.'

'All right, Angus. I'll try to explain. But let's sit down. Let's talk like honest men. Let's argue as hard as we can, but at the end of the day let's drink to a truce because neither of us knows the whole truth. And if we're honest men that should be enough. OK?' Garlyck paused and looked round. 'We have an audience of intelligent observers who cannot be fooled. They can be frightened, but they cannot be fooled. Let's let them be the judge. Fair enough?'

Despite himself Angus grinned. 'Fair enough,' he said, glancing round the motley crew. Intelligence was not the quality that would have first sprung to his mind in trying to describe them. But then Angus noticed that everyone was paying attention. There was quickness about their eyes, an interest, a shrewdness even. Angus wondered just what made the difference. He was aware that people looked away when he talked about his grand

46

plans. 'So what do you propose we do at the end of our debate? Do we have a vote, or what?' he asked.

'Well we can have a vote to see what people are thinking. But let's not pretend that a simple majority gives one of us a mandate. Either I convince everyone or I fail. Either you convince everyone, or you fail. And if neither of us succeeds then we have stalemate. And that means we keep on talking.'

'Sounds like a lot of talk.'

'Oh it is. But how much better to talk than to do something wrong. Shall I begin?'

Angus nodded. 'I'm waiting. What's your "better" idea?' he said.

Garlyck sat down opposite him. He cleared his throat. 'Well, the first thing we have to do if we want to be truly radical is to imagine a new universe with different rules ... Nothing too grand you understand, but something that we can all agree is desirable. Our task will then be to see what we have to do to move from where we are now to where we want to be. Strange as it may seem, if you want to overthrow the Roman state the first thing you have to do is stop worrying about trying to overthrow it. Because the more you worry about it, the less chance you have of succeeding.'

Angus glanced round the small assembly and shook his head.

Garlyck did not pause. 'Now let's keep things simple. Let's imagine this new universe I'm talking about has just got two rules. The first rule is this. "Don't kill people." Pretty simple, eh?'

'And what's the second rule?'

'"Seek happiness." And that's not so simple. You see by and large we've never been told much about happiness. We don't know what it is. Happiness occurs when we're not thinking about it. Happiness happens when we are just being and if we think about it too much we run the danger of destroying it. But we can see happiness in others. We can see it in old women when they are teaching their grandchildren how to knead dough. We can see it in children when for a moment they stop and let the newness of the world flood into them. We can see happiness in you, Angus, when you're down on your back under your Dragon, black with oil and swearing at a piece of machinery

47

. . . but when you take that piece of machinery out, you handle it with such care and love.'

Angus grunted. 'Come on, get a move on. So how does being happy help you get rid of the Roman state?'

'Well. Happiness is a bit like a drug. When you are in it you don't want to leave. You see when you are happy you are actually really living, and any other state is less than living. Sometimes we get trapped by thinking in dualities: high, low; big, little; happy, sad. But sadness is not the opposite of happiness. In fact, when you think about it, sadness can be a part of being happy for it completes the picture . . . it is just an emotion. Happiness can embrace sadness. Hasn't it ever struck you that sometimes you can be sad for no reason . . . well that's just your body getting rid of a bit of vapour, that's all. And if you are happy, then the sadness passes away like the mist does in the morning.'

'So how does it help us get rid of the Roman state?'

'Because when you are happy, the Roman state ceases to matter. And when you stop caring for something it'll soon start to wither. Stop caring for yourself and you'll die. Stop giving the Roman state your energy and it'll die.'

'Ignore it and it'll go away you mean.'

'Not quite. Ignoring it can be a deliberate act and that will give it energy. But happiness is a creative act and happiness starves badness.'

'Rubbish. All that is necessary for the forces of evil to triumph is for a few good men to do nothing.'

'But we're not doing nothing. We're being happy.'

Angus scratched his head. 'You're bloody barmy you are. I can see it now. There you are on a hillside, being happy looking at a tree or a sunset or something, and some Roman squaddie comes up behind you and says, "What are you doing, sunshine?" And you say, "I'm being happy thank you." And then he smiles and chops your bloody head off.'

'Well he might. Then again he might not. He might scratch his head, like you are doing. He might think, "I wonder what this guy's talking about? I wonder why this guy's not afraid of me? I wonder what this guy's seeing and what I'm not seeing?" And you know, Angus, asking questions is the start of all learning. Once your squaddie starts asking questions, he's on his way.'

'A clever answer.'

'A true one.'

'So come on. What do you do when a soldier wants to stab you? Do you just sit down and let it happen? Bullshit you do.'

'I've faced this. More than once.'

'And . . . ?'

'And once I killed.'

'Ah . . .'

'And I knew I'd destroyed something in myself when I did it. But Angus, I think there is a difference between the man who fights to protect himself and the man who sets out to kill? I've touched the limits of my tolerance and felt myself sweep over. I'm a man like you. I can feel anger. I don't claim to be good or noble or . . . I just want to tell you, the man who turns and kills when he has a choice not to, damages himself and violates another.'

'There are some men who are happy when they are killing,' said Angus, suddenly defensive for Garlyck's words had again reminded him of his last confrontation with Pozzo. Angus had turned back. Angus had killed when he didn't have to.

'No,' said Garlyck. 'That I have never seen. And I have stood in the torture chambers of the Caligula. I have watched the torturers and there is one thing I can tell you. They are, without exception, consumed with self-hatred. They are at the furthest remove from happiness. And they know it. They are trapped. And they will turn to anything – booze or clever arguments – to escape that knowledge or justify themselves.'

For a moment Angus had no reply.

'You see, Angus, men like you, men who will contemplate killing as a solution, are finally stupid. I'm sorry to put it so bluntly. You may be very clever, but finally you are stupid because you place argument before truth. You manipulate abstractions and you forget that you are human. To be human is the measure of all things. Any man can be reduced to a killer. That is not difficult. Starve him. Pervert him. Beat him. Strip him of dignity. Isolate him. But do not think that because men can be made into beasts they are beasts in their nature. What

49

is the best of humanity that you can imagine? Eh? Start from there and put that into your new universe.'

Silence.

For the first time Angus had a glimmering of what Garlyck was driving at – but it was a truth he did not want to accept. 'So have you finished?' he asked.

'For the moment,' said Garlyck. 'You can only say so much of these things before you reach the limit of words. I've said enough for the moment. But I've only just begun, Angus.'

Perol had been following the discussion closely. 'Well I think we've all had enough talking for today,' she said. 'Now are we going to have a vote, or what?'

'Er . . . what are we going to vote on?' asked Sean.

Everyone looked round waiting for someone else to speak. Finally Garlyck said, 'Angus and I only differ about the means. We both want to get rid of the Roman state. Let's simply vote on whether us Dragon Warriors should go on as we are as Angus wants or whether us Dragon Warriors should work on some new ideas. OK?'

Everyone nodded.

Angus frowned. He felt the initiative had been wrested from him but there was nothing he could do. 'So who is for action?' he said and raised his arm.

There was a pause and then Sean and Perol lifted their hands. They were followed by Wallace Duff, Betsy, Ada, Ruth, June and Estelle. Two of the children giggled behind their hands and then voted.

'Eleven,' pronounced Garlyck after carefully counting. 'Now who thinks we need a new idea?' He raised his hand.

For a few moments he was the only one and then Deric the Lame after a guilty look at Angus lifted his hand. Peter the Scribe followed him and then Gargamelle and Edna. Lastly, two of the people who had been driven witless by life in the Caligula raised their hands eagerly as though they had been offered sweets. The child that had been asleep on Gargamelle's lap woke up and copied her, lifting one hand while rubbing his eyes with the other. No one else voted.

Angus counted loudly, pointing at each voter in turn. 'Eight.'

'You win,' said Garlyck. 'But remember, a majority isn't a

mandate. So this means that we go on talking. We are divided.'

Angus groaned, but before he could say anything Drummer stood up and beat his drum in a series of bright hard taps. Drummer could not stand to his full height in the room and so had to stoop and this gave him a terrifying ape-like appearance. 'Hey, Ang-oos. You good wolf-killa, man. But we're not wolves, eh? You wear wolf-skin not rat-skin. We're not rats, eh? We're . . .' and at this point Drummer lapsed into his own old language for he did not have the words. Sean listened keenly for he had been trying to learn some of the old tongue. As Drummer spoke he nodded, catching the drift. Drummer finished speaking and hit his wooden drum with his hard horny knuckles. He turned to Sean and jabbed him with a finger the size of a child's arm. 'You tell them what Drummer say.'

'I'll do my best.' Sean faced the assembly. Some of the children, frightened by Drummer, were crying and had sought safety under the table or in the arms of the men and women. 'So what Drummer is saying is that we have the heart of a bear and the eyes of a hawk, the hunger of the tiger and the cunning of the fox – but we are more than all of this. We have this . . .' Sean pointed at his head, 'and this.' He pointed to his heart. 'We are half-way to the gods.' Sean paused. 'I'm not quite sure I know what he's talking about, Captain, but I rather have the impression he distrusts politics.' Drummer beamed and beat his drum. And then he stretched his arms wide and roared like a beast, showing his yellow teeth. Finally he ran straight at the open window and dived through. Outside he landed and rolled and then ran away under the trees. 'And I think he's trying to tell us we've done enough talking for the day,' concluded Sean.

Clearly everyone agreed with Drummer. People stood up and with a sudden eruption of conversation made their way outdoors and back to whatever occupation pleased them most: Wallace Duff and Edna set off for the machine-shop where they were stripping down a generator, Eric the Lame with Betsy, Ruth, Ada and June went back to the gardens and Peter the Scribe joined Estelle and the others at the playground, for though he could no longer see to write, he had a fund of stories and was a great favourite with the children.

Finally Garlyck and Angus were left facing one another. Perol

51

and Gargamelle remained too, Perol with her hand resting lightly on Angus' arm.

Angus was caught in a dilemma. He didn't know what to say and his face was screwed up in thought as he stared at Garlyck. One side of Angus wanted to reach out and punch Garlyck, but the other side, the side he had developed during the time he was at Roscius' Academy, couldn't help but respect the mind of the man facing him. *Why are there so many clever people in the world?* he thought. *Just when I think I've got things sorted out along comes – a problem.* Angus could feel the heat of Garlyck's enthusiasm and vaguely sense the vastness of the idea that had been presented to him. Finally, he banged his fists down on the table, stood up and walked out. 'You coming?' he called to Perol.

'I'll stay,' she said. 'I've a few things to say to this one.'

'Suit yourself,' said Angus, and was gone.

Angus did what he always did when he felt confused: he climbed a tall tree. There, perched among the top branches, he stared out over the forest canopy and tried to think. He knew he had been challenged by Garlyck, but this was not like a normal challenge where two stags lock antlers and puff and bellow until one retreats, this was altogether softer and stronger, and he did not know what to make of it.

It was while sitting there in the tall tree that he heard the branches below him creak. Moments later the giant hairy form of Drummer heaved itself up beside him. The rich feral smell of Drummer – a smell of dung, compost and wood-gum – engulfed Angus. It was like being wrapped in a sack that had been trampled in a stable. Angus realized that Drummer had been running in the forest, burning off the energy that had accumulated like water in a bucket while he had been sitting still.

'Ang-oos,' said Drummer. 'You look sad, man.'

'In which case I must be happy,' said Angus, 'according to our enlightened philosopher friend down there.'

Drummer shook his head. 'Drummer not understand.' Then he pointed downwards. 'Him Garlyck. Hey, him one tough bugger, eh? Goooood man.' This was said with such a simple frankness that Angus was caught completely off-guard. 'Good

52

man to have at your back when wolves come calling, eh.' Drummer nudged Angus and grinned. 'Drummer know. Drummer see these things.'

'He's a problem,' said Angus. 'To me he is.'

'Ah,' said Drummer, and he tore off a twig and began to pick his teeth. 'Tell Drummer.'

Below, in the dining-room Perol sat opposite Garlyck. She was in a tumult. So much of what Garlyck had said had touched her. She'd voted with Angus of course – how could she not – but yet the young man Garlyck had opened her eyes to something new, something she realized she'd been wanting to hear. Now she sat and stared, aware of the processes at work inside her, aware also of the new life that had started within her. This was something else that she had not told Angus: she was by her own calculation two months pregnant – it could be longer – but, with all the ups and downs of the past few weeks, she had not found the right moment to tell him.

'Where do you come from?' she asked finally.

Garlyck shrugged. 'No idea,' he said. 'The Caligula. That was my home. I was born in the Caligula. I grew up there. That's all I know.'

'Tell me. Tell me about your life. Tell me a bit. You are a very strange man.'

'Anyone who grew up in the Caligula's bound to be a bit strange,' said Garlyck. 'But if you were to ask me, I'd say I'm quite ordinary. And I don't know anything about my background. I was told once that a woman gave birth prematurely in the torture rooms. That was me. The guards didn't know what was happening when I came slithering out. Somehow I survived. Believe me, strange things happened in the Caligula. I don't think my mother did though. I was handed on from mother to mother, father to father. That became my early years. The farewells as parents departed for the Battle Dome. The arrival of new parents. They came in numb and stunned and looking for courage and something to love. I was always there. I grew up torn between misery and love. It seemed normal, and of course I was useful in the prison. One of my jobs was to swab out the Schoolroom with disinfectant. I dug holes in the

53

ground outside. Sometimes I worked in the kitchen. There was always work to do.'

'Where did you live?'

'When I was little I had a small place with sacks on the floor between the coal store and the dog kennels.' Perol's face wrinkled. 'Hey. It was a palace. I loved it. Warm in winter when the fires were on. Plenty of food, they fed the dogs well. I learned to talk Dog before I learned to talk any other language.'

'Did you work for the guards?'

Garlyck looked at Perol closely. 'If you are asking me did I help torture anyone, the answer is yes.'

'What changed you?'

'I began to ask questions. You see I didn't understand any-thing. First I thought I was just a lump of coal. Then I thought I was a dog. Then I thought I was a bellows for blowing up a fire. It was a big day for me when I discovered I was me. And then I started asking questions. Can you imagine what a strange school the Caligula was? Everything was back to front. Love and hate, clean and dirty. See, that's when I began to doubt opposites.'

'But where did you learn ... all your ideas? You seem so confident. I've never known anyone shut Angus up before.'

'I never went to a proper school. But I listened. There is a lot of talk in prison. People reaching their end always want to pass on what they know. And I saw a lot. It does strange things to you, watching people in pain. You can feel a cry go right through you, like a knife, and come out the other side. You get so you can smell fear, taste grief, touch anger ... all your senses become different. You see the dead, and they are pathetic – just lumps of meat: and you see the living, and they are so wonderful, full of ... I didn't know what to call it, life, spirit. And the guards! They were sick in every way and finally I didn't know who to pity, the victim or the gaoler. And then ...' Garlyck paused and grinned at Perol. 'I'm going to disappoint you, I'm afraid. I think you want to discover something profound, but I have nothing profound to offer.'

'Go on,' said Perol. 'Disappoint me. "And then ..."' she prompted.

'And then I started to listen to a new voice. A different voice, a voice that was inside me. It was me talking to me. And it made me independent. Suddenly the Caligula didn't contain me. I started to act on my own, think on my own, helping people when I could. That was very instructive. You see when you do something, other people react, and you can watch their reactions. You learn a lot about them. I gave a starving prisoner an extra potato and I was tortured.'

Perol's eyes narrowed. 'You were?'

'Yes. Many times. Do you think my hair is this colour naturally?' He grinned his crooked grin. 'Ah were a bonny lad once,' he said affecting a thick accent. 'But somehow they just couldn't bring themselves to kill me. They kept me, like some people keep old boot-laces or razor-blades in a tin.'

Perol grinned and shook her head. The more Garlyck talked the more he became an enigma. 'You were tortured?'

'Yes. But it is no good asking me what it was like because I can't remember. I can only remember the colours.'

There was a long pause while Perol absorbed this thought. 'How old are you?' she asked finally.

'No idea.'

'Twenty? Twenty-five? Thirty?'

'Older I think. Much older. But I don't think years have got much to do with it. I've always been there in the Caligula. That's the only world I know. Everything else I've discovered by looking out through other people's eyes.'

'So what do you think you'll do now, now that we've demolished the Caligula? I have the impression you're not too keen on the Dragon Warriors.'

Garlyck shook his head. 'Well you know that's a funny thing. I quite like the Dragon Warriors. It could be quite a good organization. Someone's got to look after the kids and the ones who can't look after themselves and Angus is pretty good at caring if he lets himself. I think Angus has got his thinking all arse about backwards, but I like him. He's so full of anger you could boil a kettle on him sometimes. The way I see it, Angus needs me. He doesn't know it yet, but he needs my help. So I think I'll be his shadow for a while.' Garlyck stood up and stretched. 'And now if you'll excuse me, I'm going for a walk. Even us shadows need to take a leak now and then.'

'One last thing,' said Perol hurriedly. 'Why are you called Garlyck?'

'That's easy. I used to nick cloves of garlic from the kitchen and distribute them to the prisoners to suck on like sweets. Then they'd rub the spittle on their wounds. It's a great little plant. Lovely smell. Hundreds of uses. Give it a go. You never know, maybes the little one you're carrying'll get a taste for it too.'

'How did . . . ?' But Garlyck was gone.

Perol was left wondering. She looked at her figure – as far as she could see she was little different. Nothing showed. And she hadn't told anyone. Not even rude-tongued Gargamelle who'd been a dancing-girl before she became too fat and who now was looking at her as though to say, 'I knew all along.' *Must be male intuition*, Perol decided. Then she laughed. There was something very comic in the idea of Angus needing Garlyck. She wondered what Angus would have said if he'd been a fly on the wall and had heard their conversation.

Gargamelle shifted her bulk and spoke for the first time. 'Have you told Angus yet?'

'No.'

'Well you'd better.' Then she cackled. 'Tell him there's a new little Dragon Warrior on the way.'

That night in bed, Perol wrapped her arms round Angus and cuddled him tight. He was grumpy and ill at ease but couldn't say what was wrong. They made love, and afterwards, when Angus was almost asleep, Perol whispered, 'I'm going to have a baby.' She felt Angus come awake in her arms. He turned until they were almost touching noses.

'Eh? You're what?'

'Going to have a baby. That's not a problem, is it?'

Silence.

'No. Of course not,' said Angus finally. 'It's not a problem. It's just . . .' and there he had to leave off, for he didn't know what to think. Small bombs had begun exploding round his world, changing its shape completely.

3   In Memoriam

The Caligula camp had attained a certain beauty. The blackened stumps of masonry sticking up from the low heather had already been colonized by numerous trailing plants and lichen – they had achieved the timelessness of all ruins, at home in the wild windy landscape. But now, standing up in the middle of what had once been the inner courtyard leading to the prisoners' cages was a new monument, its outline stiff and angular, but its colour and detail hidden beneath a shroud of red silk that rippled in the morning breeze.

Drawn up in close formation facing the monument was a detachment of the Imperial Guard in their best dress uniform. To one side were buglers, their instruments twinkling in the sunlight, their helmets securely buckled under their chins, and at the foot of the monument, his hand resting on a wooden lectern, was the imposing stern figure of Marcus Augustus Ulysses. A fire burned close by, its flames erratic in the wind so that white-robed priests were kept busy making sure that the ashes did not get scattered.

The occasion was a dedication. Marcus Ulysses, as acting Praefectus Comitum, had decided not to rebuild the Caligula – other prisons could serve the needs of the Battle Dome and certainly one closer to Eburacum would be more convenient. Instead he had decided to declare the site a memorial park, to be tended and protected like an outpost of civilization amid the wild heather. Waiting behind the nearby tumuli were gardeners with their heavy equipment, trucks of soil and selected shrubs. Such parks were common throughout the Empire, marking places of particular importance, battlefields and the like.

Marcus Ulysses' address was almost ended. '. . . and so, in memory of the men and women who served here, I hereby dedicate the Caligula Memorial Park to be a reminder for all times of the . . .' At this moment a gust of wind carried the last page of his speech away and sent it dancing over the ruins and up into the blue and white patched sky. Marcus Ulysses watched it go and then drew himself up tall. 'To be a reminder for all times,' he concluded forcefully, and nodded to the leader of the buglers who had been following his own copy. The leader put his bugle to his lips and blew a single clear note, high, loud and shimmering. The others joined in a fanfare after which there was a moment of silence while the notes faded and the priests dropped incense into the flames. The air was pungent with the aromatic smoke. Then old Ulysses tugged a scarlet rope and the silk drape covering the monument flapped and fell away. It was quickly gathered by attendants before it too could vanish over the moors. Revealed was an obelisk of polished black marble. At its top was a large bust, an idealized portrait of Emperor Lucius, staring blank-eyed and pitiless across the moor. Below the head was incised writing, brightened with gold, which told a brief history of the Caligula camp.

Marcus Ulysses stepped down and this signalled the end of the ceremony. Orders were shouted. The Imperial Guard broke ranks and marched away. The priests dowsed the fire. Attendants began clearing away the camp chairs while the gardeners powered up their machines.

Marmellius Caesar, as old Ulysses' deputy, stood for a moment staring up at the black obelisk. 'Fine words, Marcus. Good words.' He wiped a tear from his eye. 'Damned smoke.'

Marcus nodded. 'Now, Marmellius, we have a busy day. More inspection. I've received a report from the foreman in charge of building the holding camp up in the hills. They're well ahead of schedule. Thought you'd like to see it with me. I remember you have an interest in such things. I tried to get Calpurnia too, but she's indisposed. Come on. Let's get out of this damned wind.'

The two men hurried to a small but well-appointed flyer which stood ready at a rebuilt transit station not far from the new park. Emblazoned on its side was the insignia of the Emperor.

Behind them the gardeners moved out. Soon the rough heather would be smoothed, the ruins would be cleaned and trees, well staked, would be planted out. To preserve the view, the tumuli would be bulldozed flat.

*

Marmellius stood to one side to let the senior man climb up the ramp and into the flyer. Over the weeks during which they had worked together, Marmellius' relations with Marcus Ulysses had undergone a subtle change. He had moved from a position of deep distrust to a grudging admiration. Marmellius was no fool, he saw the vanity and the deviousness of the Ulysses, but he also saw the man's energy and sadness. Had he been in possession of all the facts, had he been able to sit in on some of the Ulysses' private conversations with the Emperor, he would have been outraged. But as it was, he saw an old man trying to do a difficult job. He considered Marcus Augustus Ulysses old-fashioned in his thinking, but he couldn't hold that against him. Where Marmellius Caesar and Marcus Ulysses were in complete agreement was in their belief that the interests of their families were synonymous with the interests of the province.

Marcus heaved himself into the ship and took his seat. Moments later Marmellius joined him and the flyer went through its uncomplicated departure procedures. As the most important man in Britannia, Marcus Ulysses' flight took precedence over all others. The flyer slid smoothly up the power gradient and joined the small sky-road which linked the Caligula camp to the main roads. The pilot and navigator had their instructions and could be heard defining their route to the central road-monitors who made sure their way was clear. Soon they had descended from the moors and were gliding through the deep forest. They passed within a few miles of the supply depot at Castra Skusa where the drums of liquid phlogiston and Cretan fire water stood ready. A few minutes later they joined the sky-road which connected Eburacum with Derventio and after some brief pitching and tossing as they moved from the charge of one road-monitor to another they came to a vast intersection and headed south. They flew past the large state farms which supplied Eburacum. Looking out they could see the elegant villas bordering the River Ouse and then, further back, the rough green wall of the interminable forest.

'And how is the Emperor?' asked Marmellius after several minutes' silence.

'Seems well. Still preoccupied with this damned pestilence. The gods show no mercy. At least he's able to say that he is doing something. But it keeps the pressure on us of course.'

Marmellius nodded, 'And what of the Emperor's plans for Aegyptus, are they advanced?'

Marcus laughed. 'No idea. I doubt he has much time to think about his pleasure garden.'

Both men settled back to enjoy the short journey south of Eburacum and up into the Pennine hills, but they were interrupted by a spate of messages transmitted to them from the Imperial Palace at Eburacum. Most were for Marmellius and were concerned with routine administrative matters, but one message made him sit forward. It was from the Chief of Gate Security in Eburacum and read:

File 127B XXV

A man and a woman, both now identified as escapees from the Caligula camp, were apprehended this morning by a routine security patrol, close to State Farm 52. Both were suffering from exposure and starvation and the man died before he could be brought to Eburacum for questioning.

Under interrogation, the woman stated that they had both been captured and held at a camp in the forest by a man she identified by the name Angus. She also, several times, mentioned a dragon in connection with the attack on the Caligula camp. No further details are available. The woman is suffering from concussion and has multiple abrasions, the result of a fall in the forest. She is not expected to survive.

The mention of a dragon is significant and led me to forward this report to you.

Awaiting further orders.

Marmellius read the report and then handed the paper to Marcus who frowned as he read.

'Angus,' said old Ulysses. 'Wasn't that the name of the mechanic fellow who stole my Dragon?'

'I believe it was.'

'Mmm . . .'course, people say anything under interrogation. They say what they think you want to hear. Even so . . . Order her to be kept safe. No duress. We'll look into the matter later. Find out where they're keeping her.'

Marcus' words were mild and did not reveal the sudden tumult he felt. It was not the mention of the Dragon that had excited him, but the possible link to his son Viti. However, he'd been excited before, and had learned patience. Privately he decided to visit the woman in person that day, as soon as they got back from the visit to the holding camp.

Their vehicle turned west from the expressway and began to travel more slowly. They were again on a small road and travelled at a height just under the forest canopy. Eventually this road terminated at a military depot in the hills and here Marcus and Marmellius disembarked.

A surface transport craft was waiting for them, and this would carry them up into the hills, beyond the trees, to the building site.

'Do you have a name for the camp?' asked Marmellius, settling into the cushions.

'Camp Lucius,' said Marcus Ulysses without hesitation. 'Has a nice ring to it, don't you think? A sense of optimism.'

Two hours later, after a lurching ride, they reached the top of a hill and pulled up at the Camp Lucius reception centre. Waiting for them was the officer in charge of construction. They climbed out of the cramped and stuffy vehicle and breathed the fresh air. The scenery about them was not unlike the moors, but was gentler and the air was filled with the smell of wild flowers. After greetings, the officer led them inside the reception centre where refreshments were waiting.

This was a spacious building which still had the smell of sawdust about it. It was built of white pine and the planks had been rubbed with linseed oil until they had a deep honey-coloured sheen. In the centre was a large dining area surrounded by a balcony. Bedrooms led from the balcony. The rafters were exposed.

Marmellius was impressed. He had not expected anything so well designed and elegant. 'And the Emperor is paying for all this?' he asked quietly.

Marcus grinned, winked and nodded. 'I thought we might turn it into a hunting lodge later.'

The most prominent feature in the dining-room was a large window which gave a panoramic view of the hills to the east. Directly below them were the buildings of Camp Lucius. An area of several acres had been cleared and was defined by watch-towers and an electric fence.

The place was a hive of activity. Platoons of soldiers were moving about, shifting timber, erecting walls, laying drains, sur-veying roads, shifting rock. A mason's shop had been set up and there the local stone was being shaped into blocks for roads. In another quarter was a smithy which belched black smoke.

Despite the activity, there was no sense of confusion and the plan of the camp could be easily understood. It had been designed on the familiar pattern of a barracks. Separate oblong huts joined by neat walkways were formed into units of ten, and at the centre of each unit was a larger building which would serve as a communal washing place, latrine, kitchen and dining-hall. The different units were separated from one another by high fences.

While no one could call the accommodation elegant, it looked substantial, in no way temporary and altogether larger than Marmellius had expected. He expressed his surprise to Marcus who merely shrugged. 'We don't know how many of them we have to house here, and the Emperor wants them in good shape for his building project. To be honest, Marmellius, I don't care. If this is what the Emperor wants, so be it. It's no skin off my nose. Anyway, the plans were drawn up by architects from Italia. Not to my taste, but there we are. And as for their being solid, well, we're looking at a seven year plan, remember. We don't want something that blows down after the first winter gale.' With that Marmellius had to be content. What Marcus had not revealed to him was that the buildings they were looking at were intended to become accommodation for shearing gangs and meat processing workers as soon as the burning programme was under way. He and the Emperor had considered the plans carefully.

The chefs at Camp Lucius had done their best to provide a banquet. Marcus dined and wined well. He insisted on visiting the kitchens after the meal to compliment the chefs personally. Then it was time to visit the huts. The officer in charge drove them down to a small vehicle park, beyond which they had to walk.

Again Marmellius marvelled at the care that was being taken with the construction. The huts were family quarters! There was a play area for children. There were even small gardens planned and the officer took pride in explaining how the camp could be more or less self-supporting in vegetables and how he intended to establish machine workshops and install windmills to pump water. The man was a visionary.

But Marmellius was baffled. 'Surely too well appointed for a transit camp,' he said to Marcus as soon as they had a few moments alone.

'That's what I thought when I first saw the plans,' said Marcus. 'But look at it this way. I'm sure we can put the place to good use at the end of the project. I could certainly use some of those huts on my estates. And I'm sure you could too. They can all be disassembled. Don't worry, man. If the Emperor is paying, who are we to complain?'

'But he does not have a reputation as a kind man or a considerate one. Are you asking me to believe he has provided this standard of accommodation for savages? I mean, those huts make our barracks look like slums.'

Marcus shrugged. He had not expected this close level of questioning.

'Are you sure he's not trying to pull a fast one?' asked Marmellius.

'Like what?'

'Like . . . I don't know. It just doesn't make sense, that's all.'

Marcus forced a laugh. 'You have a suspicious mind, Gnaeus Marmellius Caesar.'

'I inherited it from my grandfather.'

Marcus decided to play the innocent. 'Well I don't have the same fears you have. I don't see anything sinister in all this. To be frank, I think old Lucius was probably far too busy with domestic problems and with protecting his backside from the likes of Trismagister Neptuna. He probably told an architect to draw something up and left it at that. This is some fancy architect's dream-child. It is not a realistic solution to a problem and you are giving yourself fears without reason.' He paused to see how Marmellius was receiving his words. 'But . . . well, if I can't convince you, I'll take the matter up with Lucius next time I get a chance to talk to him. Or you can talk to him yourself if you like.'

'My fears were for your ears only,' said Marmellius hurriedly. 'You are right. Perhaps I am a bit too jumpy.'

'No. No. No. I'll talk to him and I'll find out, without giving any names. You leave it with me. You've made me curious now.' Marcus stared at the younger man seriously.

And Marmellius smiled. 'I would be grateful, Marcus. We can't be too careful.'

And there the matter was left.

A short time later they climbed aboard their vehicle, thanked the officer in charge for his hospitality, and departed down the hill.

Arriving in Eburacum, Marcus lost no time in contacting the senior gate warden. He discovered where the woman from the Caligula camp was being held and arranged to visit her in person.

An hour later he was underground, marching down one of the corridors which connected the different underground security stations. The woman had been transferred to a small military hospital near Foss Island.

The door clanged open and the Ulysses entered.

He saw a frail emaciated shape on the bed. The face was gaunt. The eyes were huge and stared up at him dully. The head was bandaged. There was no evidence of breasts and the arms which lay on the cover were thin and skeletal. He could no longer call this a woman.

A doctor was waiting at the bedside and saw Ulysses' look of astonishment.

'We think they ate some herbs or berries in the forest. They were starving but they chose the wrong food. It was toxic. It dehydrated them.'

'Surely there's plenty of water in the—'

'No. No. I mean physical dehydration. When the body

can't retain fluids. Internal bleeding, diarrhoea, that kind of thing.'

Marcus raised his hand. He had heard enough. 'Can she hear us?'

'She can. But whether she understands . . .'

Old Ulysses pulled up a chair close to the woman's bed. 'Can you hear me?' he asked, speaking slowly. The figure blinked again. 'Tell me, this camp you were in, was it run by a man called Angus?'

There was a pause and then the head nodded briefly, and a whispery voice said, 'Angus. Big man.'

'Was anyone else with him?'

'Black woman. Perol. She . . .' The voice faded away.

Marcus looked at the doctor and the doctor shrugged as if to say the woman could be raving.

'No. No. Not a woman, a man. Not a tall man. A young man. With dark hair. Very strong.'

The figure stared at the ceiling for a long time and her chest lifted fitfully. 'Sean,' she said finally.

Marcus frowned. 'Shorn?' he said. 'What does that mean?'

'Could be a name,' offered the doctor. 'Could be something to do with his appearance.'

'Funny name for a man,' muttered Marcus and he returned his attention to the woman. 'This . . . er . . . Shorn. Was he a Roman?'

The woman coughed. As she coughed her head nodded. Then she whispered, 'Strange . . . accent. Him and Drummer. Strange talking. Face like a tree-root. Drummer.'

'Drummer? Who's Drummer?' But there was no answer. The woman had drifted away. The eyes closed. 'Wake up,' said the Ulysses, poking the bone of the shoulder. 'Tell me about the Dragon. Did you see a dragon?'

No response. Old Ulysses looked at the doctor pleadingly. 'This is worse than no news. Will she survive to tell her story?' he asked, standing up.

'Hard to tell. I don't know what's keeping her alive now. She may not see out the night. We have incense burning and the moon is favourable, full tonight, but she has not taken any food, and the concussion . . .'

'Well if she does come to her senses, I want to be the first to know. All right?'

'Yes sir.'

'And see if you can find out a bit more more about this Shorn fellow and this Drummer – could be a sort of adjutant . . . oh yes, and ask about the dragon . . . I know it all sounds like nonsense, but we have to follow what clues we can.'

'I understand, sir.'

'Keep her alive.' With that the old Ulysses left the hospital room. He was conducted up to the office of the chief gate warden.

'Commander,' said Marcus Ulysses, 'I want your forces to go on special alert. Double the security at the city gates. Find any more of the escaped prisoners that might be wandering about. Use whatever spies you have. Find what this camp is. And where. Move with caution. We don't want to give the game away – that we're on to them. I have reason to believe that my son may be being held prisoner, by this Angus and someone called a Drummer.'

'Yes sir.'

'But don't rush things. If my son is in there, I want to catch him this time.'

'Yes sir.'

There matters were left.

It was late when Marcus returned to the Imperial Palace.

He was confused. For a moment, while listening to the woman he had seen in his mind's eye a vivid image of his son's face – a bit of a beard, his hair long – and speaking with a strong accent. But what was all this about a drum or a drummer? Marcus shook his head. 'Dark things move 'neath the dark, dark trees,' he said, quoting an old poem that he had learned from his nurse.

Tiredly he pulled the communication console towards him.

Minutes later he heard the energetic voice of Emperor Lucius. 'Hello, Marcus. A bit late for you, isn't it?'

Marcus groaned inwardly. *Doesn't the bugger ever sleep?* he thought. Then he said, 'Yes, it is a bit late, but I thought you'd like the good news. Went to the transit camp today with young Marmellius. Excellent progress.'

The Emperor Lucius Prometheus had many gifts not the least of which was a fine intuition which enabled him to sense feeling which lay beneath words.

'To hell with the transit camp. You sound tired, Marcus, and worried. Has something happened? Have you had news of your son?'

Marcus was astonished by the directness of the question. But it shook something loose in him. 'Well, to be honest . . .' And then the story just tumbled out: the woman, the camp, the young man Shorn . . . And he spoke of his hopes, for in the journey back to the Imperial Palace, he had begun to let his hopes grow, imagining the wild face of his son under the trees. But he pulled himself back. 'Nothing is certain of course, but I have this feeling, gut feeling if you like, that it was Viti the woman was talking about.'

'And you must always trust those feelings,' said the Emperor. 'I always do – saved my bacon many a time, and look where I am now. So listen. If you do catch up with him, be easy with him, man. Be proud of him. Clasp him to you. Give him wine and not a lecture. Then send him out here to Roma to spend a few weeks with me. A bit of real sunshine will soon bake the mildew out of him. I'll see he has a good time and send him home a new man. Remember, you asked me to care for him if anything happened to you. Well that will be my pleasure.'

Marcus felt a surge of gratitude. The Emperor had spoken to his deepest hopes. 'I will,' he said. 'I will.'

'Now tell us about the transit camp and that milksop Marmellius.'

Marcus helped himself to a glass of wine and then launched into a description of the day. He dwelt on Marmellius' suspicions. 'I think he's beginning to trust me, but still he thinks that something strange is going on,' he concluded.

The Emperor laughed. 'Well I must give him more credit. And as for you, my dear Marcus, I think you handled the matter brilliantly. You make me sound like a bungling philanthropist. Ha! I like it. But what this all means is that we must move quickly. I suggest you put Marmellius in charge of investigating this hideaway in the woods you've been telling me about. That'll take his mind off things. And if he does discover your son, that's good. If he doesn't, then you can always give him a good dressing down for incompetence. Meanwhile, let us advance our plans. It's high summer now and the camp is nearly ready. OK. We'll begin the round-up at the next full moon. That'll be perfect. Catch the woodlanders by surprise at the beginning of harvest. Given luck we should have them moved into the camp by the end of autumn. That gives us the winter to finalize details. And listen, Marcus. I've had a brilliant idea.'

'What's that?'

'Have you seen any of these new-fangled flying machines? They don't need a magnetic track? Mmm?'

Marcus grunted. 'Don't trust such things,' he said. 'The sky-road is high enough for me. Calpurnia's the one. She likes high flying. She had a crazy bat-like thing she tried out at the Battle Dome. Kept crashing it I remember.'

'That's the kind of thing. Well I think they are very interesting. All the rage in Roma now. I went up in one a while back. I thought they'd be brilliant for spotting.'

'I don't . . .'

'If we'd had these in the old days we could have captured the world in no time. Not much good over forest of course and they can't go very far, but where there's grass, like on your wolds . . .' The Emperor's voice trailed away, waiting to see if he had engendered some excitement in Marcus. He hadn't. 'Ah well. Just a thought. I try to do anything I can to help. I'll send you one over just in case. We mustn't live in the past, Marcus. Mustn't live in the past. That way lies stagnation and death.'

'Talking of which,' said Marcus, hoping to change the subject, 'how is that pestilence that was killing the sheep? Any improvement?'

'Nothing. Terrible. Worse than ever. We rely on imports. And that is why I'm so grateful for the sheep you send me. But that is also why I am keen to press ahead as quickly as I can with our little project. There is no time to waste. I'll send over some of my lads to beef up your forces. They'll help with the mopping up. Remember, Marcus, the Reformed Lupercalia is our deadline. I want the first fires on that day. It'll be a big party. We burn from Eburacum to the sea. *Ciao*.'

Marcus was about to say more, but the contact was ended.

Old Ulysses sat for an hour after the conversation, staring out over the city to where the dark trees rose beyond the city walls. The night was quiet and warm and the full moon lit up the clouds. It could have been a painting.

Marcus was dreaming again. Thinking of Viti. Idly, he held his old hand out into the moonlight to see if he could feel anything. Could he feel the moon? Nothing, neither warm nor cold: just a hard steely light that blanched his hand and brought no comfort.

4 *The Destruction of Stand Alone Stan*

It was a month later, and the same cold moon stared down, casting Miranda's shadow across the dark, shifting water. She was standing on a flat stone a few feet from the water's edge and the cold and the damp made her shiver though the night was warm.

Miranda edged forwards until her toes were in the cold water. She knew there was no retreat. She breathed deeply. She thought of her mother and of the women who were gathered in the darkness round the pool's edge. Watching and waiting in silence.

And she thought of Lyf who stood behind her in the shadows. She could feel his fear.

And if it achieved anything, Lyf's disquiet simply strengthened her resolve.

He had arrived, riding into Stand Alone Stan, two days earlier, his horse flecked with lather. Immediately she was aware of a change in the man. The playfulness was gone, and in its place was an earnestness. Usually Lyf could be relied on for jokes and crude good humour, now his face was drawn and his eyes had a haunted look. But he would not answer questions. He had sat holding Miranda's hands, staring at her, looking into her eyes as though trying to read her in some strange way, insisting that she tell him of her experiences, of her flights in the night and the powers which sometimes possessed her. And at the end of his questioning he spat into the palms of his hands and rubbed his hands together. She did not know what that meant but there was something ominous about it. She remembered seeing men do this before they slaughtered sheep. 'We have run out of time,' said Lyf. 'It is as simple as that. They are coming. They'll be here soon. Everything is breaking up.' Lyf stood then and began pacing. 'If I could see what's to come I would tell you. But I am at the end of my knowledge. A bit of magic, a bit of fun, a bit of bullshit . . .' He paused and then turned to Miranda. 'But what do we do when the laughter stops, eh? What do we do when we deal with men of no reverence?'

'Why are you so angry?' asked Miranda. 'Come back here. Sit down. Tell me.'

But Lyf would not sit. 'So much is incomplete,' he said, still pacing. 'Everything always botched in this life. Only chaos lays careful plans . . . we come running afterwards, unprepared when the time comes.'

'What are you talking about? You are frightening me.'

Lyf paused and took a deep breath. 'We have yet to conduct the Moon Ceremony,' he said slowly. 'I'm not the person for that. Old Mcg would have been the one . . . Gwellan isn't capable . . . There are so few left. Just tired old men and children . . . So I suppose it's got to be me.'

'What Moon Ceremony?'

'Your ceremony. The marriage of Moon and Water. You are not yet complete. Don't you know that?' Suddenly he shouted in anger. 'Grow up, woman. There's no more time to be a child. Take charge. Please.' Miranda saw his fear. For a few moments he stood with his head in his hands. Then when he looked up, he was himself once more and the fear was under control. 'Tomorrow night, Miranda, at the full moon. Stonewater Spring's the place. Gwellan knows it. She'll call the women. We'll all do what we can. I'll come early and get everything ready. Let's hope we have a clear sky and a few lucky stars.'

For a moment there was the ghost of a smile. Two quick paces. He bent over and kissed Miranda. Then he was gone. Minutes later she saw him ride out through the hospital gates, riding the old road that led down to the woods, his cloak flapping.

Miranda watched and was aware as calm spread through her. She had hardly understood a word that he had said, but she had understood everything that mattered. She felt relief, as though bad news, long delayed but always expected, had finally arrived bringing an end to hope and speculation.

Lyf rode deep into the wood. He turned off the path and let the horse pick its way through the trees until he came to his small camp, a cave hidden by bushes.

71

After tending to his horse he crawled into the cave and lit a fire. He brewed tea and then he sat, his arms clasped round his legs, staring into the embers.

Lyf was facing the greatest trial of his life. A few days earlier he had observed the Roman preparations as soldiers fresh from Italia were moved to base camps south of the Wolds. But more importantly, he had received a vision of his own death. The prospect of the pain terrified him. And he could not see beyond the pain. It waited, red and black, getting closer. He found the dealings with Miranda almost intolerable and could not prevent a bitterness rising in him. He could cope alone, just. But thoughts came to him – grey shapes of smoke that paused by the cave mouth and stared in and whispered.

'You've fallen in love with living, haven't you?'

'You can still get away. Mount up and ride, man.'

'You've done enough. It's not fair to ask you to do more than—'

'Everything passes . . .'

'. . . long time since you bedded a woman.'

'Sleeping out in the damp's no life for a man . . . A small farm, good wife, rollicking kids . . .'

'No man can be strong all the time . . .'

'. . . then the Romans'll see you scream and they'll laugh.'

'. . . soon . . .'

And so it went on, all through the night, until finally Lyf's head drooped and he slept while outside the green light of day strengthened.

Gwellan ran from door to door, and spoke quietly to women with flour on their hands or holding babies. Mother told daughter. Sisters whispered together. Men were told to make their own meals that night.

During the day Lyf slept and in the late afternoon he prepared himself. For days he had not eaten and had drunk only the herb tea. Now he warmed water and began to shave. He cut the hair from his head and shaved his scalp. He shaved the hair from his entire body. Several times he cut himself and dabbed the blood away. Then, for a while, he sat naked by the fire while the woodland darkened. Finally he unrolled clean clothes, his white robe of office, and dressed slowly. His last act was to seal the cave, levering a stone into place. He would not be returning.

Later he rode into the hospital grounds. He bound a white bandage round his eyes so that he would not see Miranda. He gave instructions that she was not to speak in his presence under any circumstances.

Lem and Sulla wanted to help, but Lyf found their presence disturbing. This was a ceremony for the human and the elemental – Lem and Sulla could cause harm, and so he sent them away. 'Go back to your own world. Your time to help will come. Go away. You are not needed here.' Lyf spoke harshly, deliberately. 'Go.'

Sulla began to protest and her eyes gleamed but then Lem took her arm and together the two small exquisite creatures climbed up to their room. Moments later Miranda was aware as Lem and Sulla slipped into their own dimension and flew high into the sky. Moments later they were gone.

Now, with only Gwellan in attendance, Miranda bathed in the hospital spring. Then she dressed in a simple white dress and bound her hair tight. Over everything she threw a dark cloak with a hood that completely hid her face.

When evening had fallen and the moon was rising over the hills, they formed a small procession. Gwellan led, guiding Lyf who walked blindly. Then came Miranda, her eyes staring down at the hem of Lyf's robe. After her came women from the hospital.

They walked through the silent village where all the windows were closed and shuttered. One by one women from the village slipped from their houses and joined them. No men peeped out. No dogs barked, though an owl hooted as they turned round the tall standing stone and made their way past the communal dining-room and on down the path which led to Moorpath bridge. Close to the bridge they turned off the path and followed a narrow way which led back up into the hills.

Soon Miranda would step down into the water, feeling for the stones that Lyf said were there, steps leading downwards, placed by the same men and women who erected the standing stone.

She would feel the water rise up her legs, soaking her dress, up past her hips, starting to lift her while the dress billowed filling with air. She blanked from her mind thoughts of eels and toads and slippery moss and hard stones underwater.

The moon blazed above the pool and its surface rippled where the spring-water came welling up. For a moment a wisp of cloud passed before the moon and the pool darkened. Miranda felt dizzy and spread her arms. But then the light came back.

There seemed to be a shining on the face of the water. A moon path. When she looked down she could see the first step under the surface, green and glimmering, and surrounded by darkness. There was a cloudiness too in the water.

'Now,' called Lyf softly. 'Take it. It is yours.'

Miranda stepped down. Her foot entered the water and found the first step.

A crying of many voices, women's voices, rang out round the pool. It was a sound of keening. Women stood with their hands joined round the edge of the water. They watched and sang.

Another step, and Miranda heard roaring. She looked up and suddenly the moon span like a ball in a socket scattering shards of light which fell down through the sky. And where the light landed it ignited a white fire which blazed without heat.

Another step and Miranda reached down and pulled the heavy waterlogged dress off and flung it away behind her. The pool sparkled where the drops fell. Miranda looked up and the moon was close now. It spread across the sky, still turning, and its light reached down. She could feel it, silver and blazing. It was like silk on her skin.

She heard a deep chortling song which came from the pool itself.

Another step and Miranda felt the rising water of the pool lift her and carry her from the stone steps. She lay still in the water while it turned her ... and lying there, staring up in the white moonlight, she felt herself dissolve away, spreading out into the water, until she became the water ... and yet she remained conscious and powerful. Now, suddenly she knew exactly what to do. There was no uncertainty.

74

She held the moon and made it stand still. She dragged it down from the sky and took it inside her.

That was the moment of marriage. In that moment Miranda shifted realities. She lifted and was aware of her brothers the hills and her sisters the rivers, and her mother the earth and her father the sky. And she was in everything. She was herself and everything.

She rose up, a shimmering presence of moonlight that cast no shadow. Below her the earth was barren. This was a time before life.

Lightning flickered in the stone hills and tore the sky.

Thunder rolled about.

Somewhere brother fire poured like a river down the hills and entered the sea like the scaly back of a crocodile that swims away from the shore.

Below Miranda was a lake with a troubled milky surface. As she watched, the snout of a beast reared. She had seen this creature before. It had come to her that night when she slept beneath a holly tree and Angus had fought off the wolves. She watched as the beast threshed about, dying. It heaved on the surface of the water and plunged and tried to swim, its body twisting and turning.

She heard, or thought she heard, its rattling cry. She saw its staring dark eye in which she had once seen an image of herself as a man, and she saw its jaw open and the forked tongue flicker.

In kindness, Miranda reached down and with one touch killed the snake. It curled and blackened. She felt its energy flow into her, returning. The simple thing that it had been slowly fell to dust until it was just a pattern floating on the pale water. And finally that pattern too was lost as the water churned and turned.

Miranda felt such peace and joy. She was at time's end.

But there was still a keening. It was a calling to action. Much as Miranda would have liked to stay in her own time and spirit, there was work to do. Another dimension, the dimension of the temporal and living, was calling to her.

She could stay or she could go. The choice was hers. But Miranda the Spirit of the Lake, because she was also Miranda the Woman, turned in the air and fell like rain. She settled low over the hills and relinquished the moon. She let Miranda the woman encase her again, gradually pressing the spirit down through the vegetable senses and the animal senses until she found herself, warm-blooded once more, floating on a cold pond of water in the moonlight.

There were fires round the pool. The women were standing, holding burning torches which sent flickering patterns of flame over the water. They were calling and waving their arms. Miranda swam to the side of the pool and grabbed a clump of grass. She pulled herself from the water easily, treading in the soft mud without fear. Nothing in Nature could affect her if she so chose.

Waiting was the woman Gwellan with gleaming eyes. She had a large white towel which she flung round Miranda, and up over her head. She began to dry her vigorously.

'That silly fool Lyf,' said Gwellan. 'I warned him. The moon ceremony won't work if he's about. Men don't know about such things. You could have been killed out there, drowned. Or worse . . . driven mad. Driven out of yourself. And then where would we have been?' She rubbed on for a few moments in silence. 'There, now are you warming up? We'll soon get some hot soup inside you.'

'But I'm not cold,' said Miranda. 'Tell Lyf the child has grown up.'

Lyf was no longer there.

When Miranda stepped into the pool and the keening started he covered his ears. He tried not to watch for he knew the danger, but something, some force outside himself, made him pull the bandages from his eyes.

He felt the light of the moon like heat that made his skin prickle. Still he watched as Miranda took her second step. He heard the gurgling song of the pool. He saw the surface ripple and next the shape of an old woman rise from the water of the pool like smoke. Lyf knew this was a vision for his eyes only. The pool was teasing him, yet it was serious too. Finally the shape of the hag towered above the pool. Her back was towards Lyf. She began to turn, her thin hand pointing, and Lyf knew that if he once saw that face, or if once the fingers pointed at him, then the joke would end and he would be destroyed as

76

surely as Actaeon was torn by the hounds of Artemis. This was his boundary.

Lyf threw himself back and dived into the soil. He burrowed into the leaves and twigs. He crawled away under branches. He found the path, hitched up his robe and ran.

Lyf had seen enough. He had seen more than he dared to hope.

Miranda could hardly speak. In her every move she was aware of the raw energy which now turned in her and she was afraid to speak lest she release that energy inadvertently. As a woman she felt time pass in the dying of her cells and the shifting of blood: as a spirit of Water she saw time like a wheel that turned round her while she remained, calm and still, at its centre. The woman knew that she would need time to adjust, to discover how to carry herself in this strange and vulnerable world. And she felt merry too in a way that she couldn't explain – merry as a dog that rolls on its back in the grass or a cat that arches its back after sleep, and is ready for hunting.

They returned silently to the town of Stand Alone Stan.

One by one the women left the group and returned to their homes. Each had seen her own truth. They would talk together the next day, comparing notes.

At the hospital, Miranda declined the soup that Gwellan offered. She was amused that her body felt tired. *What silly things these bodies are*, she thought, as she lay down in her room.

It was habit more than anything that made her send her mind out through the hospital, bringing comfort and healing. She discovered Gwellan down in the water chamber, on her knees and weeping. Miranda withdrew.

The moon set.

Stars shone out, bright and hard, and a pair of shooting stars blazed briefly over the moors.

Clouds gathered with the dawn and the sky was streaked with fire . . .

. . . and then came the soldiers.

They approached from the south. First came assault craft

77

laying down magnetic paths. Behind them, silent and menacing, the troop carriers glided through the gathering light and settled in the fields of ripe barley close to the village. Soldiers fanned out and occupied the sleeping town.

When the men of the place threw open the windows to smell the air and check the weather, they found assault troops waiting at every corner.

A siren began to wail, jarring the women and children awake. At a signal from the officer in charge of the occupation, the soldiers moved in. They began a thorough eviction. Each house was broken into. The occupants were given an hour to gather some belongings. Any who tried to argue were enclosed in a gag-mask and marched away to a prison freighter which had landed not far from Miranda's hospital. Then the houses were closed while soldiers set incendiary charges.

Each of the occupants was made to parade in the street and give their name to a soldier who wrote it carefully in a ledger. When the name was recorded, the person was given a number and marched down to the barley field. There, large transporters with empty wombs had begun to arrive and received them.

None of the people knew what was happening. They wandered about in a daze. Was it a bad dream? A nightmare? Who were these men? Why had they come? What was the cause? What were they doing here?

There were no answers to the questions. The officer in charge, high in his battle-car, looked on impassively. The soldiers moved with a calm efficiency as though they were doing nothing more demanding than shifting logs or kegs of beer. There was no killing. The instructions had been dinned into them. 'Take the people alive. Burn only the houses and temples and priests.'

Perhaps it was the soldiers' calm routine which stunned the townsfolk of Stand Alone Stan most, for only when the first house was set alight and the flames were coming from the windows did the people finally wake up to what was happening and begin to resist. Suddenly there was a cry of anger. Then anything that could be moved became a weapon. A chamber pot hurled from a top window brained a soldier who was harassing an old woman. Rolling-pins became truncheons. A man pulled a pitchfork from the roof of his barn and hurled it two-armed over his head so that its tines nailed one of the guards to the barn door. Two horses, harnessed together, were set galloping down a lane, their chains flailing and sending a patrol diving for cover. Ladles and pans were clashed together. And then, gathering momentum, began the wild war-shrieking as the men and women urged themselves to battle-frenzy.

Everywhere people began to jostle and shout. The soldiers, forbidden to use their weapons, fell back in confusion.

From the different colleges came men and women, servants and children, students and grandmothers. Some students fought with staves, probing for throat and midriff. Women and men used their fingers and teeth. Some people fought with their voices, making the sounds of beasts so that the soldiers paled under their suntan. Others pulled the props from the washing-lines which straddled the streets. Slackened, the lines became trip-wires, catching the retreating soldiers at the knee and sending them sprawling in a heap where the advancing women beat them with ladles. One woman, braver than most, took the paper ball of a wasps' nest into her arms and threw it down into a courtyard where the soldiers had made a stand.

Finally discipline broke and the first shots rang out. The commanding officer died with an arrow through his throat, his whistle in his lips. He had been waving to signal retreat and re-group. Any vestige of formal authority was now gone. The soldiers fired at random into the advancing men and women. They fired into the houses. They fired at anything. Blood ran in the streets. But still the people came.

One man tore off his clothes and ran naked towards the guns. The bullets stripped his flesh at arm and shoulder and waist and cheek . . . but still he came. Those who saw him when telling the story later spoke only of his eyes which seemed to blaze and his screaming mouth. Dead, his body still had enough momentum to slide on the slippery streets and crash into the front row of soldiers.

Nor was this mere bravado. For while the soldiers were entertained by the warriors, others of the people were slipping away from the colleges carrying valuables or helping the sick and the aged.

*

But the improvised weapons of the house and barn could not for long prevail over the guns of the soldiers. Before long the soldiers were able to advance over the bodies. It was like walking on rubber. As they advanced they fired and nothing could withstand them. The screaming died away to be replaced by the crying of the injured begging to be killed. The officer who was number two in command, a battle-hardened man called Piticus, arrived in his battle-wagon and took charge.

As soon as all resistance had been crushed, Piticus ordered the soldiers to withdraw. There was almost rebellion at this for the soldiers were angry and wild. They wanted to loot and burn. But Piticus ordered them back in the name of Emperor Lucius and to give force to his order he trained the guns of his battle-wagon upon them. None of them doubted his intentions and slowly the troops withdrew.

When he was sure that he had control of the situation, Piticus gave orders that any townsfolk who had a chance of surviving be given medical treatment and then taken aboard the transporters. At the same time, he arranged for the bodies of the soldiers who had died in the fighting to be prepared for the brief journey back to their barracks.

And only when all this had been accomplished did he allow the corpses of the townsfolk to be pillaged for rings, torcs and ornaments before being dragged to the large communal dining-room where they were piled up. Finally, when there was absolute silence save for the sighing of the wind in the trees, he shouted, 'Prepare for burning.'

The soldiers set to with a will. They set the incendiary devices and scattered fuel among the straw. They were awaiting the order to fire, when suddenly a cry went up. Emerging from one of the side paths which led away from Stand Alone Stan were three soldiers. They were leading a bedraggled man in a white cloak.

While the shouting and fighting was at its peak in the streets, Gwellan ran up to Miranda's room. She found Miranda sitting deep in trance.

'Come on, Miranda. You must wake up. We're under attack. Wake up.'

Miranda looked at Gwellan and she spoke calmly as though from many miles away. 'Help me now, Gwellan. I cannot yet trust myself. One wrong move and I will destroy everything.'

Gwellan did not understand but she did not stay to ask questions. She threw a cloak round Miranda's shoulders. 'We must get away,' she said. 'Now. There is no time for delay. Come on. Stand up. Follow me.'

She guided Miranda down through the hospital and out into the garden. There they met some children who were milling about and crying. Miranda held out her hands and the children fell silent. 'Come on. This way,' said Gwellan. 'We'll use the back gate where the hawthorn grows.' She led them across the garden and out through a small gate. This opened on to a path which plunged down between high hedges into one of the valleys on the eastern side of the village.

They were hurrying as quickly as they could and had gone about two miles when suddenly three Roman soldiers, members of a patrol that had got lost in the woods, stumbled out on to the path in front of them. It is hard to say who was the more surprised, but the Romans reacted quickly. They surrounded the women and children and shouted at them, ordering them back up the path, back to Stand Alone Stan.

All this was observed by Lyf who was hiding in the bushes. He had been there since running away from the Moon Ceremony, and he had heard the shouting when Stand Alone Stan was attacked. Lyf saw the women turn and begin to trudge up the hill. He was aware that there was a strange rightness about his being in that place at just that time. It was as though he were being offered something, a choice.

Lyf knew he could lie still and let the women and soldiers walk away from him back to Stand Alone Stan. Then he could escape. Or he could step out now, make himself known, and try to save them.

'Not much of a choice,' he muttered and stepped out. 'Hey, Romans,' he called. 'Where you going with those women?'

The soldiers stopped and turned. They saw a bedraggled bald tramp in dirty white robes come shambling towards them.

Lyf had no idea what he was going to do. In all situations he relied on his wits and a kind Providence that stood at his elbow in times of need. Usually he was able to charm people or make them laugh and so gain his way, and there was no doubt that he had skill as a healer. But Lyf's power was always something granted to him by those who heeded him. These soldiers eyed him coldly.

Lyf began to run down the path towards them. As he ran he started to dance, hopping from leg to leg and weaving his arms about like snakes. The soldiers stared at him in surprise. Lyf had gained his first advantage: he had their attention and, more important, they did not now see him as a threat. He stopped a few yards in front of them and peered at them as though short-sighted. He could see that the soldiers were in poor condition. They had stumbled through the woods since losing their way shortly after dawn and the blackthorn and gorse had torn their hands and faces. Their uniforms were stiff with mud. One cradled his arm in a way that suggested it was dislocated at the shoulder. Another had fallen into a nettle patch and his arm was a mass of puffy white pimples. The third was badly scratched about the face and eyes. There was blood in his stubble. Moreover, they had all lost their weapons except for knives.

'You look a mess if I may say so,' said Lyf cheekily, speaking in pidgin Latin. 'I'm a healer, one of the best. What say we strike bargain? I give you healing and you let these women and children go?'

The leader, the man with a dislocated shoulder, showed interest and it was obvious that the others were not averse to a rest. 'So what can you do, old man?' he asked.

Lyf displayed his hands. 'You see these,' he said. 'These can set bones, ease blisters, rub away warts, deliver babies, pick pockets, charm snakes and get rid of that nettle rash for a start.'

While he was speaking Lyf was also observing the women. Miranda seemed to be in a trance. Her face was white and unmoving, her eyes unfocused. Lyf had no idea what she was seeing or where her mind was and he doubted that she would be of any help. But Gwellan, he was glad to observe, was very present. Her eyes were alive and she was looking at Lyf, trying to read his intentions.

'OK, old man,' said the leader, with a wink to his mates.

'Show us what you can do. We'll let the women and kids go if you can bring us some ease.'

Lyf nodded and grinned like an idiot. 'Can do. Will do,' he said and shook hands with himself to signify the bargain. Then he held his hands out in front of him, palms down, and moved in a circle as though feeling for some special vibration from the earth. 'Aaah,' he said after a moment and his hands trembled above some big green dock-leaves that were growing at the edge of the path. With great reverence, Lyf knelt down in front of the dock plant. 'These will help the nettle rash,' he said, speaking his poor Latin. 'But first I sing to them.' As he picked the dock-leaves he crooned in his own language. 'Gwel-lan he rea-dy. Pre tend to help me. Then when I at-tack them. You all run away, away, away.' When they heard him some of the children laughed and nudged one another. They all knew Lyf and his antics. Gwellan hushed them. She had heard.

Lyf pressed the dock-leaves, extracting some of the juice which he rubbed on to the nettle rash gently. It brought instant relief as he knew it would. The soldier nodded as the prickling pain receded. 'Hey, this old bugger does know a thing or two,' he said.

Lyf handed him the crushed leaves. 'Here, you rub on. You heal yourself.'

Next Lyf turned to the soldier whose face was scratched. He inspected the cuts and shook his head. 'Very bad,' he said. 'You will lose your sight if not treated. You have been touched with the mujjug-jugjiboogie plant. You lucky me here.' He held up his finger and touched each of his nostrils in turn as though performing some private magic. Then he moved into the undergrowth by the side of the path. There, close to where water was seeping down he found a small attractive red flower. He pulled up the entire plant and crushed it between the palms of his hard hands. He rubbed it into a paste. 'Red rattle,' he said. 'Good medicine. This'll help. Now keep still.'

The soldier with the scratched face was wary but Lyf calmed him. Then he dabbed some of the herb juice on to the man's face, carefully avoiding any cuts. Already Lyf could feel the juice of the plant starting to sting his hand. Gwellan had seen the plant he had picked and knew what to expect.

As soon as he had the man's confidence, Lyf rubbed the paste directly into his eyes and scratches. The man screamed and began clawing at his face. At that same moment Gwellan swung round and punched the leader on his dislocated arm so that he shouted out in pain and sat down.

'Now run,' shouted Lyf. 'Get off the path. Get into the woods. The place is crawling with Romans.' And run they did, Gwellan leading Miranda, down the path, as quickly as they could.

While they ran Lyf fought.

The soldier with the nettle rash grabbed him round the legs, toppling him, while the leader struggled to his feet and kicked Lyf in the stomach. It was not much of a fight, but it was enough. As he blacked out, Lyf saw the women and the children dive off the path and into the trees. No Roman would catch them now.

One eye was closed and breathing was difficult. Lyf found himself flung down on his knees in front of Piticus. 'So what've we got here then?' asked the officer eyeing him. 'One of their priests, eh? Wondered where they'd all cleared off to.'

'We caught him trying to escape.'

Piticus nodded. 'Yeah. They always run away when there's trouble. String him up. No, better, tie him to that big stone. We'll give him a ringside seat. He can watch his town burn. Let's see if his gods come and rescue him then.'

Rough hands grabbed Lyf and dragged him over to the tall standing stone. He was hoisted up on to a platform made of tables from the dining-room and his hands and feet were chained to the rock. As a final indignity his robe was torn open revealing his flesh and water was poured over him to slow the burning.

It was all as Lyf had seen in his dream.

Piticus and his attendants withdrew to the hillside. It was the place where Miranda and Coll and Angus had paused when they first arrived at Stand Alone Stan. From here Piticus had a good view of the entire town. He settled back comfortably into the seat of his battle-wagon. 'Burn the place,' he ordered. 'Burn everything.'

Immediately soldiers stationed round the town threw burning brands up into the straw roofs. There was a short delay while the flames caught and then gradually a pall of smoke began to rise. The houses started to burn. Roof-trees and purlins, dry for many seasons, caught fire quickly and the houses collapsed inwards sending up fire and sparks.

The wind fanned the flames so that within minutes they leaped from house to house. Soon the flames were reaching the inner parts of the town where the colleges were located. These buildings, taller than the houses and well protected by trees, resisted but soon smoke could be seen pouring from the upper windows. The college where musicians had trained burned first and suddenly seemed to explode with fire. Next it was the quiet place with gardens where ancient lore was studied. Then the dancing-halls and the silver- and goldsmiths' college began to smoulder. Soon the flames, now roaring like animals, caught at the roof of Miranda's hospital. Trees exploded into fire. The flames raced through the roof and entered the wards and ran down the ancient corridors. Miranda's room burned and an old skull toppled from its secret niche above the door and fell into the glowing ashes.

Gradually the fire worked its way in towards the centre of the town where Lyf was chained to the standing stone. He felt the hot wind fan his cheek. The smoke made his eyes water. He could feel the drag of the air as it fed the fire and saw with surprise that steam was already rising from his torn robes. In front of him, the wall of the nearest building blackened and then fell outwards with a belch of flame and sparks. The fire ran towards him. Now the pain began, a pain he could not avoid. He tried to think of Miranda – it was for her sake that he was here – but he could not remember her face.

Under his feet the tables started to smoulder. Lyf tried to turn away but the chains held him firm. He felt the skin on his chest burn and frizzle. He could smell it too. And then the first tongue of flame licked him and Lyf screamed.

His body reddened as he threw himself back and forth and his skin tore in the chains. When he tried to scream his tongue burned and his mouth dried. When he tried to look his eyes burned. The last thing he saw as the flames closed over him was the dining-hall with black billowing oily smoke and high above it, in the sky, a lone bird turning, riding the up-draught.

Lyf was blind but he was still standing and the flames beat at him and the noise roared in his ears. It was a kind of music and the flames were like cold waves coming in from the sea. In his last moments Lyf knew that he had been here before, in the flames. He saw this life and earlier lives unfolding like a seamless web. For a moment he saw other worlds he had known, and then the black and red waves broke about him and tossed him and battered him till at the last there was nothing . . . not even silence.

The fire burned for an hour and at the end there was just charred stumps and grey ash stirred by the wind. The buildings were gone. The trees were gone. Only the standing stone still rose, unmoved and unchanged except that its surface was completely clean of lichen. The chains had melted, but of the body of Lyf there was no sign. Not even the charred skull.

Where the hospital had stood a lake was slowly forming. Ash and masonry had blocked the outflow from the spring and now the water, swirling and black, was filling the depression where the hospital had stood. Soon it would break out and a new river would begin.

Trumpets sounded. The soldiers who had burned Stand Alone Stan re-grouped. Their numbers had been swelled by fresh troops from Petuaria. To the rear the giant transporters lifted, carrying the remnants of the population of Stand Alone Stan away to Camp Lucius.

Again the trumpets blared and the assault craft ground into motion, laying down their magnetic track.

Some days earlier, the spotter plane which had carried out a survey of the region had reported sighting a strange assembly of buildings to the east of Stand Alone Stan. It looked like a secret community. No one had suspected its presence or had any idea what it was.

Piticus was interested to find out. He gave the order to advance and his battle-wagon lurched and moved forwards.

Post scriptum for Lyf

A salmon leaps and crashes down into the water, thrashing with its tail to gain advantage before the river can hurl it back.

Above the rapids, a lone angler waits, rod at the ready. He

86

sees the fish tear the water seven times, each leap carrying it higher, until finally it swims exhausted into a deep pool. It holds close to the bank, its tail and fin trembling, keeping it steady against the flow of water. A fly on a thread snakes through the air to land a few feet from the fish and drift, a tempting morsel for a tired creature.

The salmon looks up, darts and stops.

Then it turns and swims lazily away. It will not be caught today. No nor tomorrow either. Not if Lyf has his way. He has earned his rest.

5   Luck

'Shut up. I'm trying to listen.'

Angus speaking, bent over the small radio transmitter. He'd been getting ready to make his monthly 'Mikos' report to Roscius' headquarters and while he was waiting had tuned in to the military wavelengths. This was something he did every day, scanning the radio frequencies to pick up what bits of news he could. Usually all he heard were reports of troop movements or command units exchanging banter. But this time he encountered what sounded like live action with shouted orders and the crackle of gunfire in the background. At first he thought it was a manoeuvre in progress. But then he heard a reference to the tall standing stone and realized that Stand Alone Stan was being attacked.

Perol joined him and then Sean and Drummer.

It was Drummer, tapping on his drum when he heard the gunfire, that made Angus snap. Together they listened to the shouting and the panicked call for reinforcements. They heard the call for Piticus to take over on the front line after the death of the commanding officer. Confusion. A lot of shouting. Then an ominous calm. A man described as wearing a tattered white robe was captured. He was to be burned alive, chained to the standing stone. Angus recognized Lyf. Later they heard the roaring of the fire, the dry commentary as the buildings were consumed, the clinical details as the fire reached the stone.

Angus turned the volume down.

Perol's eyes were wide with horror. 'That was terrible. Worse than being there. Did you know him, Angus?' Angus nodded. He spun the dial, tuning in to Eburacum HQ, and was just in time to catch a summary of action prepared for unit commanders. It seemed that several attacks were in progress. Across the entire Wolds, small communities were being attacked and the people transported. There was fierce fighting.

'I didn't hear any word of Roscius' house,' said Sean. 'That seems strange. I thought they might be looking for Roscius.'

'I got the impression they didn't have too many clues about what they were supposed to be doing,' said Angus. 'What a shambles! They're taking things as they come. They probably don't know about Roscius' place. He was always very careful.'

'But they soon will,' said Perol. 'What the hell is going on?'

Again Angus shook his head. 'No idea. They called it Operation Clean-up. Did you hear that? Whatever that means.'

'Do you think Roscius knows that he's in danger?' asked Perol.

'How the hell should I know?' said Angus. 'Why does everyone keep asking me questions? I only tuned in by chance. You all know as much as I do.'

'Forgive me, Captain,' said Sean, 'but do you think you ought to call Roscius and warn him? It'd be a neighbourly thing to do, considering we've been enjoying the hospitality of his camp for the past few months.'

'Sean's right,' said Perol. 'Warn Roscius. I can't bear the thought of his house being burned and what about the books and the paintings and the vases . . . and that wonderful greenhouse with the grape vines, and the . . .'

'All right, all right, all right, I'm doing it,' snapped Angus as he tuned the transmitter to Roscius' wavelength. 'He probably knows all about it – he had spies all over – but here goes.' He tapped out the coded call sign from Camp VI.

They waited. There was usually a short pause while the operator verified the incoming call. It was just one of the security procedures.

The seconds became minutes. There was no reply. Angus put out the call sign again, and again there was no reply.

'Are you sure you're on the right wavelength?' whispered Perol. 'Roscius keeps the transmitter attended night and day. There's got to be someone there.'

'Of course I'm on the right wavelength. There's no one replying. That's all.'

'Try again. Try a live call.'

Angus opened the microphone link. He affected the thick accent he used to imitate old Mikos. 'Hello. Mikos calling from Camp VI. Calling Roscius. Come in now.'

Silence, save for a distant whispering sound like steam escaping from a kettle. 'Hello. Mikos here from . . .'

Sean reached out and closed the transmitter down. 'Excuse me, Captain. But we've been in open transmission for five minutes and that can be a dangerous thing when we don't know who might be listening on the other end. I think we must fear the worst. Either Roscius has escaped and his house is deserted – or it isn't.'

They stared at one another as the implication sank in.

Twenty minutes later they were gathered in the dining-room. With them were most of the older inmates of the camp including Garlyck who, since his debate with Angus, had rather been accepted as one whose opinion was worth heeding.

'How many people knew about the different escape camps?' asked Sean.

'Well Roscius of course,' said Angus. 'And I suppose one or two of his top people. Marcus probably and that Danea woman. Not many.'

'But enough. If the Romans moved fast enough they might have caught one of them alive. I think it is probable they did.'

'Why?' asked Perol.

'Because I reckon that if Roscius had got wind of what was happening then he'd have contacted all his secret camps to get them ready. That's logical isn't it? And he didn't contact us did he?' They shook their heads. 'So, I conclude he was caught with his toga off. And if that is the case the Romans may know all his secrets. Could Roscius hold out under torture?'

'No one could hold out,' said Garlyck.

'Then there we are. Let us plan for the worst. Let us plan on the assumption that the Romans know about the escape camps. It is only a matter of time before they come looking.'

'But where can we go?' asked Wallace Duff. 'If they know about all the camps, then . . .'

'We'll have to live wild,' said Perol. 'We can't go back. And we can't go to one of the villages, we can't put them at risk. So . . .'

Drummer had been listening, his brow furrowed in concentration. Now he tapped lightly on his drum.

'Hey up. The big fella's got something on his mind,' said Sean.

'Drummer knows a place,' said Drummer pointing out of the window. 'Some walk from here. Caves. Old caves. Home of wolves. Very safe. Good water. Dry in winter.'

'If I didn't know better I'd think he was trying to sell them to us,' said Sean.

'Enough room for all of us?' asked Perol, gesturing round.

Drummer nodded. 'Room for everyone. Long ago, men and women live there. After the big ice. Drummer show you.'

'Sounds promising. Could serve us *pro tem* while we're sorting things out.' Angus glanced round the table. 'Has anyone got a better idea?' There was no reply. 'All in favour of moving to Drummer's caves?' Everyone nodded.

'I like caves,' said Gargamelle. 'Let's go.'

Within two hours they were packed.

'Shame about the Dragon,' said Wallace.

'Aye well,' said Angus, 'I've got plans for that.'

Perol overheard him. 'You are not taking that Dragon,' she said. 'I thought we'd agreed.'

'I'll come back and shift it when we've settled in,' said Angus.

'Away, Captain,' said Sean. 'It'll be a dead giveaway. If the Romans do come, then all they'll have to do is follow its tracks. We were lucky once up on the moors, but you can push your luck too far.'

'I'm not planning on taking it to Drummer's caves,' said Angus. 'I'll use it as a decoy. I'll lead them in the other direction. I'll dump it in a swamp or something. I'm not leaving it here. I can't.'

Perol's eyes flashed. 'Oh, I've no time to argue with you,' she said. 'Do what you want. Come on, let's go.'

Drummer tapped lightly to gain attention. Perol conducted a roll-call. Then Drummer hoisted two of the children up on to his shoulders and set off.

The small party headed down to the river and then on into the forest. The trees closed about them. They walked in silence following a narrow path.

From time to time Drummer led them away over stony ground

or up a stream-bed. He led them carefully, sometimes making turns for no apparent reason, sometimes pausing with his head back as though listening to the forest.

Occasionally he stopped and peed unselfconsciously into the undergrowth, spraying wide.

Angus looked at Sean. 'I've seen a horse be more delicate,' he whispered.

Sean nodded. 'If anything following us gets a whiff of that it'll back off sharpish. And do you mark the way he's following animal paths. If the Romans bring dogs and try to follow us, they'll soon get confused.'

When he had finished, Drummer led on, but Angus held back pretending that he too wanted to relieve himself. Then, when the others had passed and no one was looking, he trailed the end of his wolf-skin through the wet grass.

Drummer led the small party through dense thickets, through stands of briar and through small damp ravines.

By late afternoon they came to a lightly wooded hill. Suddenly Drummer stopped and signalled for everyone to be quiet. They listened. Faintly they heard the blaring of sirens. The sound seemed to come from the direction of their former camp. Then they heard shooting.

'Lucky eh?' said Garlyck.

Sean nodded. 'They moved quickly. Quicker than I'd have guessed.'

'Aye,' said Angus, 'but that means those buggers'll have found the Dragon by now.'

'Better the Dragon than us,' said Perol. 'Come on, warrior. No regrets.'

The people looked from one to another, aware how narrowly they had escaped. When they moved on they hurried, drawing close.

Some time later, Drummer led them between two thick-trunked oak trees which guarded a narrow cleft between rock-faced cliffs. They found themselves dropping down into a small valley fringed with birch and ash and rowan. It was completely enclosed by hills and trees. The air was still and warm, and sweet with the smell of grass. A stream spilled from the rock-face and ran over stones down to a small lake before meandering the full length of the valley and disappearing into the trees. Everyone stopped and stared. Tall meadow grass came high up over their knees so that some of the little children almost disappeared when set down on their feet.

'Boy oh boy,' said Gargamelle, 'this is for me.'

One side of the valley was a rocky escarpment and there they saw caves. They also saw, standing proud and staring down at them, a giant wolf.

'Aye well, we might have to do some negotiating first,' said Angus.

Drummer motioned for the group to stay still and quiet. Then he tapped his drum lightly and began to walk towards the wolf. It drew back its lips and growled. Other wolves appeared, and stared down.

'I hope he knows what he's doing,' said Wallace.

'He does,' said Sean and Angus in unison.

As Drummer approached the wolves, the tempo of his drumming increased. The sound seemed to mesmerize the wolves so that they lowered their heads and their tongues lolled out. Finally Drummer was among them. He took the leader of the pack and worked his fingers in its scruff. Then he led it down away from the caves. The other wolves followed.

When he was half-way to the stream, he stopped and suddenly began beating a furious rhythm on his drum. The wolves howled. Their ears flattened against their heads and their lips drew back. They ran in a circle round him and then the leader charged away. He ran like an arrow and leaped the stream at a bound. The others followed. Drummer watched them go and when they had left the valley he turned and strode back to the small group.

He gestured up the hill to the caves. 'Yours now. Wolves gone, eh? Drummer talk to them nice. Not like your wolves, eh An-goos?' Drummer laughed and slapped Angus on the shoulder. Angus staggered. 'You like?'

'We like,' said Perol.

'You move in now. Get fire. Get food. Drummer go runabout, eh?' He beat his drum briefly and snuffled the air and then loped away.

*

93

The caves were ancient homes. They felt solid and safe, and most had been extended and shaped by the first men and women to dwell in the land.

Gargamelle went exploring. She gave a whoop of delight. At the back of one of the caves, high on the walls and well away from the light, she had found drawings. Men hunting. A big woman giving birth. 'Looks like me,' said Gargamelle. 'Any offers?'

Before long the caves were cleaned and the accumulated rubbish of the wolves – mainly gnawed bones – was carried away. People moved in, claiming the cave of their choice. They found them comfortable in simple ways: smooth sandy floors, niches for oil lamps, raised sleeping areas near the fireplaces. Several were linked by passages deep in the rock, with cool back rooms where food could be kept.

Perol imagined skins hung over the low door and a fire burning. She was thinking of the coming winter when she was due to give birth.

As evening fell everyone gathered round a fire lit by Sean. He had cooked their first meal – a small boar brought down by his cassik during the hike through the woods.

Suddenly Angus laughed as he tore the meat with his teeth and everyone looked at him. 'I was just thinking about the Romans,' he said, licking his fingers. 'I bet they got one hell of a shock when they found we'd gone but the Dragon was there.'

Angus was right. Marmellius did get a shock.

Appointed to investigate the dragon and the mysterious camp in the forest, Marmellius set to with a will. He felt that he had failed somewhat with his investigation into the Caligula camp. He wanted to make amends, and he took pride in his efficiency. Within days he had established his own network of spies and informers.

The woman that old Ulysses had spoken to died that same night without regaining consciousness. But then, just a few days later, a woodlander – a former inmate of the Caligula camp who had come to Eburacum to sell wood carvings – was picked up for brawling in the street. As luck would have it, he was caught by the same trooper who had arrested him a few months earlier for the same offence, and he was recognized. Under normal circumstances he would have been taken straight to the cells beneath the city. But one of Marmellius' agents, himself a woodlander, intervened. He decided on a new tactic. He got the man drunk. He encouraged him to boast about his courage and finally got him to tell the story of how he broke out of the Caligula. As it turned out the man did not know much but the agent was able to get an idea where the the secret camp was hidden. Equipped with this information, he led a small troop into the forest and after a couple of weeks came upon dragon tracks where Angus had taken the beast for a run some weeks earlier. Before long they found Roscius' Camp VI and radioed back a message giving its location as accurately as they could.

This was very wild, completely unmapped terrain and rather than risk the attack misfiring, Marmellius ordered the small force to return to Eburacum, taking close note of their route so that an easy return could be negotiated with a larger force. He decided to lead the assault himself. He hoped that he would discover the secret of the dragon and capture the young Ulysses son and have the pleasure of bringing him back to Eburacum.

So it was that one morning Marmellius, disguised as a woodlander, led a division of his best assault troops into the trees. Being unfamiliar with the forest and its ways, they travelled slowly. After four days they were close to Roscius' Camp VI and one of their scouts reported that the camp was occupied.

Marmellius decided to attack the next day at dawn. He drew back and gave strict orders that no one was to do anything which might jeopardize the surprise. But the next day coincided with the assault on Stand Alone Stan, an operation which Marmellius had not been told about, and he lost valuable time when he had to report back to Marcus Ulysses in Eburacum and receive a briefing. Thus it was that by the time Marmellius had the small camp surrounded and the sirens began to blare, the small band of Dragon Warriors had already departed. He missed them by just a few hours.

When they stormed the camp with siren and gun, they found the place deserted. One of the soldiers saw the head of the

95

Dragon reclining on the ground outside the workshop and began firing wildly. He, like all the other soldiers, knew about the dragon that had attacked the Caligula and it filled him with fear. Others joined him in panic and it was several minutes before Marmellius could regain control. In that time two soldiers had been wounded by ricochets.

Marmellius, of course, recognized the Dragon for what it was, he had seen it often enough at the Battle Dome. He approached it and banged its side with the butt of his assault rifle. It boomed hollowly. Hearing this unmistakably metallic sound, the soldiers approached sheepishly. For the first time they saw the Dragon, not through the eyes of superstition, but as it really was. They saw the dented scales, the scratched paint, the broken tail mechanism and the holes in the beast's sides where scales had been ripped away revealing the chains and couplings. Finally they clambered about, inside and all over the machine, touching the levers and knobs and hydraulic pistons. They smelled the hot oil and they heard the humming.

'Hey, it's fully charged,' called one who had worked in the Battle Dome and knew about such things. 'Look at this.' He pointed at the improvised electric motor which Angus and Wallace Duff had set up and which cut in whenever the fly-wheel revs dropped. 'Clever eh?'

As soon as Marmellius had established that the camp was deserted he sent soldiers out with tracker dogs to see if they could pick up the trace. It was obvious that the inmates had not been long gone. They quickly found the route but the dogs would not behave and kept turning aside.

'Something in the scent they don't like,' said one of the dog handlers and then he pointed to the ground. Clearly visible was the giant imprint of Drummer's foot. They called Marmellius who looked closely at the print and then stared into the dense wall of trees, his eyes narrow with concentration. 'If it's not dragons it's giants,' he said, shaking his head. 'We haven't a clue, have we? We don't really know what is out there.'

Evening was falling by the time the troopers completed their exploration of the camp. For all of them, the experience of living in the open under the groaning and creaking forest had been unnerving. They were glad to be in this outpost of civilization, no matter how small. They took over the kitchen and one of the dormitories. They found what was left of the wine store. They began to make themselves comfortable.

Before he retired for the night Marmellius set guards at the corners of the camp and near the Dragon. He did not expect any trouble, but he was a cautious man by nature. Then he withdrew into what had once been Sean's room. He did what many military commanders have done when they find themselves stationed at an outpost, far removed from their normal secure haven: he read the classics. Marmellius thumbed through his ancestor Gaius Julius Caesar's book of military exploits, *On the War in Gallia*. Finally, heartened by this tale of courage and military genius, he extinguished his candle and lay back, listening to the noise of the forest. A wind had got up during the evening and it shook the trees so that the branches heaved and tapped at the walls.

Angus too heard the wind.

And he heard Perol snoring gently beside him.

Quietly so not to wake her he slipped from their improvised bed and pulled his clothes on. He left a note propped against the wall where she would see it. Then he tiptoed from the cave.

The night was very dark. Clouds had gathered, driven by the wind, and there was a hint of rain in the air. Angus sniffed deep, drawing in the raw night air. The forest at night could still fill him with fear – but he was determined. He had prepared his plans carefully during the walk to the valley. He intended to rescue the Dragon. He wouldn't bring it back to the caves, of course, but he would deny it to the Romans. He knew that if he'd told Perol his plans she would have stopped him, and so he decided that a *fait accompli* was the best tactic.

Wearing his wolf-skin and with a pack over his shoulder, Angus made his way along the face of the escarpment and came to the narrow entrance into the valley. The wolf-skin stank. Apart from Drummer's urine, Angus had carefully trailed the hem in the wolf droppings. If anything happened to him, he didn't want the Romans to come back-tracking.

At the end of the valley he unpacked a small charged lantern.

Its beam was not strong, but sufficient to reveal the low branches which could reach for his eyes, and the raised roots that could trip him. Angus plunged into the gloom.

He had memorized the route well, but even so, travelling at night was difficult. Several times he took the wrong turning and had to retrace his steps. He felt as though the trees had eyes and were watching him. He also experienced the feeling of being followed. Occasionally he turned quickly and shone his lantern, hoping to catch whatever might be following him, and then he berated himself when he could see nothing. 'Make myself jumpy if I'm not careful,' he muttered. Once he definitely heard sticks break behind him and he hid for a few minutes with the lantern extinguished, but nothing came by.

The walk took longer than he had hoped and he did not reach the outskirts of Roscius' Camp VI until dawn was breaking. He crept through the familiar bushes and came upon a guard asleep beside one of the sheds. He was big man with a scarred face and he had made himself a small bivouac. The man's throat was visible as his chest heaved. Angus paused, as though indecisive, and then he slipped his knife into his hand and crept close.

'Don't kill.' The voice was soft but clear. Angus spun round, and there was Garlyck no more than a few paces from him.

'What the hell are you doing here?' he hissed.

'Keeping an eye on you, that's what.'

'Well bugger off. I don't need you.'

Garlyck pointed his finger at him, like a schoolmarm with a naughty pupil. 'Yes you do. Left to yourself you'll muck everything up. Don't kill, remember. Or I'll raise the whole bloody camp.' So saying Garlyck rested his hand on one of the mobile hand-crank sirens.

The guard grunted and yawned and his eyes opened. He stared in surprise at the two men and was about to shout when Angus punched him. The guard fell without a sound. Garlyck caught him.

'Now there's luck,' said Garlyck. 'Just your size.' Quickly he stripped the guard of his uniform and sat the man up with his head over his knees. He handed the one-piece uniform to Angus.

'Here, you've got yourself a disguise.' Then he uncoiled a length of rope from his waist and tied the guard up expertly and put a gag in his mouth.

Angus watched with surprise at Garlyck's speed and expertise. 'Do you always carry lengths of rope?'

'On a stunt like this? Yes,' said Garlyck. 'And I use whatever advantage fate deals me. Put the uniform on. It might gain us a minute's advantage. Come on.'

Angus did and Garlyck pulled the buckles tight. 'Now you look like you mean business.'

Angus reached for the gun but Garlyck put his foot on it. 'Away, Maestro. You don't need that. You're with me now.' And so saying he kicked the gun away into the bushes.

'Just bloody well keep well out of my way, that's all,' said Angus.

Garlyck grinned. 'Lead on. You're the boss.'

They moved into the grey camp slipping from building to building silently. Angus glanced at the sky where heavy grey clouds were now rolling past above the trees. The wind blew gustily. 'Going to be a hell of a downpour before long,' he muttered.

'Could be to our advantage,' whispered Garlyck. 'Come on.'

They sprinted between the last two buildings and came to the machine shed. Just inside the door was another guard and he too was dozing, sitting on an upturned bucket with his back against the wall.

'Watch this,' said Garlyck. He approached the guard and took him in a head lock. He worked his arms back and forth and the guard, who had at first struggled and tried to stand, slowly relaxed and slumped with the whites of his eyes showing. Garlyck grinned at the surprise on Angus' face and unwound more cord from his waist.

'You'd better be careful your pants don't fall down,' was Angus' only comment.

The side door to the Dragon was standing wide open. 'What's your plan now?' asked Garlyck, sitting the guard up and beginning to strip him of his uniform.

'Power her up. Drive her out. Do as much damage as I can and ditch her.'

'Sounds like you, Angus.'

'Do you have a better idea?'

'Why don't we take a few more things we can use. Wine, medical supplies, extra bedding, a few more pots and pans, seeds. I reckon we've got ten minutes before this place comes alive. Let's do it.'

Angus agreed grudgingly. Not only did the plan make sense but it appealed to his sense of adventure. 'OK,' he said, throwing his wolf-skin into the hold of the Dragon. 'Ten minutes, and then we go.'

'You're on.' Garlyck fastened his uniform tight. 'How do I look?'

'Daft. Come on.'

It was a quick ten minutes. Both men moved like shadows through the camp. Only the kitchen showed signs of life where the sleepy cook was preparing a vat of porridge. He grunted at Angus as he strode in and started removing pans, ladles and knives. 'Captain's orders,' growled Angus. Then he was gone.

Garlyck collected bedding which he flung into the Dragon. Then, while Angus was assembling tools and coils of wire from the machine bench, he slipped away. 'You've only got two minutes,' whispered Angus.

Two minutes later Angus heard a commotion of clucking and a stifled cock-a-dood — Garlyck was back carrying chickens in a sack and a cockerel that he held by the feet. In front of him he drove a flock of goats. He released the chickens once he was in the Dragon. They clucked and scampered and shat with fear. The goats were more of a problem.

'We can't . . .' began Angus.

'Bloody can . . .' said Garlyck. 'Think of the cheese. Help me.'

They caught the goats and urged them into the Dragon. At that moment they heard the whine of the alarm siren.

'Time to go.' Angus swung up into the control compartment while Garlyck slammed and bolted the lower door.

Angus brought the Dragon alive quickly. He waited impatiently while the systems warmed and the relays clattered. Finally the screens cleared and he had a view of the central compound. Soldiers were milling about. None seemed quite clear what had happened and why the siren was wailing.

'Here goes,' called Angus and he engaged the tractor mechanism. He fed power to the hydraulics which raised the head and neck. The Dragon's eyes blinked open and glowed red. One of the soldiers saw this and pointed. Some ran back in panic. Others knelt down and began firing. Inside the Dragon the sound of the bullets cannoning off the plating made the goats jump while the chickens set up a squawking and one keeled over with a heart attack.

Angus tapped the power of the fly-wheel and the Dragon lurched forwards. He raised it so that the arched back tore away the roof of the workshop. It trundled into the open. Seeing it advance, the soldiers began to scatter, diving into the bushes or running between the buildings. Angus drove the Dragon in a tight circle, destroying the balcony in front of one of the dormitories. This was the kind of manoeuvring the Dragon was built for. If it had had a tail he could have sent it snaking out like a whip to break windows and walls – but Angus had to be content with crushing whatever buildings he could reach. He brought the big rear legs into action and drove the belly of the Dragon right over the kitchen. Next he made the beast rear and scamper and he used the head to smash into the front of the villa. He heard a shouting and realized it came from within the Dragon.

It was Garlyck, down in the hold. 'Hey, hey, hey,' he shouted. 'Think about us. We're rattling about down here. Stop pratting about and get the hell out of it.'

Angus looked down. Garlyck was clinging on for dear life while the chickens hopped and ran and the goats nipped at his legs.

Angus brought the Dragon down and set it to run between the trees towards the river. He took it through a sharp ninety-degree turn until it was moving parallel to the river, and then guided it up a grassy slope. In front of him he saw a tall thin man in a singlet emerge from the bushes at the side of the path. He came jogging down the slope directly towards the Dragon. He tried to stop but slipped on the damp grass. His arms flailed and he managed to dive to one side as the Dragon charged past.

*

Marmellius, unable to sleep, had gone for an early morning run.

He was sitting on a log, catching his breath, when he heard the commotion in the camp. He began to sprint back. Half-way down the bank he saw the Dragon turn out of the woods and accelerate towards him. He could not believe his eyes. Rational as he was in all situations, he felt a thrill of terror as the Dragon turned and its neck arched and it raced towards him, its giant rear legs clawing the ground. At the last moment Marmellius dived to one side and landed face-down in a muddy puddle. The claws of the Dragon tore the earth only a few feet from where he lay.

As the Dragon passed he heard, or thought he heard, the sound of clucking.

The Dragon reached the top of the hill and was greeted with a sudden flash of lightning followed by a long rolling roar of thunder. The rain came hissing down.

Angus had a rough plan. He knew there was a swampy area to the east of Roscius' Camp VI and he decided to make for there. He avoided the deep forest but skirted round, driving the Dragon over the scrub and small trees. To be driving the beast again felt good. He trimmed the rhythm of the rear driving legs until they were delivering maximum thrust. He fed more power from the spinning fly-wheel to all the systems and the Dragon leaped forwards, scampering like a giant frog.

The rain sliced down and the ground turned to mud. Visibility declined.

Eventually he came to a place where two rivers pouring down from the moors encountered a flat depression. This was the swamp, and it became a lake whenever there was heavy rain. It was here that Coll and Gwydion had almost drowned on their journey to Cormac.

Angus cut the power and began looking for a place where he could enter the margin of the swamp. He knew that if he was lucky, he would be able to drive over the shallow water and then find a place where he could abandon the Dragon under the trees. After which he and Garlyck could take a leisurely walk back to Drummer's caves with their chickens and goats and whatever else they could carry.

Without any warning they came to the bank. Before he could do anything about it, the Dragon lost traction and skidded down and into the water. Angus hit the emergency full power switch. Instead of trying to stop the Dragon he accelerated so that the Dragon drove forwards, planing over the tops of the rotting logs and reeds. He dared not lose speed lest the Dragon start to sink.

Garlyck climbed up and joined him.

'What's it like down there?' asked Angus.

'Bloody wet. The chickens aren't happy, I can tell you. Where are you heading for?'

'A way out of this. The water's rising.'

Together they scanned the surface of the swamp trying to find the best course, never letting the Dragon slow for an instant.

'There, to the right,' shouted Garlyck. 'It looks like a shingle bank or something. Drive up there. If we can get to higher ground . . .'

The Dragon lurched as the drive feet suddenly clawed into the bed-rock, sending up a shower of stones and mud. Then the beast heaved out of the water and pulled itself up on to the high ground. Angus cut the power quickly and lowered the tractor mechanism. The Dragon lurched and began a steady climb.

For half an hour it ground its way up the slope, tacking back and forth to avoid high rocky outcrops. At the crest it teetered for a moment before plunging down on the other side. But in that moment both Angus and Garlyck saw in front of them the hard profile and high pylons of a Roman road. It was the small road which led to Castra Skusa. A heavy arched bridge had been built at the place where the road crossed a ravine. Luckily there were no vehicles on the bridge at that moment and Angus took the Dragon crashing down through the scrub and undergrowth and finally brought it to a halt directly under the bridge. He manoeuvred until they were partly hidden by the shrubs and ferns growing on the side of the ravine.

Methodically he began to close the Dragon down.

'Are you going to leave it here?' asked Garlyck.

'Good a place as any. Under the road where they can't see it. Out of the rain. And I doubt that they'll be able to follow us here. This rain'll wash out our tracks.' What he did not mention was that he had parked directly under one of the road power points. 'Now come on. Let's get back. Perol'll skin me alive for this little enterprise.'

The journey back took a day and a half.

When they finally made it down into the valley they were given a tremendous reception. And Angus was right, Perol did tear strips off him. But he weathered it and when she quietened down he pointed at the goats. 'Think of the cheese,' he said.

Marmellius was not so fortunate.

He stood to attention in full regalia and made his report. Old Ulysses listened, looking at the ground, nodding patiently.

At the end he let Marmellius stand for a minute. Then he said, 'So they escaped from the camp, stole back the Dragon from under your nose and you didn't capture my son. How would you rate the success of your enterprise, Marmellius? Out of ten?'

'Er, pretty low.'

'I agree. Thanks be to Mithras we had at least one triumph to show that we're still competent fighting men. We captured that rat Roscius. Dismiss, Marmellius.'

6   The Library

Two soldiers, nicknamed Romulus and Remus by their mates, were lost.

After the assault on Stand Alone Stan, they had pushed ahead faster than the main detachment, hoping to find some small settlement to pillage. Dropping down from the high Wolds, they had come to a zig-zag path at the bottom of which they found themselves stumbling about amid pine trees.

'We'd better head back,' said Romulus nervously, thinking of bears and wolves and dragons. 'We don't know what might be out here.'

'Bit of path here,' said Remus, paying no attention, and lifting his assault rifle. 'Must lead somewhere. Come on.'

Cautiously, with rifles advanced, each surveying the territory to front and sides, they moved through the dark wood.

They came into the sunlight as though they had passed through an invisible door, and there they gawped in astonishment. Where they had expected to see more trees and grass or a hovel with thatched roof, they found instead a stately mansion nestled beneath tall beech trees with brightly coloured outbuildings, gleaming windows, neat fields, an artificial lake, terraces and windmills. They had never seen anything like it. It was completely silent. It was like a painting or a stage set. Nothing moved.

Facing them, just beyond a stone bridge, was a gateway above which was a sign that said, ONLY FOOLS ALLOWED WITHIN.

'What the hell's that supposed to mean?' whispered Remus and he lifted his rifle and fired at the inscription sending chips of stone flying. The noise of the shot was loud and echoed round the hills, sending birds clamouring from the trees.

'Quit it,' said Romulus hurriedly, glancing round. 'Better be careful. Might be some fancy retreat for the top brass. We go stumbling in there, we get our arses kicked.'

'Looks deserted,' said Remus. 'Look at them fancy towers and that house. Tell you, Rom, we won't get a chance like this again.'

No more they would, but at that moment they heard an explosion. Dust and smoke rose from one of the hills. 'Hey, what's—' began Romulus but his voice was cut short by another explosion. They saw some trees close to the house shake.

'Someone's got there before us,' said Remus. Moments later they saw smoke begin to rise from the white and grey villa at the centre of the community.

'Come on, let's get in there,' shouted Romulus breaking cover and running out on to the path. 'Come on. They're burning the place.'

For years Roscius had remained secure at Stand Alone Stan, aware that he was vulnerable but trusting to the network of informers and sympathizers who sifted the news and gossip which leaked from the Imperial Palace in Eburacum. He had also been protected by the innate conservatism and lack of curiosity which characterized the Roman state.

But even the best systems fail when the rules change.

Where in the past the emperors had secured their power by maintaining shifting alliances among the many military leaders who managed the Empire, Lucius Prometheus Petronius was different. He kept things to himself and never revealed his mind. He was unpredictable, and that was part of his strength. An order was given and carried out without reference or consultation. The wider plan was not revealed. The attack on Stand Alone Stan was one example.

Roscius heard about it only the day before, though he had been alerted some weeks earlier that something strange was going on.

On a fine blue day, a flyer was seen wobbling in the air over the high Wolds in the direction of Stand Alone Stan. At first Roscius thought it might be Angus coming back, but the machine vanished over the hills without coming close. It might not even have been aware of them.

The portly philosopher Marcus, whose classes had had such

an influence on Angus and Perol, puffed on the stub of his cigar and watched it go. He shook his head.

'What do you think it means?' asked Roscius.

'The end,' said Marcus and he threw the stub of his cigar into the bushes. 'Begin to pack up your books, scholar. Nowhere is safe any more. Time to retreat to the dark woods. Or better still, to Africa.'

Danea, standing close, scooped up the cigar butt with her trowel and handed it to Marcus. 'Here. Dispose of your rubbish yourself,' she said. 'Not among my flowers.'

Roscius smiled. 'No need to be alarmist, Marcus. I'm sure we have time to make a proper decision. I agree we are no longer secure. But there's been no hint of trouble. I'll start some enquiries.'

'Well you have my warning,' said Marcus looking at the remains of his cigar with disgust. 'Everything comes to an end. Consider cigars.' And with that he wandered off holding the trowel.

Roscius did take action – he had not survived so long without taking heed of warnings – but his heart was not in it. Too long he had trusted to his old methods of defence. He could not believe an attack on his house might be coming. He had heard not a word.

He began a slow packing. The most valuable and ancient texts – an eyewitness account of the end of the Trojan War, some songs of science from old Atlantis and a strange text printed on gold which Roscius was trying to decode – all were taken down to the secret library underground and enclosed in copper-bound chests which were then pumped free of air. Meanwhile, the security staff combed the radio frequencies for any signs of danger. But they heard nothing. The only report of any concern related to a small band of soldiers on some sort of reconnais-sance outing in the woods north of Eburacum. Otherwise every-thing seemed normal and Roscius relaxed.

At dinner on the night before the attack on Stand Alone Stan, Roscius dined with his closest friends and students. He spoke about the sighting of the flyer. 'It was probably some young fellow out from Petuaria – skylarking. I see no immediate danger to us, but as my philosophical friend warns, we must take action. Our time at Stand Alone Stan is coming to an end. I have decided that our villa here will be closed down over the next few months. Slowly. Carefully. Protecting what we have. I propose a gradual withdrawal.'

'Where to, Roscius?' asked Danea. 'Down into the forest?'

Roscius shook his head. 'Not unless we have to. I was thinking of somewhere further afield – warmer and not so damp. Perhaps the Western Empire, perhaps the Southern Ocean, perhaps Africa.' There was polite laughter. 'I am not getting any younger,' he continued, patting his pot belly and running his fingers through what was left of his red hair. 'And what's more these damned ulcers on my legs keep coming back. I don't want to keep running away ... the life of a fugitive lacks glamour. I know we've had a good time here ... but I would like to find somewhere where we could be really secure. I thought we should discuss the future, now, while there is still time.'

At that moment an attendant hurried in and whispered urgently to Roscius. Those round the table, enjoying the late harvest wine, saw Roscius grow suddenly pale. He drank his wine quickly and when next he spoke his voice trembled.

'It would appear from a report just received that assault troops are massing at Petuaria. What this means is not clear except that our departure may be sooner than we hoped.'

During the night everyone worked, carrying the books, the manuscripts, the paintings and valuable vases down into the underground chamber and stacking them against the damp-proofed walls. Gradually the shelves filled up, and the floors were covered. The people saved what they could, working quietly.

In the middle of the night Roscius contacted his security camps, selecting numbers I, III, VII and IX only. The messages were brief, a pre-arranged code, alerting the custodians to prepare the camps, that people were on their way.

The windows of the villa were covered with heavy curtains and no lights were allowed outside. Look-outs were posted in the tallest of the towers.

'They won't come till dawn,' said Hetty, packing her journals into an oak chest. The journals represented a lifetime's study of mythology and Nature, for Hetty was an inveterate note-taker. 'They won't try to attack in the dark.'

Dawn came and the look-outs reported no movements in the hills. There was a feeling of unreality as the light brightened and the birds sang. Everything so normal!

But then the radios went crazy. Troop movements were occurring on several fronts, moving up the east coast, moving inland, establishing a base close to Stand Alone Stan.

Before long, carts piled high with belongings were trundling away from the villa and down a narrow lane which wound back and forth beneath the trees dropping steeply down to the forest in the plain below.

Some of the students wanted to fight, to stay and make a stand, but Roscius shooed them away. 'No. Fight with your pens not with swords. Go now. Help the people down below. Protect the knowledge you have. Away. Away.' They protested, but they left.

Danea kissed Roscius. 'See you in Camp III,' she said. 'Now don't delay. Don't linger. We've done what we can here. I'll make a poultice for that leg, for when you arrive.' She turned to Marcus. 'And you be careful too.' Then she was gone, perched atop one of the carts among her seeds and bulbs and plants, her handsome face grave and tired.

As the cart creaked down the slope, they heard the distant rattle of gunfire.

Next it was Hetty's turn to depart. 'I'll take my chance on foot,' she said. 'I know the woods well and the gods of the green wood are kinder than most men.' She shook hands with Marcus and Roscius in a formal manner. 'I hope we meet again. If not now, then in another place and another time.'

Then she too was gone, walking into trees beside the lane.

Finally there was only Roscius and Marcus left. They gathered on the marble terrace and stared up at the sky. They watched appalled as a column of smoke rose over the hills.

'What would you consider the legitimate limits of non-violence?' asked Marcus, lighting a cigar.

Roscius looked at him. 'Not now, philosopher,' he said. 'Not when the darkness is at our door. I've yet a few things to stow down below. Excuse me.'

Roscius hurried away and left Marcus staring up at the column of smoke. 'I was thinking of poor Angus,' muttered Marcus to himself. 'He'd have been a handy man to have with us just now. Him and Perol and that other one . . . what was his name . . . Sean.'

Behind him the radio telephone rang. Marcus reached out but then stopped himself. 'No. Too risky. It's all too late anyhow.' He let the apparatus ring and then he pulled its cord from the wall.

Roscius walked through the empty rooms. There were still valuable carpets on the floor and rich curtains at the windows but there was nothing he could do to save them. The big chamber underground was full.

Suddenly Roscius heard a shot. It had come from the pine woods near the gate. He hurried down to his study where he found Marcus waiting for him. Quickly Roscius opened a panel in the wall. Facing him were two sets of shiny copper contact plates – a bit of Angus' handiwork. 'Farewell the past,' said Roscius and he closed one of the contacts. Outside there came a muffled explosion and the room shook. 'Welcome the future,' said Marcus and he closed the second contact. Nothing happened. The two men looked at one another and then a second explosion, nearer this time, shook the windows.

Marcus heaved a sigh of relief. 'I thought the bloody thing wasn't going to blow.'

Roscius wiped away a tear. 'If it hadn't then I think I would have answered your question.'

'What question?'

'About violence. Some things leave us no choice. We have to defend them. No matter what.'

Marcus slapped him on the arm. 'Young Angus would be proud of you,' he said. 'All's done. Come on. Let's go.'

He ran outside to the back of the house. Two horses were

waiting. Marcus heaved himself on to the larger one, released its bridle from the wall and urged it towards the covered lane.

It was some minutes later when Marcus was already half-way down the hill and riding through the dappled shade that he realized that Roscius was not with him. He reined in and turned in the saddle. He was about to call, but then he heard shooting.

'Romantic,' he murmured, shaking his head, and urged his horse into a canter.

Roscius had not meant to delay, but with the library buried, he felt a bitter rage sweep over him. Any of his students who could have seen him would have been horrified. This mild somewhat clown-like figure with his red nose and frizz of carrot-coloured hair stood rigid and beat his fists on the desk.

Then he ran from the study and out to the dining-room. Moments later he was holding a lighted candle under the fine curtains. The flame ran up the fabric like a snake. He set all the curtains alight. He broke a sandalwood screen and piled it over cane chairs and set them alight in the doorway. The flames caught. The wooden building began to burn. Soon the fire would spread, leaping from building to building, consuming the old pagoda and the minarets and tall towers.

Satisfied, Roscius hurried to the door to the stables and there he met the black-uniformed Romulus and Remus.

All three were startled, but Romulus the trained assault fighter, veteran of many skirmishes, reacted by instinct. He jabbed upwards with his rifle catching Roscius in the stomach and then slammed the rifle butt into his face.

Roscius fell without a sound.

'Why the hell was he smiling?' asked Remus.

Outside two columns of dust were still rising.

Beneath them, trees were canted over where a long low depression had formed.

Deeper, beneath the roots, the iron doors which protected the library were locked in place, and buried under several hundred tons of rock. No sign of the library or the access road that led to it now remained.

Inside the black chamber only one bookcase had canted over

when the charges went off. The books slipped off the shelf one by one and landed with a heavy thump. The echoes died. The air became still. Then there was silence.

Post scriptum for Roscius

Romulus and Remus had no idea what a prize they had captured and it was only the strict order that people were to be taken alive that saved Roscius. When the main assault force arrived during the afternoon they duly handed Roscius over to Piticus, explaining that he was the only person found on the premises and that he had set fire to the house.

Piticus sniffed. 'Saved us a bother,' he said looking at the charred ruins. 'Must've been a big place.' He turned to Roscius who had been thrown down on the ground in front of his assault car. 'So what's your name and what were you doing here?'

Roscius could hardly speak his face was so swollen.

'e-sceeus.'

'Eh?'

Roscius made signs that he wanted something to write on and the back of an order form was duly produced and a pen. He wrote, 'My name is Roscius, the writer and historian.'

Piticus saw the educated style of writing. He read the message aloud so there could be no mistake and Roscius nodded.

Piticus knew the name of Roscius though he had never read any of his books. For those who served in the military, the name of Roscius was synonymous with a traitor, a corrupter of youth, a man dedicated to the overthrow of civilization. Piticus looked at the pathetic clown-like creature that lay at his feet. Something didn't add up.

'If you are joking . . .' he began. But then he wondered why anyone in their right mind would claim to be Roscius, for the fate was certain to be a slow and painful death. Crucifixion perhaps – upside down.

Word of the capture was sent to Marcus Ulysses in Eburacum along with a description of Roscius.

Word came back immediately. 'Save him. Send him to Eburacum. At once.'

This they did. Later Romulus and Remus were given promotion 'for services to the State' and the reward for the capture was divided between them and Piticus.

In Eburacum, Roscius was held under twenty-four-hour surveillance. In the evening he dined with Marcus Ulysses for though he was a renowned enemy of the State, he was nevertheless a high-born Roman and hence given special treatment. Under interrogation Roscius insisted that he had only been visiting the area of Stand Alone Stan, and that he had spent most of his time as a fugitive living on a ship anchored off Manavia which would by now have sailed away. When asked about the house where he had been captured he said, the report of Romulus and Remus notwithstanding, that it was a crude imitation of a Roman villa, built by 'savages' who had run away at the first hint of trouble. He span simple lies with just enough truth to make them credible.

Word was sent to Emperor Lucius that the famous traitor Roscius had been netted. 'Capital,' effused Lucius. 'Liked his prose style. Always have. Terse and no nonsense. Shame about the content.'

Three days later Roscius was dispatched to Roma. There he dined with the Emperor and the next day he was shaved of all his body hair and put on display, in a cage suspended in the forum.

Copies of his works, seized over the years, were brought to a nearby temple. The plan was to ignite them under the cage in which Roscius was held and cook him slowly.

But the night before the burning, when Roscius was brought his evening meal (for he was fed well and given certain comforts) the man who brought him the food said, 'The wine has a taste fit for the gods. Drink deeply.'

Roscius sniffed the flask which contained the wine and smelled the unmistakable odour of hemlock. 'Thank you,' he said. 'To all of you. *Ave atque vale*. Hail and farewell.'

He ate and then he drank. He felt a numbness begin to rise through him and then he called for paper and wrote his epitaph. 'No debts.'

7 Coll the Singer

As soon as his decision to become a singer was made, Coll's training began.

Cormac was a strict master. In the mornings Coll learned to play the cithara. He practised until he could string the instrument in the dark. He learned the different tunings which matched moods. He improvised, sitting by the marsh, under the trees, in the sun and in the shade. He learned strict songs while Cormac tapped out an exact rhythm. His wrists ached and sometimes his fingers bled – but slowly he learned to play and his hands hardened.

Coll did not find the learning easy and his voice was harsh.

When he was not playing the cithara he was learning the other arts of the singer and these took him into strange worlds. 'When we sing we move out of this world,' said Cormac. 'We join other worlds.'

'How many other worlds?'

'Hundreds. You don't count them. This is not something mathematical. You learn how to live with them. When we play we bring worlds together, one foot over here, one foot over there. As living creatures, born of the earth, we have a place in those worlds too – well, in most of them. You're called Coll. That means you have a place in the world of the trees. But what place do you have in the animal world?'

Coll looked at him askance. 'I haven't a clue what you're talking about.'

'Yes you have,' said Cormac. 'You just haven't recognized things yet. You don't quite trust it. You will.'

One evening they sat outside the tree-house.

'Close your eyes,' said Cormac. 'Now watch.'

Cormac began to play the cithara and after a few moments Coll felt a small animal jump up on to his leg and scamper up to his shoulder. He heard noises in the bushes.

Coll did not want to open his eyes but a force greater than his will made his eyes open. The glade was brilliant with light which flowed from the trees.

Animals stood round as they had on the night when Cormac summoned his powers. Opposite, Coll saw a stag with a magnificent spread of antlers. It dipped its head and the antlers rattled the branches. Coll became aware of the breathing of a beast at his shoulder and he turned and found himself staring into the bright amber eyes of a tiger. The head was huge and he felt its breath on his cheek. It stared back at him and then returned its gaze to Cormac.

Cormac had transformed into a giant vole with whiskered face. He was pounding the cithara, striking at the strings with his claws. Then all the animals started to howl. They turned, opening up an entrance. Coll became aware of a clattering in the bushes. Some creature was approaching, running through the forest, and it burst into the middle of the ring just as the vole that was Cormac struck the strings for the last time. It was a pig, with stiff hair on its back, curving tusks and mighty shoulders. It looked round grunting and squealing in a state of high excitement and then it saw Coll and lowered its head and approached him, nosing the soil.

The pig spoke. It said, 'Come on.' Coll squealed and squirmed off the chair. Moments later he was running through the forest aware of tremendous power in his legs: aware too of scents which came at him sharp and colourful, and branches which scratched down his back. He was racing and he twisted and changed direction without slackening speed. He ran down to the edge of the marsh and turned on his back and rolled in the mud, arching his spine and grunting with delight. Then he was up again and splashing through the water and bounding up the bank towards where Cormac sat at the foot of the tree.

Cormac was asleep with the cithara cradled in his arms and his head resting on its string board. Coll butted him with his head and the old man started awake. He reached down and scratched Coll on the back of his head and Coll jumped back up into his vacant chair.

'So you're back,' said Cormac. 'Have fun?'

'I've had a hell of a funny dream if that's what you mean.'

'Oh aye. Tell me.'

'I dreamed I was a pig.'

'And?'

'That's all.'

'It wasn't a dream. You were a pig. Now if you'd asked me, I'd have guessed you would be a ferret or an otter perhaps. But no. You turn out to be a right noble beast, full of wit and magic. A pig eh? Fancy that.'

'But . . .' began Coll.

Coll became aware that Cormac was gradually leading him into stranger and stranger territory. 'If you are going to be a singer, you must have sympathy for all creation,' he said. 'You must go to places which are new and difficult.'

Once Coll dreamed – for he still felt safer if he called his experiences dreams – that he was a woman giving birth. The pain was enormous and it seemed to engulf him in waves. In one small part of his mind he heard a tiny voice which cried, 'This isn't happening. Not to me.' But it was and the pain washed over him and he tried to push it away from him. And pushing so, he felt delirious as the baby slithered out. Later he gave milk and felt strong and tender and infinitely tired.

When he awoke he would not talk of his experience and Cormac thrust the cithara into his arms. 'All right, if you won't tell me, tell the instrument. Play the feeling into the instrument. It can take it. It has coped with worse and better. It doesn't get embarrassed.'

And play Coll did. For the first time he felt that the cithara bent itself to him so that he played with ease, the instrument tucked into his arm.

'That's more like it,' said Cormac approvingly. 'Whenever we learn something new, we have to give away old understanding. That can be hard. Look at me. I'm very old in your years . . . but I'm still learning. It never stops . . . it doesn't get much easier either,' he added thoughtfully.

One fine morning Cormac took Coll down to the stream. Coll was a true apprentice now and he carried the master's cithara while the old man leaned on his shoulder. They talked easily too in a light banter which allowed difficult things to be said.

'I'm going to introduce you to an old friend,' said Cormac. 'The most beautiful woman you'll ever meet, but don't fall in love with her. Play to her and listen to what she says.'

Coll sat down by the tumbling water. 'I drank here before I decided I wanted to be a singer.'

Cormac nodded. 'I know. No wonder you were so clear-headed. Go on, play.' Cormac strolled away to leave the young man on his own.

Coll re-tuned the cithara until he felt the notes were right. Then he played, trying to find a melody which would match the water and the sunlight. Nothing happened. Try as he would, he could not make the music feel right. He stared into the water and felt powerless. He tried to play again but the sound was harsh and finally he gave up and just sat by the stream looking at the play of light on its surface. He could see his own reflection staring back at him.

When Cormac came back he asked what had happened.

'Nothing,' said Coll. 'I began to feel useless. I just sat here. I couldn't get the music right.'

'Ah well. That happens to the best of us sometimes. She didn't want to see you, that's all. Perhaps next time. We can only ask. But they decide.'

'Who is she?' asked Coll, picking up the cithara.

'The spirit of the stream. She came when the stream did. Quite a lady when you get to know her. But strong too. Very strong. Were you happy, lad?'

'I was. When I started to play, I thought this will be lovely.'

'Ah,' said Cormac, mock serious with his hand across his chest. 'Youth. What a splendid thing. But listen to an old man. When you are happy, play sad. You won't be diminished. And when you are sad, play sad, it will relieve you.'

'But when can I be happy?'

'Don't think about it. Ask your companion, there at your side. Ask him what he knows of happiness.'

Coll thought of his Death which walked beside him at all times.

'Here's a riddle for you,' said Cormac. He held out his skinny brown hand palm up, and then he turned it palm down, showing the back. 'Now, which one of those is the hand?'

If his visit to the stream showed Coll the limit of his powers, a later visit showed him the strength that was waiting.

For this stage of his training Cormac took Coll far away from the tree-house to an ancient burial mound visible from the main Roman road which connected Eburacum with Caledonia – the very road which old Ulysses travelled when journeying to and from Farland Head. Coll had travelled it often.

He paid it hardly a glance as they scrambled down a bank and came to a small group of standing stones. Gwydion remained behind on guard.

Close to the ring of stones was a long low hill. Cormac squatted down at one end where twin stones supported a heavy lintel. He made Coll sit opposite and breathe in the juice from some crushed herbs to relax him and clear his head. 'We're going to contact the guardian spirit of this place,' he said. 'Remember, nothing is ever lost. The old wisdom is all here,' he gestured round, 'in the stones, in the remains of the old wanderers. But you must not be afraid. Fear is the enemy of knowledge. We will play and sing together. Follow me.'

Cormac held the instrument between them. He began to tap out a rhythm on his small hand-drum. Coll plucked the strings while Cormac changed the pitch. When the music was established, Cormac began to sing in a droning monotone. It was a song with words but the words were lost to Coll – still he tried to join in.

They sang for an hour during which Coll's arm became tired and his back started to ache. Cormac seemed to feel nothing. The old man had drifted into a trance almost immediately.

When Coll could hardly bear the pain of plucking the strings any more, Cormac struck his drum twice and laid the cithara to one side. He began speaking and chanting. Coll relaxed and felt himself falling asleep. He tried to keep awake but there was a force working on him and he leaned back against the old burial mound.

Immediately it seemed the sky brightened. Coll found himself standing in a place of long grass where a wind blew steadily, pressing the grass into waves. Standing beside him was a tall warrior with scars on his face and tattooed arms. He wore a head-dress of feathers and a necklace of desiccated mice. Cormac. He pointed, and Coll saw in the distance a figure which was hopping towards them, first on one foot then on the other and carrying a long spear, crowned with a tuft of feathers.

Coll lifted his hand to shade his eyes. His wrists were brace-leted with tusks from a wild boar. He felt a weight on his head and knew that he wore a head-dress which incorporated the skull of a pig.

'Such things protect in this world,' whispered Cormac. 'But this warrior approaching is our friend.'

The hopping man was now close. Coll saw that while he was perfectly proportioned, he was quite small. Smaller than Coll. He wore a long woven cloak which flapped in the wind. It was decorated with eagle feathers. On his head was a crested head-dress. He held his spear in front of him and called a challenge.

Cormac answered him. The warrior seemed satisfied and moved his spear until it was pointing directly at Coll. He shouted his challenge again and Coll said, 'I come in peace.' It was all he could think of to say. It seemed to be enough.

The warrior hopped closer. When he was no more than two yards away he suddenly raised his spear and plunged it deep into the ground. Then he stripped off his outer cloak and hung it on the spear. He spread the garment until it enclosed three quarters of a circle and placed stones on the hem. He crawled inside and Coll and Cormac joined him.

A conversation began which to Coll's ears seemed to consist of snatches of song, moments of laughter and long pauses during which Cormac and the small warrior sat looking at one another with no sense of embarrassment. Occasionally Cormac trans-lated what was being said. He introduced Coll and the warrior nodded, neither smiling nor frowning. Coll saw a brown face, very tanned and wrinkled, with high cheekbones and a wide, flat nose. The eyes were bright and birdlike and studied Coll with the kind of frank curiosity which in the Roman world would have been considered rude. The man's hair was thinning and his beard was wispy – but the face did not seem old. It was a noble face and, the nose apart, it could have appeared stamped on a Roman coin.

'I have told him you do not yet speak the language,' said Cormac, 'and he says that if you come back he will teach you.'

Coll nodded. 'Tell him that he is very kind.'

Cormac grinned. 'He wouldn't understand. He is not being kind in the way you mean. He is being sensible. He knows you will need his songs. His knowledge is in his songs. And it is your knowledge too. It is your birthright. He will teach you so that the knowledge is not lost. But he *is* kind too, you are right.'

'Tell him I will come.'

'Tell him yourself.'

But the warrior had understood. He nodded, and for the first time he smiled. The years fell away and Coll could have been facing a young man little older than himself.

Cormac and the warrior were in conversation for a long time, speaking quickly. Coll sat and listened trying to guess what they were saying. Then Cormac held up his hand while he translated. 'He tells me that next year he will be dedicated protector spirit of this place. He will be killed near here and his spirit will enter the land to remain until the land is no more. So you must come to him soon.'

Outside the tent the wind moaned softly.

Cormac picked up his cithara and together he and the bird warrior shared a song. But before they had finished, the wind suddenly gusted and the sides of the tent billowed and lifted.

'Time to go,' said Cormac. 'The wind is telling us.'

He crawled out of the small tent and stood up. Coll joined him. Without a word the small warrior lifted the cloak away from the spear and threw it round his shoulders. He pulled the spear from the ground and hopped back. He called some words and then he turned and started to run, loping over the ground with an easy run.

'He says he will look forward to your meeting.'

'Me too,' said Coll. 'Why isn't he hopping?'

'He is no longer in the power of the eagle.'

And with that darkness fell.

They woke up to the smell of wood-smoke. Gwydion had started a small fire and was warming water. He had baked some bread cakes. He also had a flask of wine. Coll was starving and thirsty but Cormac insisted that the first corner of the bread be scorched and then placed outside the burial mound and likewise that some wine be poured on to the ground. Only then could they eat and drink.

'You know why,' said Gwydion. 'Not for what the food is, but for what the action means. Remember?'

And Coll did. Little by little this new world was starting to make sense. 'Is he buried in there?' he asked nodding towards the burial mound.

'Yes. With several others,' said Cormac.

'Who was he?'

'A man at home with his world. Afraid of nothing, because nothing could hurt him. I envy him.'

Gwydion poured the wine.

Cormac continued. 'You see, in those early days everything was a message – the wind, the rain, the sunrise and the phases of the moon and he lived by those messages. He was part of them. The rivers and the trees and the hills were as valuable as he was. No more, no less, though he wouldn't have thought of it like that. He was closer to everything.'

'What were his songs?' asked Coll, nibbling bread.

'Ah. His songs. Now there's a puzzle for you. His songs are his understanding. In his songs he names things, he reaches out. You'll feel them buffet you, and pull you apart – and when you feel like that, you'll know that you are human. Do you understand?'

'A bit.'

'Well he will teach you, not by telling you things for there is nothing to tell. But by letting you feel things, by letting you see through his mind: and you'll be there, back where it all started, this ... this ... adventure. And when you can sing his songs, his power will be yours. You'll talk to the trees and the birds and the hills in their language – and you won't feel daft. But remember two things, Coll. The first is that song is more powerful than the singer. The second is that if you stay away too long in the song, you will never come back.'

Coll had more questions, but Cormac shook his head. He was tired. The effort of building the bridge back through thousands of years had taken its toll. He rolled himself up in his cloak by the fire and fell asleep.

Coll sat for a while with his back to the burial mound, his eyes reflecting the firelight. In those few moments he made a decision. That he would come back to this place, many times, for it was his place. He would learn. This was what he wanted.

Eventually he too dozed.

He was awakened once briefly in the night when a Roman convoy passed down the road, travelling fast. As chance would have it, the lead vehicle was the *Ithaca*. Old Ulysses was travelling south to Eburacum. It was just two days before the attack on Stand Alone Stan.

The next day they returned to Cormac's house under the oak tree.

That evening and all the next day Cormac sat cradling the cithara and rocking back and forth, singing to himself while Coll beat the drum. Cormac was reaching out to Stand Alone Stan, bringing the comforts of a singer.

Late that night, Gwydion returned with news. He had visited one of the neighbouring villages and had been drinking in one of the inns when a runner arrived telling of the burning of the town. 'Lyf is dead. Burned.'

'And Miranda?' asked Coll.

'Escaped. They reckon Lyf got her out. Her and a woman called Gwellan and some kids. That's when he was captured.'

'Events are moving quickly now,' said Cormac. 'Remember the wave that is coming to a crest? I told you about that. Surely you can feel it now?'

Coll nodded. He was starting to feel something akin to the nervousness he had known when he was a junior officer at the Military Academy and binding his knuckles before an appearance at the Battle Dome.

*

Cormac stepped up his training. He decided that despite the unrest, it was time for Coll to do his first singing in public. He named a village that Coll had never heard of but which made Gwydion laugh. The performance would be a few weeks hence.

Cormac drilled Coll until the young man felt dizzy. When they relaxed, he explained the protocol. 'First they'll feed us and we behave as the mood strikes us. You don't have to be funny or sad or grateful or anything. Just be yourself. Then will come the singing. You can sing a few songs everyone knows – the song of the magpie, for instance – old favourites. But then they're going to want something more. They'll want you to go back, to sing of the start of things and that's where you must try to visit Dark Eagle, or think of one of the places you have been with him. Go there willingly, forget the present, bring back whatever you receive. But don't worry if you flounder about. We all do. I did when I started and I'd had much more training than you.'

'And then?'

'Then do whatever you like. When I was your age I used to cast my eye round to see if one of the girls had that special look. And I'd go after her. Good singing always generates lust. But it is over to you. It is your night. You're in charge. It'll be your first night of singing, so enjoy it and then it'll be back to the learning.'

That night Coll begged leave to return to the burial mound alone. Cormac looked at him hard, and then gave his permission. 'Go for two days. And if you're not back after two days I'll send Gwydion to get you. And remember my warning.'

'I will.'

Coll returned after two days. He seemed in good health but was quiet and reserved.

'Well?' said Cormac, anxiously. 'How was it?'

Coll sat for a few moments, as though trying to remember. 'OK,' he said finally. 'Good.' He nodded as though agreeing with himself. 'Right, let's get back to the practice, eh?'

And with that Cormac had to be content.

*

The day of the first singing came too soon for Coll.

On the morning of his performance he woke early and felt sick. He wanted to lie in bed and wondered if he could sham an illness. But he heard Cormac and Gwydion moving about in the small house talking about the coming journey and knew that he could not avoid his fate.

After food, they packed up a few belongings, loaded up Aristotle and set out. Gwydion led, followed by Cormac on the donkey. Last came Coll carrying the instrument in its black bag, staring at Aristotle's behind.

They travelled south, following a path which meandered under the trees. Already some leaves were turning brown and falling and the air smelled damp.

The small procession passed through several villages. Wherever they paused, people came running out of their houses to speak to Cormac, asking him when he was coming to sing. And always Cormac replied with a jest and introduced Coll as his apprentice and told the people to make him welcome too and invite him. Coll felt uncomfortable when people looked at him without smiling and whispered behind his back. More than once he heard the names Viti and Ulysses.

They also received news. The first attacks on Stand Alone Stan and other villages had ended. But there were rumours of new attacks being prepared, of Roman forces moving into the green woods without warning. Many people had already moved away but others were arming themselves. And there was talk of plans that were afoot to burn the forest, but no one knew when or where. Everywhere people were skittish.

Eventually, late in the evening, after a long hike over moorland and down into a valley, Gwydion led the donkey through one of the wide gates which blocked the road at the entrance to a village. A bell rang in the trees when the gate opened and people came hurrying with lanterns on poles.

People gathered round them, jostling and calling for favours and offering gifts of wine and baked sweetmeats. Suddenly Coll felt himself seized from behind and swung round by a pair of strong arms. Before he could protest he felt himself enveloped and kissed firmly on the mouth. 'Welcome back, Coll,' said a warm voice. 'It's grand to see you.'

By the light of one of the lanterns, Coll saw Bella, the mother of Gwydion and the owner of the inn where he and Angus and Miranda had stayed when they first escaped from the Battle Dome. She looked bigger than ever with her mane of red hair standing out from her head like a crown of snakes. She held him at arm's length. 'Let me look at you? Ee. You've lost weight but I like your beard and you've got a real woodland smell about you.' Coll was not sure what this meant. 'And what a turn-up, eh? You the apprentice of Cormac! Mark you, I always knew you had something special, the way you charmed the animals and all – not to mention the women.' This was news to Coll.

Bella took Coll and Cormac by the arm and led them into her new inn. 'Not as big as the old one or as comfortable, but not bad. This is a small village – all of us who live here are refugees of one kind or another – but we make do. There's not much trade, we're off the beaten track, but that means we're safer too. Can't see the Romans wanting to poke their noses in here – we've got nothing worth taking.'

The dining-room was set up for a performance, just as Coll remembered. A table was already laid and covered with a white cloth to keep the flies off the food. Cormac took his place at one end of the table and gestured for Coll to sit at the other. Bella whipped off the cloth and revealed a feast of pickles and beer and ham and fresh bread and cheese. The small room was already crowded. People kept their distance but sat round and watched every movement as the two men ate – how they tore their bread and cut their cheese – and whispered to one another.

Coll was in a kind of dream. He ate automatically. He was tempted to drink deep, but he resisted and sipped his beer. Not so Cormac. He tucked in and sat cracking jokes and asking questions of the people sitting round. He knew most of them by name and asked questions seeking gossip and news – which couples had joined up, who'd had babies, who had died since his last visit.

But the end of the meal arrived and Cormac clapped his hands for silence.

'This is a special occasion. I've been walking these woods since before your great-grandmothers were children – and I was old and ugly even then.' A mock groan went up from the people sitting round. 'But every good thing comes to an end. I'm getting so daft these days, I can't tell one end of the cithara from the other and my voice is getting hoarse.' He held out his hand and someone passed him a beer mug. 'So I have taken an apprentice in the time-honoured way – that is to say that this young man, Coll of the forest, found his way to me, with a bit of help from his friend, big Gwydion there.' This was greeted with a round of applause. 'And he has showed himself worthy. You are all very privileged to be here at the start of a new singer. It doesn't happen often. We singers are made of flint and leather and we don't wear out easily. Now, the reason I chose this village for the first singing was because I know you are all the fiercest critics, the wisest judges, the kindest souls and the biggest drunkards in the whole wild wood. Ladies and gentlemen, friends and comrades, allow me to introduce Coll.'

Coll stood up and bowed.

Quickly the tables were cleared and a seat was set up in the middle. Cormac moved to a big chair set to one side. He whispered to Coll, 'Give 'em a good show, lad. Lots of heart, lots of tickle. Be yourself.'

Coll sat down. Across from him he saw Gwydion and Bella. Gwydion stuck up two thumbs and Bella raised her fist in encouragement.

He cleared his throat and immediately one of the children stepped out and offered him beer which Coll accepted. He sat for a few moments looking round. He saw the faces, all full of excitement, kids nudging one another and giggling, old men chewing on some remnant of food. He heard himself say, 'This first song I want to dedicate to my teacher Cormac – one of his favourites, I know.' Then Coll performed the old song about a magpie that fell in love with a swan and went to a river to try to wash away the blackness from its feathers. It was a song with very complicated rhythms representing the water and the washing. There was one passage where the instrument was used to imitate the call of the magpie and although Coll faltered and muzzed some notes, the effect was not too bad and the audience – all of whom knew the song backwards and had heard Cormac play it many times – gave him a round of applause. Cormac nodded.

So far so good. Next Coll sang a comical song with a chorus and the audience joined in. Coll was pleased to see feet tapping. The audience were beginning to relax and he started to feel more confident. He sang a teasing love song, deliberately singling out a couple at the back of the room who were obviously in love, and who blushed.

Coll was experiencing the power of the singer. The more he sang the stronger he felt. He began a rollicking bawdy song into which he wove verses dealing with life at Bella's Inn where he had first met Cormac and Lyf and Gwydion. He got people laughing as he described some of their adventures. He looked at Bella, expecting to see her laughing and protesting at his exaggeration. But she was crying. Gwydion had his arm round her and was comforting her. For a moment Coll lost the melody. The momentum dropped away. His nerve failed and the song died. There was a terrible silence, filled only with Bella's sobbing. Some people comforted her: most looked away, embarrassed for Coll. One or two glanced furtively at Cormac to see if he was angry and about to intervene. But he sat back with his eyes closed.

Coll struck a chord fiercely. 'It is hard to remember the happy times when there is so much sadness now. I don't want you to think I am apologizing, but there are some things you should know.' Coll began to play chords and then began telling the story of who he was, how he grew up and his father. He ended with the story of Bella's village being attacked and how he came by the name Coll. He told the story simply and the audience sat, their faces still and serious and attentive. They already knew the bones of the story, but now it was becoming real as part of their tradition. Coll finished with the same chord with which he had begun, sounding each note separately. There was no applause. Nor did Coll want any. He did not want to delay. He was feeling hot inside. He drank quickly and spat into a bowl. There were feelings he needed to get out, and only the music could do it.

'So many died then. And it is still going on. So now I want to sing a song for a man who gave his life recently, who was known to you . . . for Lyf.' He saw Bella look up when he said this and knew that he had touched the cause of her weeping.

'And for Bella who loved him. I'll sing it in the old way if I can.'

Coll began to re-tune the cithara, letting the new relationships of pitch open his mind and heart. He willed himself to ·drift back to join Dark Eagle. He let his fingers wander and heard a voice singing in his head. Cautiously, carefully, like one who walks on slippery stones, he joined the song. It began with a howl and was a keening song about a man, a deer hunter, who was lost in the snow when a storm came from the north. Later, his wife went looking for him and found him frozen beside the carcase of a deer he had killed. The song was about her grief.

As he sang, Coll became the woman, wiping the snow from the dead wanderer's face and crying aloud so that the whole valley would hear and know. The grief was fierce and tore him open, like a bear ripping open a honeycomb.

It ended and the last chord died. Coll sat for a moment while Dark Eagle withdrew from him. When he opened his eyes he found everyone sitting still, staring at the ground. The silence continued. No one wanted to break the spell. Finally it was Bella who stood up. She walked forwards and kissed Coll. 'Thank you. You sang my grief exactly. You did the real work of a singer. I feel lighter already.'

Coll called an interval. He was shaking and could not remember what he had sung though the feelings were still alive in him. He sat at the table and let someone pour him a drink. He was left alone, except for an old woman, who needed two sticks to walk with and who was supported by her granddaughter. She spoke to Coll but her accent was so broad that he could not understand. But her meaning was plain enough. She too was saying thank you and she pressed a small piece of amber into his hand.

Then one or two of the other old people came up to Coll and told him they had seen Dark Eagle sitting with him during the song and it was one of the best 'steppings' they had heard.

'Am I doing all right?' asked Coll of Cormac.

'A bit too sentimental for my taste,' said the old singer. 'But yes. You are doing all right. But don't let them be gone for too long. Hold the magic. Now get them dancing. But I have a word or two to say first.'

Coll struck two chords to gain attention. Cormac lifted his hands. 'There's a ceremony which none of you have seen but which has to be performed before the eyes of witnesses. It is not much. But it is important.' He whistled and Gwydion carried in a leather bag and set it down on a small table to Cormac's side. Cormac undid the catches. 'You know we singers are always sticklers for tradition. Well there is a tradition about the first singing of an apprentice: he is given a singing robe. And here it is.' He lifted the stained green cloak and shook it out. A mouse fell to the floor along with several beetles and a dead moth. The mouse rolled and before any of the inn cats could take an interest, it scampered to Cormac and ran up his leg, finally to appear, nose sniffing, at his neck. 'Well all I can say is I wish I'd had as many gaudy nights as the times I've rolled myself up in this mucky old thing and slept under the trees while the wolves howled. It is a good cloak for a beginning. An honourable cloak. It was given to me by my teacher on the day of my first singing; and my teacher received it from his and so on right back to when Coaly was a pup. So you take good care of it. Chances are it will see you out and maybe another after you. Come here, lad.' Coll approached and Cormac slipped the cloak over his shoulders. He said a few words of the old tongue which Coll was able to understand. He said, 'Here's a new master, starting his learning. Serve him with honour, all courtesy due. Save him from shaking, when cold winds are blowing. Let him sleep easy by frost and by dew.' Then he added in the language of the woodlanders, 'It is I Cormac the Singer who gives this cloak to Coll of my own free will.' Then he clapped his hands. 'That's all. I said it was simple. Now I think a dance, young Coll. Show us what you have in your bag.'

Coll obliged. He played a lively jig. Next he and Cormac shared a round, passing the cithara back and forth between them, each building on what the other had done. Then Gwydion jumped to his feet and danced a stamping dance while the people clapped. It was during this dance that Coll took a few moments to glance round the audience. He saw a young woman with auburn curls who swayed with the rhythm of the dance. She smiled when she saw him looking and then looked away.

'Do I get a chance to dance?' Coll asked Cormac.

'Yes, you can dance. But you must sing the last song. No sloping off now . . .'

But he didn't get the chance. Just as Gwydion ended his dance, there came the sound of a siren whining in the air. The music stopped. The clapping stopped. People listened. They heard the harsh sound of a loudspeaker ordering everyone to stay calm and moments later there came the first sound of gunfire.

Coll looked at Cormac in disbelief.

'No. It's not you they want this time,' said Cormac. 'It's everyone. Keep close to me.'

Even as he spoke they heard the sound of voices in the street. 'Outside,' they shouted. 'Everyone outside.'

Gwydion and Bella were with them in an instant. 'This way. There's a back way . . .' began Gwydion, but Cormac hushed him. 'Go with Bella,' he whispered. 'She needs you now. Don't worry about us. Your work with us is finished.' As he spoke there came pounding at the door. Cormac lifted the cithara and struck it three times. Then he shouted in a huge voice that filled the room. In response, the people began to shout back, building to a battle-anger.

'Now keep close to me, Coll. Never let go of the hem of my cloak. Come on.' Cormac seemed to glide over the floor. Coll followed. At the back of the inn, they came to steps leading down into the darkness. Behind them they heard the door break open. There was a brief patter of gunfire.

Gwydion was set to fight. There was a light in his eyes which anyone who had ever tangled with him knew to fear. But he moved to Bella's side and protected her. The door gave way and three soldiers tumbled into the room. They looked like giant insects in their masks. One fired his gun into the ceiling as a distraction while the others sprayed the room with gas. Even Gwydion wilted like a cut flower, and fell to the floor with a thump.

At the bottom of the steps Cormac began to play, holding the cithara under his cloak.

There were soldiers on guard at the back door as they opened it, but strangely they all turned away and Coll and Cormac slipped past.

Further on they had no option but to pass in front of some high-intensity lights that had been rigged and filled the small town enclosure with their glare. But no one was looking or seemed to see their shadow. Still Cormac played, a monotonous repeat of notes.

In the same way they slipped through a line of soldiers who were all intent on watching the bodies being carried from the inn. Nor were they challenged at the village gate. They hurried past and out into the dark lane. After five minutes they were up on the hillside and the sounds of the tumult in the village seemed distant. They hid at the side of the road and only then did Cormac stop playing. 'You can let go now,' he said.

He whistled softly and a few minutes later they heard a steady clip-clop as Aristotle the donkey made his way peacefully up the lane towards them.

Cormac was mounted.

As they climbed the path from the valley, they heard behind them the siren howl briefly. Turning, they saw the first of the transporters nose its way through the dark trees and depart south.

8 *The Horribles*

After the last of the big Roman freighters departed, the people of Cliff Town enjoyed a brief respite. Fishing resumed. Life returned to normal. The bay became quiet except for the keening of seagulls when the fish were gutted, and the steady, unnoticed because always present, hissing of the sea on the rocks. During the long warm days of summer, men and women sprawled on the flat headland or hung the new-caught fish on smoke racks while the kids chased crabs. Memories of the dark freighters with their cargoes of chemicals faded.

Then one morning, the people heard the throbbing of many engines, and when they looked out through their windows they found the bay filled with all manner of craft. First were giant troop-ships with high decks and thousands of portholes. Landing-craft, small and wedge-shaped, were plying between them and the shore, ferrying soldiers. Already camps had been established at the base of the cliffs. Fires of driftwood were blazing. There was a smell of cooking and latrines had been dug in the sand above high water mark.

But there were other ships too, navigating carefully between the troop-ships and the landing-craft. These were ungainly flat-bottomed barges towed by squat tugs with pounding engines. From the noise of horns and the flashing of signals, not to mention the shouting between ships' crews, it was evident that a blunder had taken place and two separate contingents had arrived in the small bay together. The people of Cliff Town gathered on the headland and watched. This had all the makings of an entertainment that would be told and re-told during the long nights of winter. Some even cheered and called encouragement as one of the barges just sneaked past the prow of a troop-ship and came in to dock.

Minutes later it berthed at the wharf with a heavy thump. The officer in charge, Gaius Daedalus, whose bald head shone with perspiration, lost his footing and fell over. This was greeted with hoots of derision. But one old man was not amused. 'More barrels of that stinking phlogmajig stuff,' he said. 'Fish'll be bad for the winter. You mark my words.' But he was wrong. When the tarpaulins came off the barge, it was not drums of chemicals that were revealed, but two gleaming brass cannon.

'Now what the hell do they want those for?' asked one of the women.

'Maybes they want to put out a fire,' answered another.

At that moment, heavy transport vehicles, their hooters blaring, emerged from the valley woods and followed the road round to the wharf. 'Hey up. Here come the cavalry.'

The vehicles drew up in line just as they had when the drums of liquid phlogiston were being unloaded. Soon the cannon had been hoisted out of the barge and trundled down the wharf and winched up into the transporters. They were placed on beds of hessian and straw before being covered with heavy tarpaulins. Officer Daedalus ran round the transporter making sure that everything was secure. Then he climbed into the vehicle. Moments later it lifted and began to glide slowly round the bay and then climb up the valley road.

Within minutes a second barge was tied up at the wharf and unloading was in progress.

And so it went on until all the barges were empty. Heavy machinery, lengths of thick black tubing, compressors, crates of spare parts, big brass isolation valves and racks of heavy-duty overalls all came out of the holds and were transported away. Those who had hoped for a mishap were disappointed.

And soon the last transporter had gone.

The people on the headland turned their attention to the troops on the shore. While they had been preoccupied with the barges, the landing-craft had continued to ply back and forth. Now a sizeable army had landed.

'They don't look like the regulars,' said one man, a burly-shouldered individual who had once served in Germania. 'They look foreign.'

Some of the bolder among the townsfolk came down on to the shore and stood under the trees, watching.

'That's the insignia of the Emperor,' whispered a blond young man.

'Yeah and look how dark they are,' commented another.

The soldiers paid them no more attention than if they had been cattle.

'I don't like this,' said one woman. The ginger cat in her arms meowed and squirmed and jumped down and ran into the wood. 'And nor does puss. There's something bad happening. I can feel it. Why do they want all these soldiers here? We haven't got anything.'

She received her answer a short time later. The commander of the forces, Publius Pacificus, stepped from his landing-craft and each soldier on the beach came to attention.

'By, he's got them well whipped into shape,' said the blond young man.

The commander was not a tall man but he gave the impression of great physical strength. He was obviously the kind of commander who led from the front relishing the action. He carried his campaign ribbons boldly so that there could be no mistaking who he was and what he had done. And he was proud too of the soldiers who now stood stiffly to attention before him. They were part of Emperor Prometheus' military elite, battle-hardened in the Andean provinces where they had snuffed out unrest. It was their boast that they would go where no others could – to Hades if so ordered. Fierce in their loyalty, fierce in attack, they had never been defeated. And now they were in Britannia. These were the soldiers who relaxed on the word of command and silently got back to their business of unpacking arms and equipment.

Minutes after he had set foot on the sand, Publius Pacificus issued his first orders. Bugles sounded and the black-uniformed soldiers lined up. On a second command they began to advance on the small town. Those of the townsfolk who had come to watch were hustled straight down to the wharf. Any who resisted were simply pushed. The soldiers never spoke, and they moved with the silence of cats.

The soldiers advanced through the streets and houses. They gave the people no chance to return home. Their job was to evict and burn, and that was what they did. Simply and speedily.

As soon as a house was cleared, it was closed. Moments later it was smoking.

Landing-craft, having completed the disembarkation of the soldiers, arrived at the wharf and soon people were being handed on board. They could have been going for a pleasure trip, except that some were crying and all were angry and confused.

Finally an old woman broke through the line of soldiers, and threw herself at the feet of Publius Pacificus.

'For pity's sake,' she shouted. 'Why are you doing this? Who are you?'

One of the soldiers picked the woman up bodily and was about to carry her back into the line when the commander stopped him. He signalled to one of the attendants at his side, obviously requesting a translation. The attendant whispered in his ear and when the commander heard his words, his face broke into a smile. He murmured to the aide and then nodded, indicating that he wanted him to translate.

'The commander, he says, "When Emperor Prometheus says 'bark' we bite." He snapped his teeth together for emphasis. Seeing this, the commander nodded and laughed. 'And . . . um . . . who are we, you say?' The aide consulted a small dictionary. He was trying to find a single word which would translate their name which meant Dread, Terrible, Fierce, Fearful to Behold. His face lit up. 'Aha. We are horrible. Yes? That's right, we are the Horribles.'

Despite the situation one or two people laughed. But the old woman spoke up. 'Horrible are you? Well I'll show you something really horrible. This is what I think of you . . .' And before the soldier could stop her she turned round, hitched up her skirt and showed the commander her bare bottom. She was grabbed quickly and roughly, but the insult was complete.

And it was effective. The commander paled. White-faced and tight-lipped, he nodded for the soldier to dump the old woman into the landing-craft. But she began to chant 'Horrible. Horrible. Horrible' even as she was carried away. And others joined in. They began to laugh at the soldiers, jeering at them, calling them names and making rude gestures, joining finger and thumb into a circle.

Their voices could be heard from the landing-craft as they set out over the water. And even from the troop-carrier that took them on board. Their voices only faded when the troop-ship headed out to sea and departed down the coast.

Behind them the town burned.

The number of people transported away was no more than half the town. The other inhabitants, as soon as they saw what was happening, fled into the woods. Even as the troop-ship turned in the bay, villages a few miles inland were being warned.

For the Horribles, the burning of the town was merely one task that had been set them. Their real job was to enter the forest at Cliff Town and then move steadily inland, capturing villages and dispatching the inhabitants back to the coast. Eventually they were to emerge close to Eburacum, and there have a friendly and triumphal entry into the city, to symbolize goodwill and mutual support.

The plan sounded simple but it proved difficult in operation. First, the Horribles had trouble finding any villages. The people who lived in the woodland closed the lanes and opened false paths. Many times the Horribles found themselves at the end of a path facing a wall of trees or a bank of shoulder-high nettles. When they did find a village it was always deserted. They burned what they could and moved on. Wherever they went, the woodlanders faded into the forest in front of them only to emerge behind them later, and skirmish.

Casualties mounted.

Publius Pacificus became frustrated. In the mountains of the southern continent he had been able to enlist the help of native guides who innocently showed them the secret paths. Here there were no guides.

At the same time, the gloom and damp of the forest affected the soldiers' spirits. For them the dawn came late and the evenings came early. The forest was like a vast green mist in which sounds were deadened and through which it was impossible to see. The trees pressed in.

Then, to make matters worse, there was a strange encounter.

It came a week after they had entered the deep forest. The main army had branched off, some following the Roman road which led to the site of the Caligula Memorial Park, others following the road to Derventio. But a small contingent was sent to explore a network of side paths close to the Wolds.

They climbed beside a stream and came to a clearing by a river. The air was still under the tangled oak and beech trees. The only movement came from the insects which darted in the warm air and hovered over the stream. 'Here we stop,' said the centurion in charge. 'Camp for the night.'

Before long the men had set up their bivouacs. Many decided to wash their clothes, for the combination of sweat and the sugary secretions dropping from the trees made them itchy and uncomfortable. They hung the wet clothes out to dry in the late afternoon sun. Others were content simply to strip off and lie in the deep pools letting the cool water flow over them. But all were alert in one way or another. They were aware of the dangers and their weapons were never far from their hands. Round the perimeter of the clearing, guards stood in the shadows or knelt close to the bushes, listening, watching, staring outwards.

But nothing came close. The forest seemed deserted. Methodically, on the hour the guards changed and so it would be all through the night until they continued their advance after dawn.

Night fell, and many of the soldiers just lay back and looked up at the stars, seeking relief from the claustrophobia of the forest. Then they climbed into their bivouacs. They looked like river-stones on the floor of the clearing.

Shortly after the midnight watch had changed, there came a singing in the air. Men began to stir, peering about silently, hands feeling for weapons. Diving down from the sky came lights which then flowed round the clearing like patterns of ripples reflected from water. The lights took on substance, seeming to settle in the oak and beech trees and the singing grew louder until it was harsh and discordant. Suddenly twin bright lights detached from one of the trees and hovered over the riverbank. Their brilliance lit up the clearing. The soldiers stared in wonder as the lights took on shape, like molten glass cooling. Two children, or what looked like children, were left standing. The boy had a compact, neat face with sharply modelled features and pale skin. The girl's face was radiant and her hair was a golden corona which stood out round her head. They looked round the grove unsmiling, their eyes like glittering glass.

One of the soldiers started to move, crawling out from his bivouac. The girl looked at him and her eyes suddenly glowed red and the man heaved and twisted like something being burned over a fire. At the end he lay still.

No one else moved. The girl spoke to the boy, her voice high and thrilling. He set his small hands at his waist and threw his head back laughing. Then they began to transform. They began to glow as though heating. Wings sprouted from their backs and billowed in the air, their hands became barbed, they grew tall until they towered in the clearing above the soldiers. The air in the clearing became charged and hot and each of the soldiers saw whatever, in their hearts and minds, they most feared.

Those that could, struggled from their bivouacs and ran screaming into the forest. Some simply lay on the grass rolling back and forth, their hands over their eyes. Others fell into the stream, not to emerge. Many never moved but lay pale and still.

The next day, a patrol sent out from the main force encountered two of the soldiers who had escaped from the clearing. They had gone insane and could not be understood. The patrol pushed on and came to the clearing which was pretty and peaceful in the early morning sunlight – and would have been quiet too had it not been for the buzzing of millions of flies.

This event, the complete destruction of an elite fighting unit, decided the commander's mind. He had begun to have doubts about the wisdom of trying to fight a guerilla war in the deep forest. He had been told it would be easy, a simple matter of rounding up some terrified savages, but that clearly was not the case. Publius Pacificus was an intelligent man and a sensitive man. He could feel something ominous brewing in this part of the woodland. Even in the cold whispering heights of the alte-plateau, he had never felt such foreboding.

He withdrew the troops and began a forced march to Derventio. They spent the night in the military camp there and the next day they marched to Eburacum using the main road.

In his private dispatch to Emperor Prometheus, Publius

Pacificus noted: 'It may be that the burning of the trees is the only way to break the spirit of this land. But a wiser course may be to leave the glades alone, for I have felt the strength of that spirit and it is fierce in all ways.'

These words pleased the Emperor, not only for their elegance but for the metaphysical encounter that they suggested. For this was what he wanted in his heart of hearts, to provoke the wrath of the gods. And if he gained good lamb chops along the way, so be it.

He wrote back. 'Forget the woodland. Enter Eburacum as a humble friend. Win hearts. Be kind. But when the time is right, I will take up the challenge. And you will be there.'

9 A Debate in Eburacum

The entry into Eburacum was a victory of sorts for the Horribles. Citizens lined the streets, waving and calling out to them. These soldiers were famous and their campaign exploits were the source of stories and songs. Everyone wanted to look at them. And they did look grand as they marched: strong, confident, precise. The mistranslation of their name had been reported and was now regularly used, giving them a familiar, almost homely, presence.

Old Ulysses held an official welcome. The officers and soldiers were wined and dined and shown the sights of the city and taken on trips up the river. A special performance was given at the State Theatre in which their exploits were dramatized. Then after a week of festivities, they were dispatched to Camp Lucius. Publius Pacificus returned to Roma.

In Eburacum, members of the senior families gathered for a meeting.

'I for one am not happy about the presence of foreign troops on our soil.' It was Sextus Valerius Manaviensis speaking, and he was angry and emphatic. 'And especially not this crew. Did you look at them? They are the stuff that nightmares are made from.'

'Nor am I. Happy,' said old Ulysses, affecting indignation. 'I was not informed and I have made my views known to the Emperor in person.'

'And?' Calpurnia Gallica speaking.

'And he thought he was helping. Said that was why he'd sent his best.'

'Bah! I don't trust him and I don't believe him. I will not rest easy until they are off our shores.' Few had ever seen Calpurnia so angry or resolute. 'I support Manaviensis' resolution, that we get them out of Britannia immediately. What do you think, Marmellius?'

Marmellius nodded. He had recovered from the humiliation of his exploits in the forest and felt some sympathy for the suffering of the Horribles. 'I agree. What I don't understand is how they come to be here in the first place. Are you saying that the Emperor never consulted you before sending in some troops? I mean, that is invasion.'

'Well perhaps I'm at fault there. He did say something about sending us some help. Didn't want to be a burden on us. That sort of thing. But I didn't know that he was planning to send his killers from the mountains. But as I say, I have made my views known.'

'Then when will they be withdrawn?' asked Sextus Valerius.

There was silence, during which Marcus Ulysses stared at them. 'I'll arrange it,' he said finally. 'Though in my view we are being a bit hypersensitive and naive.'

'Why naive if we show the robber who has broken into our house the door?'

'Naive because at present we have good relations with the Emperor and we should protect them. Naive because while the Horribles are here we at least have them under our thumb. Naive because if the Emperor gets huffy he might just park them in Western Gallia and then how would we feel? Naive because they can be used to do any dirty work we want while we keep our own forces safe. Naive because they are, when all is said and done, a good fighting force. I liken it to our being given a scalpel rather than a pocket knife. But then, perhaps I have a more cosmopolitan view of things. I do not feel threatened.'

They looked at him. 'Only a fool opens the door to the wolf and bids him enter,' said Sextus Valerius.

'Only a fool sees wolves where there are only shadows,' replied Marcus.

'We can go on for ever quoting proverbs at one another,' said Calpurnia, 'and never get anywhere. I hate to admit it, but the Ulysses may have a point. Perhaps we are being too hasty. Perhaps there is a middle way.'

Marmellius indicated he wished to speak. 'I would like to have heard the opinion of our good friend Quintus Herculis Quinctius. I am surprised he is not here.'

Marcus Ulysses spread his hands. 'He was invited. He

141

declined. He says he will have nothing more to do with Emperor Lucius Petronius. Ha! He calls him a farm manager and he calls his soldiers sheepdogs. Now there, if you want my opinion, *is* a foolish man. The Emperor is of a peaceful disposition. But, by the gods, you only have to look at his history. If someone comes looking for trouble, they don't have to look very far.'

Sextus Valerius snapped his fingers. 'I have it,' he said. 'By all the gods I think I have it. I think the Horribles, or whatever they call themselves, are the start of an expeditionary force. I wouldn't mind betting that that's what Lucius wants. He's aiming to swat poor Quintus hard.'

'Then why not tell us about it?' asked Marmellius.

'Because he thinks we might tell Quintus Herculis.'

Calpurnia looked perplexed. 'Wheels within wheels,' she murmured.

'And all a bit too complex for an old soldier like me,' said Marcus Ulysses. 'Come on, let's make a decision about these Horribles. Shall I tell the Emperor bluntly to get them off our land or shall we parley a bit?'

'Better move slowly,' said Marmellius. 'The stakes may be higher than we thought. What say we keep them at Camp Lucius, use them for the dirty work, and meanwhile I keep a couple of my detachments on stand-by near the camp, just in case of trouble?' He glanced round. 'There, how does that sound?'

They nodded except for Sextus Valerius who said, 'Well that's all well and good, so long as you are not in league with the Emperor.'

Marmellius looked astonished. 'Me? The Caesars? In league against my colleagues? What nonsense.'

'It has happened before.'

'I resent that.'

'Gentlemen. Gentlemen,' said Marcus Ulysses in his best Chairman of the Board manner. 'Let us not fall into acrimony. We have to begin by trusting one another otherwise where are we? Sextus Valerius Manaviensis, I ask you to withdraw your last remark.'

'Very well. Perhaps I was too hasty. I just don't like foreign troops on my doorstep, that's all.'

'And Marmellius. Just give us an assurance, for the record, that you have not had private dealings with the Emperor.'

'Of course I haven't. I've never heard anything so preposterous in my—'

'That's all right then. The matter is closed. Now I suggest that we do as Marmellius suggests but that we put a time limit on the whole thing. Let's see. The Emperor wants the burning to coincide with the Reformed Lupercalia. What say we ask, nay require, that the Horribles be removed after the first burning. Does that seem fair?'

Everyone nodded. There was no more discussion.

'Meanwhile, I'll try to find out if Lucius Petronius has any designs on poor Quinctius,' said Calpurnia. 'I shall be in Roma for my daughter's birthday. I'll make myself known to him.'

There the meeting ended, and Marcus rang for refreshments.

The room had grown dark and an attendant came in with candles and the customary red wine and beer.

'Storm coming from the north-east, sir. Sky's very heavy.'

They gathered at the window looking east over the formal gardens of the Imperial Palace and out to the city walls and beyond to where the tall trees of the forest started. Dark clouds were rolling in. Leaves were piling up in the gutters and under the trees.

'First storm of autumn,' observed old Ulysses. 'Early this year.'

'By the gods, I'd hate to be out there when the wind really gets blowing,' said Sextus Valerius, looking at the waving trees.

'Yes, can be quite unnerving,' said Marmellius, remembering the night he had spent at Roscius' Camp VI.

The wind blew suddenly rattling the windows. A few moments later came the rain.

'I hope we have a white winter,' said Calpurnia. 'I love a white winter. Everything feels so clean after it.'

Prisoners

Gwydion placed the two tin bowls containing boiled oatmeal down on the table. 'They ran out of bread again, again,' he said.

Bella, seated opposite him, pulled her bowl towards her. 'There's dandelion growing at the end of the hut and wild parsley too. Here, I picked some.' She scattered the leaves on the oatmeal. 'Won't improve the flavour much. But . . .'

They were in the hut assigned to them, and lived in company with people from different villages.

A man called Temba came in with his wife Kora.

'Bird food,' he said, putting his bowl down. 'They certainly know how to insult a hungry stomach.'

His wife, sharp-featured with her black hair drawn tightly back, reached inside her bodice and pulled out a small bag. 'Here, have some of this with it,' she said. 'I've got work in the kitchens so I got us some salt and sugar.' She pushed the bag over to Gwydion and Bella.

'Any news?' asked Bella, sprinkling salt.

'Rumours. Just rumours,' said Temba. 'I just met a man who came in with the crowd from Cliff Town. He says he got talking to one of the guards when they were on the ship, and this guard told him there was a plan to send us all overseas.'

'Why?'

Temba shrugged. 'It doesn't make sense. None of it does.'

More people arrived. One woman, a mother with four small children, set down her tray with a clang. 'Look at this muck,' she said. 'I used to use stuff like this to bung up the knot holes on a winter night. We'll have to do something about it. I could cook better meals with the stuff they throw away for garbage.'

'I reckon we need to get organized,' said Temba. 'No more mucking about. Get some plans working. Make ourselves useful, then infiltrate.'

'We could break out any time we want,' chimed in another man. 'I know of six places where the perimeter wire can be pulled up. And as for that chalet . . . just let me get under it with tinder and matches.'

He was about to say more when there was a noise from outside the hut.

It was singing, and it came from the chalet above the camp that had been built for the officers, and which now housed many of the Horribles.

'Listen. They're drunk,' said Bella. 'Better be ready in case they come down into the camp later, looking for fun.'

Gwydion cleaned the inside of his bowl with his finger and licked the last of the gruel. 'That's because they're frightened,' he said. 'They don't know what they're into. I met a woman they captured north of Fox. She told me these Horribles had a big fright in the forest. They met the tree spirits. That turned them back.' He laughed. 'I remember when I was a kid, old Bella here told me to run a mile if I ever got so much as a whiff of the Faeries.' Bella nodded. 'Aye well, I reckon those Horribles got more than a whiff. Poor buggers. Driven mad, according to this woman.'

Bella didn't laugh. 'Strange things happening, Gwydion.' She paused and looked at her son closely. 'Did you ever meet any of them, in your travels?'

'The Faeries you mean? Aye often. Kissed one of them once.'

Bella's mouth opened in surprise and wonder. Then she caught her son's eye. 'Ee you lying little jade. Worse than old Aunt Polly, you are.'

'True as I'm sitting here. That was the time I nearly got turned into a horse. It were like this, see . . .'

Paterfamilias

Confirmed bachelor, scholar, polyglot and man of sundry dirty habits, Marcus the teacher found himself in a situation for which all of his philosophy left him unprepared. He was now the man of the house living with two strong-minded women who treated him like a cross between a favoured younger brother and an odd-job labourer.

He cleaned his plate with his bread and stacked his rabbit bones neatly to one side, hiding rounds of carrot.

'You have not finished your carrots,' observed Hetty without looking up. Scattered on the table in front of her were several piles of acorns which she was carefully measuring and then recording in her notebook. She was puzzled by the fact that this year the acorns were smaller than ever she had known.

'I'm saving them to feed the compost,' replied Marcus smoothly.

Opposite him Danea continued rolling some dried leaves between her hands. 'The compost is doing fine without your offering. Eat up.'

'But . . .' The two women paused in their tasks and looked at him. For a moment Marcus maintained his defiance. 'Hetty didn't finish all her cabbage yesterday,' he said weakly.

'Hetty eats a lot more vegetables than you do,' replied Danea. And this was true. Hetty was a strict albeit experimental vegetarian. The things she ate made Marcus shudder. He groaned. 'Oh all right. Anything for a quiet life.'

He cleared his plate. Danea licked the inside of one of the leaves and rolled it down, pressing firmly. 'There, try that,' she said, handing him the improvised cigar.

'Outside,' added Hetty.

This had become a ritual – a cigar in the quiet of the evening. Indeed, Marcus' hitherto chaotic life had suddenly become encased in small rituals such as finishing his food at meal times, strolling in the evening with a cigar, rising early, rubbing down the horses and tending the small garden. The grown man was experiencing a new kind of growing-up. In this house he was not venerated and pampered because of the excellence of his intellect, but was expected to conform to certain basic, almost prim, standards of behaviour. He affected a grumpy acquiescence.

'We'll have dessert after you've had your smoke,' said Danea clearing away the plates. 'Hetty. You're on dishes.'

Marcus strolled outside. He followed the small path through Danea's vegetable garden to the spiked fence which surrounded the property. The small house in which they now lived had been abandoned before the Romans arrived. Its hapless owner had run directly into a Roman patrol and hence had been shifted to Camp Lucius. The house had not been discovered and had remained empty for some time until Danea found it while driving her cart. Some days later Marcus arrived having lost his way and then finally Hetty turned up, strolling out of the woods one evening as though returning from a picnic. The house was small but adequate. Danea had the single bedroom. Marcus occupied the loft above the stable and Hetty lived in the cart. Each seemed content.

Marcus lit his cigar and coughed. 'Shite a brick,' he muttered. 'What the hell does she find to put in them?' But moments later he was puffing contentedly and looking at the leaves drifting down. He'd always enjoyed the smells of autumn, and now he was living close to those smells. His life had become unpredictable since the destruction of Roscius' villa and as a result he was aware of the immediacy of pleasure. He was grateful for small luxuries. Gone was the fine wine and cool beer in the evening; the cut and thrust of intellectual debate about abstract principles. In its place was wood-ash to be cleared, wood to be cut, water to be carried, a latrine that always seemed to need extending and a cigar concocted from whatever leaves Danea had dried over their fire. Moreover, as a result of this new life, muscles had begun appearing on his arms and back where no muscles had ever been seen before. Marcus had lost four stone in weight and while his figure could hardly be called athletic or graceful, the difference was very noticeable.

Marcus smelled crab apples cooked in their jacket and stubbed out his cigar, saving the butt for a last surreptitious smoke before turning in. Walking back to the small house where Hetty had already lit a lantern in the window, he thought of Roscius who had never appeared riding hell for leather behind him. He hoped he was well. He hoped he had escaped. There had been no news. But he feared the worst.

Over the crab apples Hetty finished her calculations. 'Well the trend seems pretty well established,' she said pointing at the piles of acorns. 'These I gathered not far from Roscius' place. These are from a few miles north of here and these are from the trees outside. They all tell the same story. The acorns are stunted. Their vitality is sapped.'

'Why?' asked Danea.

Hetty shrugged. 'You tell me. You're the one with green fingers. I'm just a recorder of folklore and mystery.'

'I take it that the acorn symbolizes virility,' said Marcus.

'Correct,' replied Hetty. 'For anyone who cares to look at one, the symbolism is obvious. In which case the miserable specimens we see before us may merely be a reflection of our current misfortune, Danea.'

Danea looked confused but Marcus, attuned to this kind of banter, replied. 'The almonds too are dry and pinched this year, I understand. Hardly worth the plucking.'

Hetty laughed. 'They probably are. But the why remains unanswered. My mythology tells me that this is not a happy omen. Plants are aware of trends in the air. Am I right?'

Danea nodded. 'One of the mysteries of Nature. They seem to be able to predict the seasons.'

'Well the acorns are telling us to watch out.'

A Dance

At Drummer's caves people were eating in silence.

Shortly before the meal, Sean and Drummer had arrived at the caves carrying a deer they had killed. They had been away for three days and when they returned they were walking slowly, Sean leading.

Children ran to greet them. Both Sean and Drummer were popular and always returned from their journeys into the forest with exciting stories to tell. But this time, instead of hoisting the kids up on to his shoulders, Sean plodded on. When they reached the fire in front of the caves Drummer threw the deer down and began to butcher it. Sean raised his arms and called for people to gather – he had an announcement to make.

One by one people arrived and squatted down in the firelight, shawls over their shoulders.

Last to arrive were Perol and Angus, hand in hand. It was evident to all that since their departure from Roscius VI, Perol and Angus had become closer and happier. Some said it was the absence of the Dragon, others that it was the quiet of the valley, most considered that it was nothing more than the fact that Perol was pregnant – a fact that could no longer be disguised.

'So what's up, Sean?' asked Perol. 'Have you got some news about Roscius?'

Sean seemed in the grip of some deep emotion, and Perol wondered whether it was his ancestors who had again seized control, but in that case . . . She glanced at Drummer who was calmly preparing the meat to go on to the spit.

Sean began to speak. His words came slowly and had obviously been prepared.

'Friends. I can no longer keep from you something that has been troubling me for some time. As you all know, I am not from these parts, but from . . . ach, a long way away, it matters not where . . . and of late I have felt such a longing to be home again that my heart is almost breaking. What is a home if not the place that you can always call truly yours and always return to? No one can take it away. You can be angry with it, you can call it names, you can walk away from it, but it is bigger than all those things. It is the one place where, for your ears, the stones have tongues and the hills voices.

'Well, I can hear their calling, and I'm too weak a mortal to resist. So I have decided to leave here and return home. I'll leave tonight. But I'm Janus-faced in sadness. For here also is my home, with brother Angus and sister Perol and all of you. But go I must.'

Drummer finished dressing the meat and slid the chunks on to skewers which he then placed above the fire. Soon they began to steam. The juices ran, dripping into the fire with a hiss and spit.

'I told Drummer while we were away. I tried to explain. But Drummer doesn't understand. Perhaps he feels that everywhere is his home . . . perhaps nowhere . . . I don't know. But Drummer said he wanted to come with me and that pleases me for there are people in my country who know the sound of his drumming though they have never heard it, and who will welcome him and treat him as one of their own. But I know it will bring sadness here, among you, and perhaps some fear – for we have all come to trust Drummer, to rely on his knowledge and his strength.'

Sean turned and looked at Drummer who quite unconcernedly was turning the meat over the fire and feeding the flames with pieces of dry wood.

'So there we are. We've decided to leave after the meal. Cleaner that way. Drummer, do you have anything to say? I'll translate.'

'Food,' said Drummer. 'Eat.'

While they were eating Sean moved from person to person, making his farewells. Finally, with some embarrassment, he sat down with Angus and Perol.

'Are you surprised?' he asked.

'Devastated,' said Angus. 'Abso-bloody-lutely stunned.' And then he saw that Sean was taking him seriously. 'Away, you daft prat. You've had a moony half-here, half-there look on your face for months. I thought you were just randy but Perol here guessed. She said you'd be off.'

'We're sad to see you go, of course,' said Perol. 'You're dearer to us than anyone. It'll take some getting used to. You'll leave a big hole, you and Drummer.'

'I didn't try to take him away,' said Sean quickly.

'I doubt you could make Drummer do anything he didn't want to.'

'Ah well. So what am I going to do for a right-hand man now?' asked Angus.

'There's always young Garlyck.'

'Spare me!'

At that moment they heard a furious burst of drumming which echoed back from the hills. 'Hey up. Big fella's up to something.'

Drummer stood by the fire, very still, with his head thrown back. After a few moments he raised his drum in front of him, like an offering. He began to tap its wooden surface. Then he began to dance. He beat his drum while he stamped with his feet. He began to step, now like a bear, now like a mouse. A heron in the marsh and a snake weaving its sinuous path through the grass at the wayside. He sang, naming the hills and the trees, all the time tapping on his hard drum with his hands like roots. He began to dance round the flickering fire, turning in circles, beginning slow but getting faster and faster until he was whirling. He stopped suddenly, and beat his drum one last time, very hard, very loud. It was a call. The echo bounded back.

'Youse see what I mean,' whispered Sean. 'Who needs language when you can talk like that.'

His dance complete, Drummer crossed to Angus and Perol and placed his drum on the ground in front of them. Then he picked up the woven bag in which he carried all his possessions, waved once to the people round the fire and walked away.

'Away you go, Sean. You're on your way.' Perol kissed him and Angus held him in his arms, slapping him on the back.

'Take good care of the little one. Hope you have an easy time.'

Then he was gone.

Soon Sean and Drummer were lost in the darkness beyond the flickering flames.

Miranda

'Try some soup. Please.'

There was no reply. Miranda lay still on her back, barely breathing.

Gwellan stood, holding the bowl, uncertain what to do. 'Well can I get you anything?'

Again there was no reply.

Outside there came the sound of furtive footsteps on the stairs. Moments later, a suppressed giggle and then a child's voice said, 'Is Auntie Miranda still not any better?' The door creaked open and two faces came peering in.

Gwellan turned and shooed the children away. 'Yes, she's feeling better. But she needs to rest. You go down now and get the others in for their meal. There's soup and bread. Then we'll have a story.' The children moved away reluctantly and then ran down the stairs shouting.

'You can let the children stay. I will not harm them.' The voice seemed to come from everywhere: from the roof and the floor and the window. Gwellan turned quickly. Miranda was still not moving but the voice continued, 'Or do you think they will be frightened?' The lips had not moved but the voice was clear.

'I don't know,' replied Gwellan. 'I'm afraid. But perhaps children cope with such things better.'

'There is nothing to be afraid of.' The voice sounded tired, and slightly in pain.

'I'd better go now and feed the kids. I'll come up later and bathe you. Perhaps then the children can come in. We'll see.'

There was no reply and Gwellan left the room and closed the door quietly.

Downstairs the children were still playing outside. They had built a small enclosure from burned timbers and within it were a pair of chickens which clucked and pecked and looked at them with bright untrusting eyes.

'Will they lay any eggs?' One of the little girls slipped her hand into Gwellan's.

'I hope so. Perhaps. We can check in the morning.' Gwellan looked round the small, ruined enclosure. The village had been burned. Almost all the houses had been destroyed and the air still had an acrid tang. The house they were living in had more or less survived and only one wall had been scorched. They had been lucky. Gwellan marvelled at the resilience of the children. They had moved in, squabbled over which corner of the house they could have as their own, and then got on with living. They had questions of course, like why had the village been burned and where were the people, but by and large they accepted the situation. They were like the grass which was already peeping up through the scorched earth.

Gwellan served the food. Then it was time for a wash and finally, with darkness falling outside, time for a story and then bed.

'Can we see Auntie Miranda?'

'Please.'

'We really want to.'

Gwellan held up her hand for silence. 'I'll go and see. I'll give her a wash and tidy her up and see if she feels like having visitors. Now you tuck in. I'll be back down in a minute.'

Carrying a bowl of warm water, Gwellan climbed the steps, tapped softly at the door with her elbow, lifted the latch and went in. Miranda had not moved. Gwellan set the bowl down by the bed and lit a couple of candles. She checked the bucket at the foot of Miranda's bed but it had not been used.

With the efficiency which comes with long practice, Gwellan rolled the bedclothes back and manoeuvred Miranda on to her side. She lifted her head and brushed her hair, pausing to remove the strands as the brush became clogged. Then she washed Miranda's face and tried to avoid looking at the eyes. She washed the body concentrating on the task so as to avoid confronting the strangeness of what had happened to Miranda. Then she changed the sheets. They smelled musty – it was a smell that Gwellan could not place. Satisfied that she had done what she could, she asked, 'Would you still like the children to come and see you?'

'Ye-es.' The voice seemed to come from a long way away.

Gwellan went to the top of the stairs and called down. 'All right. You can come up. But quietly now. And you can't stay for too long.'

The children tiptoed upstairs, holding their improvised dollies and comforting scraps of fabric. They came into the room and stood round the bed looking down.

'What's happened to her hair?' asked one child.

'She's losing her hair. That sometimes happens when people get sick.'

A little boy reached out and placed a finger on the top of Miranda's head that was now almost completely bald. 'She feels warm,' he said. 'Like when an egg's just been laid.'

'What's happened to her eyes?' asked one of the little girls. 'Why are they all red? Can she see us?'

Gwellan did not know what to reply, but then a voice spoke from the air. 'I can see you. I don't need my eyes any more. I'm all about you. Don't be afraid.'

The children looked round and nudged one another.

'Look,' said one, pointing at Miranda's arm lying on top of the sheet. 'I can see through her skin. Look, you can see the bones. Look.' All the children peered.

Slowly Miranda's hand opened and turned. They saw the

sinews which controlled the joints contract and the finger-bones move.

'There. That's enough,' said Gwellan. 'Auntie Miranda needs to rest. You can come again another day.'

Obediently the children trooped out, calling good-night.

Gwellan stayed for a few more minutes, straightening the covers and fussing about. Then she blew out the candles. In the darkness Miranda's body glowed with a soft light which could even be seen through the sheets.

Gwellan closed the door.

Downstairs the children were sitting up in bed discussing what they had seen. 'Now,' said Gwellan, 'was that all right? Are you all ready for sleep?'

'Yes, Aunt-ie Gwel-lan,' they chorused. It was one of their rituals.

'Can I get you anything before you settle down?'

One of the boys, the one who had touched Miranda on the head, asked, 'Will Auntie Miranda be all right?'

'Yes. Of course she will,' said Gwellan. 'She's going to be fine. Now who wants a drink of water?'

Lightning

Coll looked at the mess of hedgehog.

He'd tried to cook it the way Gwydion had shown, packing it in clay and then baking it. But something hadn't worked. He scooped up the remains and took them outside and threw them down the hill. Then he wiped his hands on the damp grass. A light misty rain had enveloped the marsh during the afternoon, and now, as evening drew on, the rain was getting heavier. Far away in the hills there was a flicker of lightning and then, moments later, a rumble of thunder.

Coll hurried back inside and adjusted the fur at the door to stop the draught.

To make matters worse, the small hotplate that he used for cooking had become erratic. The vegetables were hard and the water tepid.

'No matter,' said Cormac, and then he could say no more.

He was doubled up in his chair with coughing. He had caught a chill on the way back from Coll's first singing, and now a cold had settled on his chest. When he slept at night, his breathing was laboured and uneven.

The energy required to confuse the guards so that he and Coll could pass unseen had almost destroyed him. Not only was Cormac well past the time for his natural death, but for years he had kept himself going by a combination of will-power and metaphysical connivance, hoping always that his successor would show himself or herself. But every breach of natural order has its limits and every day brought its strain. During the journey back to their tree-burrow, Cormac had sat slumped on Aristotle while Coll walked beside him. And then he had started to shiver. At the end of the journey Coll had carried him bodily down into the dark cave under the oak tree. He had nursed him but gradually the illness strengthened its grip.

Coll touched the hotplate tentatively and found it was barely warm. 'Now if ever I could do with Angus,' he muttered and wondered if he could remember enough of what Angus had shown him about the black ivy when he was building his own tree-house. But there was a more immediate problem, what to do about food for the night. 'I'll walk over to the village,' he said. 'I'll get supplies. Won't be above three hours.'

But Cormac shook his head. Between coughs he said, 'Bad night coming. River'll be up over the stepping stones afore long. We'll cope. We can eat the vegetables raw. Just get me another shawl and we'll sort things out in the morning.'

Coll tucked the soft skin of a deer round Cormac's shoulders and made him comfortable. He cut the vegetables as small as he could and they sat in the gloom crunching them while the thunder outside grew closer.

Cormac ate slowly. He seemed to have difficulty chewing and swallowing. Once he dropped the food but didn't seem to notice and when Coll looked at him he saw that the old man's eyes were staring with the pupils dilated. He seemed to have stopped breathing and white spittle had gathered at the corner of his mouth. Then he had a fit of coughing that left him gasping and exhausted. Coll watched with a sudden, growing fear that he would see Cormac die, that the old man would suddenly rear up and pitch over. *What then?* thought Coll. *What the hell do I do then?*

Coll had a vision of solitude – of the vast gaping hole that would be left when Cormac died, of the weight that the man carried and the knowledge that could never be passed on because it came from experience. 'Don't die,' he whispered. 'Please don't die.'

From nowhere it seemed, a thought came to him. *Get some water from the stream. Get him to drink it.* Without waiting Coll collected the water bucket and climbed up out of the oak tree. The sky was black and the only light came from the flickering lightning. *Use some of your skills. What do you think you've been learning for?* Coll tried to focus his mind on finding his way to the spring. He tried to feel the life of the trees and the grass and the water. He was not sure that he saw anything but he set out boldly, his hand in front of him, and some sense seemed to guide him round the small hill to where the spring-water bubbled.

A sudden flash of lightning revealed the spring and the rain slashing down. While he filled the bucket Coll thought of Cormac, hunched and coughing. And he thought of Dark Eagle and asked for his help. He thought of the spirit that was the stream and asked for her help.

The bucket was full. On his way back Coll nearly slipped on the wet grass and he grinned to himself. 'Just bloody teasing me, aren't you. Just trying to make things difficult.'

Then he was back at the hole which led under the tree and feeling his way down, holding the iron-hard roots. As he climbed down he suddenly felt the hair all over his body begin to stand up. It was the strangest sensation he had ever known. He felt the hair on his chest press against his shirt and his beard tickled and stirred. He hurried inside and was astonished to find Cormac up on his feet with his straggly white hair standing out from his head like the seed head of a dandelion. Cormac reached for Coll and held him in a fierce grip. He was about to speak when there came the loudest explosion that Coll had ever heard. The air roared. There was a smell of burning. Dust rose from the floor in spirals and the hotplate glowed suddenly red. Everything shook. Cups and plates fell from the shelves and for a moment the small room became incandescent. Cormac shone. Coll's hands were bright and the water in the bucket teemed with light. The brilliance passed through them. And at that moment, all the strings on the cithara twanged and broke together.

Slowly the glow faded and the roaring receded. It seemed to be sinking into the earth, passing down through the soil and stone and on into where the subterranean streams flowed.

'Well that will have cleared the air a bit,' said Cormac dusting his clothes where soil had fallen, and this time he didn't cough.

'What happened?' said Coll. 'Was it an earthquake?'

'No. We were struck by lightning. Can't you smell it?'

Coll sniffed. And he could smell something. A clean smell. Then he noticed that a bundle of herbs had fallen from the roof where they were drying down on to the hotplate where they were now smouldering. 'No not that,' said Cormac. 'The smell of the lightning.' He breathed deeply and more easily. 'Come on. We're safe now. The storm's moving on. Let's drink water from the spring and pretend it's beer from old Bella's inn. Don't look so frightened, lad. I'm not dead yet. Not yet.'

Calpurnia and Prometheus

A blare of trumpets and a clash of cymbals announced her passage.

Soldiers of the Imperial Guard, in full dress uniform, marched in front, forcing the ogling crowd back with long spears. Then came the plumed palanquin, carried by six tall slaves. Behind came the cavalry mounted on pure white horses with bells at their bridle. The Emperor Lucius Prometheus was out to impress.

Calpurnia Gallica, the object of his attention, reclining on cushions of silk, smiled to herself as she waved to the cheering crowd.

The procession turned in at the Imperial Palace in Roma and made its way under flower-covered arches to the triclinium where the Emperor was waiting. He handed her down from the palanquin and conducted her to the place of honour.

The court poet, observing with quick dark eyes, began to pen hexameters likening the occasion to the meeting of Antony and Cleopatra.

Dancers performed to the tinkle of finger cymbals while slaves scurried about serving wine flavoured with honey. To a fanfare of trumpets, the curtains to the kitchen were pulled back and a miniature procession entered in which the god Bacchus led his satyrs each of whom carried a silver platter laden with a different dish. Soft-boiled eggs in pine-nut sauce, fried anchovies, peas marinated in garum and wine, rose petals and lambs' brains. The merry god approached Calpurnia bowing low and offered his speciality from a domed silver dish: baked dormice stuffed with pork and peppers and glazed with sugar and almonds. One of Calpurnia's favourite dishes.

Calpurnia was served by the Emperor himself. She found him a merry host, almost boyish in his delight at the theatrical display, and obviously keen to please. But she was on her guard. Calpurnia had not survived so long by being naive. She liked men, but she did not trust them. She was a passionate lover, but she was no romantic. Thus she drank little, preferring to sip scented water, while observing closely how the Emperor quaffed with seeming abandon. Calpurnia had her agenda, as also, she assumed, had Lucius Prometheus. The question was, could they discover common ground.

While the appetizers were being cleared the Emperor suddenly leant across to her and asked, 'What do you think of my little scheme for establishing a sheep farm in Britannia?'

Calpurnia was surprised at the directness of the question. 'If it is only a sheep farm you wish to establish then I see no harm.'

'What more could I have in mind?'

'The presence of your soldiers on our soil does not inspire confidence.'

'I was trying to help.'

'. . . said the butcher as he sharpened his knife.'

Lucius Prometheus guffawed with laughter. 'I like you,' he said. 'I like you. A woman who is as beautiful as she is witty—'

'And as realistic as any man.' She looked at him coldly. This one attempt at blandishment by the Emperor had alerted her. 'Lucius Prometheus, if you wish to deal with me it must be on a basis of directness and demonstrable honesty.' She made herself smile. 'I am too old for flattery and I have heard too many lies from men.'

For a moment she saw a darkness in the man's eyes, it could have been anger or contempt even, and then almost as quickly it was replaced by the winning boyish smile. But she had seen enough. *How sad*, she thought, *such a handsome man. What a shame he can't be honest too.* But at least now she knew how she should behave. She would lie as the occasion demanded. 'So let us talk as directly as we can,' she said, as though she were offering a challenge or a flirtatious invitation. She raised her glass.

'The only true course,' said Lucius, returning the toast. 'Intrigue is such a bore.'

Again the curtains drew back. Steam billowed from the kitchen fanned by slaves and through the steam, its jaws opening and closing, came a giant lizard with folded wings. It reached the table and there it stopped. An attendant ran to Calpurnia and, bowing, offered her a cord with a gold tassel.

'Give it a good sharp tug,' said Lucius. 'Let's see what happens.'

Calpurnia jerked the cord. Wooden pegs dropped from the sides of the beast and its wings started to unfold. When they were spread over the diners like a tent, they flapped once and the entire beast rose up into the air. Revealed beneath was a detailed model of a pastoral scene in which a shepherd (who bore a striking resemblance to the Emperor) played his pan pipes while sheep paused near a lake. Centaurs and dryads looked on adoringly. This was the main course. All the figures were made of pastries and the lake was chilled wine. The diners clapped in appreciation and some threw gold coins in the direction of the kitchen.

Attendants with sharp knives approached and when the pastries were cut into they revealed different meats in silver dishes. The sheep contained lamb cutlets in Marsala wine, tender strips of meat grilled on skewers and dark with pepper, rolled pancakes containing ground and spiced veal. The shepherd contained pork sausages, medallions of pork simmered in prune sauce, pork stewed with apples and lemons. When the belly of one of the centaurs was opened, an entire suckling-pig turning on a miniature spit was revealed. Before roasting it had been stuffed with a mixture of boiled brains, raw egg, pine nuts, semolina, pepper, olives and garlic. Now it ran with juices and its skin was crisp and brown. The dryads contained pigeons and quail cooked whole, roasted mullet and jugged hare.

Calpurnia found her plate filled with bite-sized morsels. She pecked and picked, eating very little but always seeming to be eating.

'All I want,' said the Emperor, tossing some bones on the floor under the table and wiping his face with a steaming napkin, 'all I want is to take advantage of Britannia's favoured status with the gods.' He hiccoughed heavily.

'And we have given our support willingly,' said Calpurnia. 'We are Romans. The old traditions live on in Britannia. Surely Marcus Augustus Ulysses has told you that.'

'He has. He has. And I and all the Empire rejoice.'

'Then why the special detachment of soldiers?'

'Ah that again. Do they worry you so much?'

'They do.'

'Do they worry Quintus Herculis Quinctius?'

'Why . . .' Calpurnia checked herself. 'That I cannot answer. Quintus was not at our last meeting.'

'He doesn't like me, does he?' Lucius looked at the roast hare that had been placed before him. He jammed his knife down into the meat. 'That is what I think of Herculis.' He turned his dark eyes on Calpurnia. He looked sultry and dark and very dangerous. Calpurnia had to check herself. 'Can you keep a secret?' he asked.

'If it is worth keeping.'

'I intend to scorch Herculis' burn.' The Emperor winked. 'That is what my men are for and I will pay handsomely if you will allow me to pass through Britannia. There, is that a secret worth keeping? And like any secret, it carries an obligation. If Quintus Herculis Quinctius finds out I will know who to blame.'

Calpurnia inclined her head gracefully. 'Some have wondered if this might be your aim.'

The Emperor leaned close. 'Strictly *entre nous*, I don't altogether trust old Ulysses. Nice enough fellow. Staunch as they come. But a bit of a duffer. And they tell me he can't keep secrets. There, now you know it all.'

'Thank you.'

'So now we can relax. Tell me about the Amazon. I campaigned there, you know. Loved it. Loved the people. Loved the . . .'

And there the conversation drifted off into tales of adventure. Some time later the tables were again cleared and the desserts brought in. Already some of the diners were past eating and lolled back on their couches. Calpurnia took one look at the honey custards, the cheeses, the peaches, the cakes filled with cream and decided to make her excuses.

The Emperor looked sad and shrugged. 'Perhaps another time,' he said. 'Perhaps a smaller meal. Perhaps something more intimate . , ,'

'Perhaps,' said Calpurnia. 'Perhaps you will dine at my house when you come to Britannia. You are coming for the bonfire, I understand.'

'I am. I wouldn't miss it. And I should be honoured to be your guest.'

Calpurnia signalled to her servants to be ready for departure. 'Just one other thing,' said the Emperor again leaning close. 'I have a favour to ask. Would you mind if occasionally I called you? I shall be seeking your advice, nothing more. I think I do not understand Britannia . . .'

'Surely the Ulysses is your adviser. That's why you made him your deputy. Surely he can—'

'The Ulysses is not a woman. I understand men, but they only tell half the story. I want to be remembered as a good Emperor. Oh I know I clown about a bit and I was a terror when I was younger, I freely admit it. But if you had seen the state of things here . . . well. There is much to do to pull this Empire together. Have no fears, I will not ask for favours or for anything which you would not give your groom or cook. Simply advice.'

'Whatever the Emperor requests, if it lies within my power and modesty to grant, I shall not be found unreasonable.'

'Capital. Those are the words I had hoped to hear.'

The Emperor stood. Everyone stood. Moments later Calpurnia was aboard her palanquin, now with its curtains drawn, and was on her way back to her daughter's city house.

Later that night, dressed in a simple loose gown and slippers, she called for a mushroom omelette lightly cooked and a glass of red wine and soda water.

Before settling between the sheets for the night she noted in her diary, 'Tonight I met a crocodile – very clever – not to be trusted. But I'm a terrible flirt.'

Post scriptum for Sean and Drummer

They travelled to Hibernia where, after crossing the island, Sean led them down a narrow path to a small village. Evening was well advanced when Sean approached one of the houses. Already a light was burning in the window. He knocked softly. Moments later the door opened, and shortly thereafter the peace of the evening was broken by a cry of joy. Mother and son were united. Brothers and sisters gathered round. Only the father was absent for he had died at sea a few months earlier when the wind changed and carried his small boat on to the white rocks.

The whole village came alive as word spread that Crazy Sean had returned – but he wasn't crazy any more. He was big and strong and handsome and . . .

'. . . and I didn't travel alone,' said Sean. 'I want you to make my companion welcome. His name is Drummer. He is outside now. I warn you, he is a bit singular.'

Drummer was the stuff of legend, a giant from the time before stories were written. There was a hush as he stepped over the threshold into the small whitewashed house, bending almost double to avoid the low oil lamp. His smell filled the small room. His face was a face that they had all seen at one time or another, in their imaginations if not in actuality, staring out of the leaves at the edge of the forest. Drummer chose a place by the window and squatted down. Even so, his head was just a few inches under the dark beams.

He was welcomed.

Samhain came and went. The gusty storms of autumn gave way to the high-breaking seas of winter. Mist came in from the sea and the smoke from the cottage fires hung low.

As the days shortened, Drummer became restless. He was hearing a call which he could not ignore. For a short time he went away into the neighbouring woods and when he returned he had fashioned a new drum from the trunk of a tree. Sean guessed his intent.

A few days later, close to mid-winter, Sean watched Drummer depart, walking up the cliff path, his drum at his side. Sean felt part of his life was leaving him. His dark intuition told him that he would never see Drummer again. He knew that that was how things should be, he knew that it was right; but it was so painful that it made him want to howl and pull his coat over his head.

But Sean survived.

Sometime in the next springtime they heard rumours of troubles in Britannia. Once they felt a Great Darkness pass over them. For seven days no man put his boat in the sea and no woman walked in the fields, though the sun shone brightly and the breeze lifted the spray from the white-capped waves and the fish were plentiful. That darkness lasted for a week and then was gone ... except that it lingered in memory, and so was never completely lost.

Sean dreamed one night that Drummer came to him and showed him his broken drum. Then he walked away, down a sombre valley into a dark forest leaving the broken pieces of drum at Sean's feet.

The next morning Sean climbed up on to the headland and there he buried the cassik he had brought from Britannia.

Autumn was distinguished by the number of flies which buzzed and hovered in the forest, attracted by the unpicked fruit, the mouldering stooks of corn and the rotting meat. For those who had escaped and survived in the forest, the coming of winter was a release from smell and noise.

A sudden cold dry spell brought silence. For a whole week there were frosts and when the ice melted, plants which had died collapsed on to the forest floor. Perol, noting red holly berries out before their time, felt glad and wondered what name she should give her child. Hetty, seeing the holly in her part of the land already showing clusters of fruit, predicted a harsh winter, and she was right.

Sullen heavy days set in, with grey skies and a steady cold which seemed to seep to the very heart of things. It was a time of death and only the very perceptive could see the new life waiting.

A Death

In the month known as Beith, the life of Cormac the Singer finally came full circle.

The old man had never completely recovered from the chill. His body fought, but his energy waned and still he intensified his teaching. He taught Coll the dark power of the cithara that can kill or cause sleep, and the tunings that make easier the passage from this world to the world of the animals. And in this Coll was an apt student who soon could surpass his teacher. 'For more knowledge than I have you must ask Dark Eagle. I have never needed to bend the trees, but you may need to. He can teach you the language of the trees.'

Then one morning at four o'clock, Cormac was gently rocked awake. Standing beside his bed was the dark companion that he had first met many years earlier, at the time of his first singing. 'It is time, old man,' said his Death. 'Make your way.'

Cormac rose immediately. There was a lightness in his step as he pulled on his singer's tunic of white trimmed with green. He busied himself in the small room making himself a brew to give him strength for the journey. Then he woke up Coll. For the last time, he and Coll sat opposite one another and Cormac sang in his wheezing tired voice. It was a song of his life and a song of farewell.

Coll cried. He could not have stopped himself had he wanted to. Sweet and bitter; light and dark; salt and honey. At the end Cormac slowly untuned the cithara letting the strings sigh and rattle and hang loose. Then he handed the instrument to Coll. 'Here. It's yours now, lad. If it serves you as well as it's treated me, you'll lack for nothing. Tune it yourself when you get back.'

Dawn was just lightening the sky as they saddled up Aristotle for the last time. Coll hoisted Cormac up and the donkey began to pick its way through the forest. They turned to the hills.

After some hours of weaving back and forth, they came to where the trees ended. They were now high, at a place of wind-sculptured scrub and stiff tussock grass. Still they climbed.

Looking ahead Coll could see a pass in the hills, a notch beneath an overhanging outcrop of rock. It took them half an hour of climbing before they reached it. There, Cormac slid from the donkey's back and the creature stood still facing into the harsh wind which pressed its ears back. Then it wandered to the side of the path. Coll and Cormac looked down from the pass. Below them, both front and back, was the same view – the forest, like dark froth, which merged at the horizon into the grey mist.

'You stay here now,' said Cormac. 'Come and look for me later. And remember, I want a clean quick fire. Too bloody damp to muck about.'

The two men held one another briefly, and then Cormac set off, climbing up the steep hillside above the rocky outcrop. He moved slowly and painfully but with a steady determination. He was like a stone moving, and his old cloak blended with the grass and bushes.

Coll stared out over the wide valley in the direction of the sea, remembering when he and Gwydion had journeyed from Cliff Town. It seemed a century ago.

When Coll finally turned back and looked for Cormac, the singer was gone.

For the next few hours he busied himself finding dry wood and building a pyre. He wove the dry branches together and stuffed crisp brown heather deep under the twigs. Finally he was satisfied. He had built a platform in the very heart of the fire and piled brushwood round it. 'So long as it doesn't rain,' he muttered. 'And with this wind blowing, the fire'll blaze like a furnace.' There was nothing to do now but wait. He settled down and made himself as comfortable as he could, leaning back on the soft tussock, out of the wind.

He fell asleep and only woke up some hours later when Aristotle nudged him with his blunt nose, seeking for soft shoots. The sky was the colour of milk. Coll blinked, for a moment uncertain where he was, and then he shook himself awake and climbed to his feet. 'Time to go, eh, Aristotle?'

He checked the funeral pyre to make sure none of the wood had shifted and then set off, climbing the hill, following the route taken by the old singer. He scanned left and right as he climbed, pushing through the bracken and heather. Ahead of him, high on the hill, was a boulder which looked like a fist emerging from the hillside. It was mottled with yellow and grey lichen. Coll climbed towards this.

He was astonished to discover that it was at least a mile away, and the climb was steep. 'Tough old bugger,' muttered Coll, 'climbing all this way.' But when he reached the boulder he understood why. The view was magnificent: the whole vale spread out.

At the foot of the boulder lay Cormac. His knees were drawn up and his head was covered in the hood of his cloak. His hands were held out in front, like little paws. He reminded Coll of a mouse he had once found that had died in the wainscot at Bella's Inn, and was completely dried out. When he bent down to pick up the body, the similarity was even more pronounced, for Cormac was light – like a bundle of straw that has dried in the wind.

Coll carried the small body down the hillside. He moved as

in a dream, stepping carefully round the rocks and gullies, aware of the hush which comes with evening. He placed the body on the platform and then wrapped the cloak over it and packed the dry brushwood tight. As he did so he heard words in his head, voices singing a warrior song before battle, and he joined with the song. Even while he was singing, he struck up a flame and blew on the sparks until they caught.

The smoke was whipped away by the wind. The flames leaped and the twigs crackled. Coll pushed more wood into the pyre, building a base of hot embers. Then the fire began to roar as it took on a life of its own. The bigger branches caught and Coll had to back away as the flames reached out and singed his beard. He watched as the inner branches fell in on themselves creating an inferno. The whole bonfire shifted, settling, and the breeze fanned the flames until they were leaping high and the embers became incandescent. The body blazed and then was lost to Coll in the smoke and flying sparks.

He turned away, his eyes streaming, and was astonished at how dark the sky was. All that remained of the day were a few streaks of light above the hills to the west. Looking down from the pass, Coll wondered what the people in the valley below would make of the blaze. They would know that someone had passed away. Some might come looking in the morning. Soon the word would spread, and soon Coll would be asked to sing about the passing of Cormac.

He settled down in the tussock, his green cloak wrapped tightly round him, and stared into the blazing heart of the fire. 'Strange this business of being a singer,' he murmured. 'You don't so much do things as let things happen, and then you do things, and then other things happen.'

Coll was woken by raindrops in the middle of the night. He crawled under a bush and made his cloak into a cave the way that Cormac had shown him and then he withdrew into himself, detaching from the present, pushing away the rain and the cold. Not far away Aristotle stamped and blew.

Dawn came cold and grey. All that remained of the blazing pyre was a pool of sodden ash in which were bits of wood, bits of bone. Coll gathered the bones, the broken skull and the fragments of pelvis, and put them in one of the saddlebags. The fire had done its work well and many of the shards crumbled to dust when he picked them up. Then he uprooted a bush and used it to sweep the ashes away. The rain would clear the site. New grass would grow. All would be almost as it was.

Coll stared up at the boulder where Cormac had died. It caught the morning light and dominated the landscape. 'Away, Aristotle, time we were gone.' The donkey protested when Coll began to lead it, tossing its head. But Coll was firm. He rubbed its ears and talked to it, and then, for the first time, he swung up into the saddle. The donkey began to pick its way carefully down the path.

They had only been going about twenty minutes when the donkey's ears twitched. Coll guided them off the path until they could stand silent and invisible within the trees. Moments later two men and a woman came hurrying up the path.

Coll let them pass and then continued on down and soon was lost amid the trees.

They did not meet anyone else. When they reached the oak tree Coll removed the few bones and carried them to the spring. This was his own idea, for though he could not see the spirit in the water, Cormac had often talked about her. He lodged the bones by the stream, said a few words in the old tongue to mark the moment, and then returned to take care of Aristotle.

Post scriptum for Cormac

Cormac lay down among the stones and damp grass. 'Let it be now,' he said.

Beside him his invisible companion reached out and touched him.

An old man, Cormac sighed as though he had just set down a heavy burden. The sigh continued as his eyes closed.

When he stood up he was a young warrior, with so much energy that he felt his footsteps would burn the land. He stared at the gleaming landscape, at the shimmering blue sky. He saw the wind come scampering up the hillside like coiling golden snakes.

Behind him the boulder was an arch of light and Cormac

168

stepped into it. Cormac joined with the stone and his spirit entered the land.

A Birth

It was at the dead time of the year, between seasons, when everything hangs for a while suspended, undecided it seems between a deeper, final rush into darkness and cold or a slow awakening, that Perol gave birth.

Nothing had prepared her for the pain.

While outside the snow fell silently, she cried aloud,

Angus held her hands and felt useless as he looked down at a woman he hardly seemed to recognize. Perol's face was beaded with sweat. She tried to smile but then her face was creased with another spasm. They were coming quickly now. She turned and squirmed and held his hands fiercely and cried out . . .

Gargamelle, vast in a tent-shaped caftan, was in charge. She seemed to know everything about birth and Angus was bemused at the change in her. Gone was the saucy flirtatious woman with a ribald comment for any occasion. In her place was a commander who gave orders in a way that brooked no delay or question. Garlyck too was there and Angus wondered just how it had come about that Garlyck was now involved in this most intimate moment. But of course Garlyck too knew about birth and moved with a calm humorous competence, wiping Perol's brow, telling Angus that he would survive and standing ready with warm dry towels.

'See here,' said Gargamelle. 'Look. You can see the baby's head.' Angus stared at the smooth blood-streaked dome which pulsed. 'That's the top of its head. It's coming now. Hold her hand. Hold her hand! Push, Perol love, push. It's coming now. It's—'

And come it did. The head emerged, and then the rest of the body slithering, to be taken and supported by Gargamelle. The baby took its first breath and cleared its lungs lustily. It was a girl and she had wisps of ginger hair and dark skin. 'Angus' daughter. No doubt about that, by the fuss she's kicking up. Aren't you then?' Quickly and expertly, Gargamelle severed the umbilical cord and wiped the baby down while cuddling it and keeping it warm. The eyes opened and looked about without focus.

'You can relax now, Perol,' said Garlyck. 'All's well. Ten fingers. Ten toes. All perfect.'

But Perol could not relax. Still the contractions continued. Gargamelle looked closely. 'Hell's bells,' she said. 'It's twins. Jump to it, Garlyck. This one'll come easier.' And it did. A few contractions later the crown appeared to be followed quickly by a bawling boy with a fine head of raven-black hair. Garlyck took delivery of this child. Perol cried with relief and lay back gasping. 'You got any more in there?' asked Gargamelle. 'Because if you have, me and Garlyck here want overtime.'

Perol grinned weakly. 'No, I'm . . . I'm finished.' She held up her arms. 'Can I have them? Where's Angus?'

They glanced round. None of them had paid Angus any attention when the babies started coming. He had fainted and now lay propped against the wall. Gargamelle eyed him like a woman of the world whom nothing can surprise. 'You mark my words. In a couple of months from now, he'll be bragging about seeing the birth with full graphic details.'

'He was never brought up to know anything about such things,' said Perol, protectively. 'It's not his fault. Take him outside, Garlyck. Pump some air into him. Then bring him back.'

Garlyck hoisted Angus expertly and got him up over his shoulder. 'Good job I'm used to shifting dead weights,' he said, grunting. 'See you shortly.'

He carried Angus to the heavy skin door and pushed his way through. Outside was an antechamber which led to the outside. Waiting were Wallace Duff and most of the other inhabitants of Drummer's caves.

'Everything all right?'

'We heard the cries.'

'Is there two?'

'How's Perol?'

'Perol's fine and so are her son and daughter. This one's not so hot though,' he said hefting Angus. 'There's a bit of cleaning up to do in there. But I think Gargamelle'll let you in in a few minutes. But don't go peeping in till she asks you. OK?'

Garlyck's warning was timely. Inside the room the afterbirth came away. Perol had not expected this and didn't know what it was. 'This we treat with care,' said Gargamelle. 'This we bury in good soil, eh? Mother to mother.'

'Whatever you say,' said Perol.

Clean pillows were in place. Covers that had been soaked when the waters broke and the babies were born had been dumped in a tub to soak. Perol lay back with the two small babies tucked in the crook of her arms. Her face was washed. Her hair was brushed. She looked like a queen ready to receive guests.

'Now you just lie there while I go and get changed. Have a few moments alone. I'll see what's happening to Angus.'

Angus was outside, breathing in the cold air. The snow swept down, seeming to come in sheets, lit by the flickering fire at the cave mouth. He was sitting on Drummer's drum which Garlyck had thoughtfully provided and the snow had plastered one side of him white.

'Congratulations,' said Garlyck.

'Bloody hell,' said Angus. 'That got to me. The pain and then the blood . . . And then that sudden . . . I don't remember anything else. Is it always like that? Is Perol all right?'

'They're all all right. Here, rub some snow in your face. Then come on in. Perol'll want you to be with her. Get to know your daughter and son.'

Angus gaped at him. 'Two of them? A daughter and a son? I thought . . .'

For a moment Garlyck thought Angus was going to faint again, but he steadied himself. Then Angus scooped up snow and rubbed it in his face and stuffed some in his mouth for good measure and spat out. The chill brought him down to earth. 'A son and a daughter, eh? That takes some beating.' He stood up. 'Now I know why Drummer left his drum. So I could make an announcement.'

He threw back his wolf cloak and picked up the drum. Drummer used his fist and knuckles to beat the drum but Angus found a knotty piece of wood that had been set out to dry. He held the drum out in front of him and began to beat it, sending out hollow boomings which the wind carried away past the cave mouths and down the valley and into the tangle of dark trees.

Inside the cave Perol heard the sound and smiled. 'Don't worry,' she whispered, 'it's just your father bubbling over. I think he's finally realized what's happened.'

Angus beat the drum until his arm ached. Then he placed it at the cave door and went inside.

He passed through the vestibule and felt hands slapping him on the back and heard voices calling congratulations.

He was in the room. Perol again looked like Perol, not the distressed creature he had seen before, and now she had a glow about her. Her eyes were very big and gleaming and she was sitting up proudly.

'Here's your son and here's your daughter. We don't do things by halves. Now give me a kiss and tell me you like them.'

Angus kissed her gently. He suddenly felt clumsy, as if with one wrong move he might break her or them. He peered at the babies. This was the first time he had ever seen a new-born baby and he didn't know what to make of them.

He didn't know what to make of any of it. But as he looked, the engineer in him responded. He saw a tiny hand, scarcely bigger than his thumb, but perfect in every detail. It opened and closed, and when he offered his little finger, the small hand closed on it briefly.

Outside the wind howled.

It howled for a week while the snow piled high against the cave walls. Within the caves the people were safe and warm behind their skin doors, moving by oil lamp and candle through the warren of passages that connected the caves.

The soldiers at Castra Skusa were not so fortunate. They were behind schedule in the building of the bunkers and firing stations for the great conflagration and so were driven out of their warm barracks to continue cutting down trees and digging trenches while the snow wheeled down from a lead-grey sky.

The storm lasted a week, and then came silence.

After the silence, the tinkle and clatter of water.

The year had turned. Though there were many storms of winter yet to come, the drive towards spring was on, and everything felt it.

When the snows finally cleared and the icy water drained away, the officer in charge of building the firing site, an old campaigner by the name of Burrus, surveyed the mess of mud and debris and shook his head. Of all the work undertaken in the autumn little remained except silted pools and sodden logs. Burrus was a superstitious man who believed he had survived in battle on account of the lucky charms he wore and his strict vegetarian diet. He had been assigned this task by old Ulysses since he was an expert in demolition, following the logic that destruction and construction are complementary skills. In addition he was renowned as a ruthless administrator with a delight in efficiency. He declared, 'For us to have this site ready for the Reformed Lupercalia in three months' time will require prayer, sacrifice, the assistance of the gods and luck – not to mention hard work – or we'll all be roasting, need I remind you.' He was addressing the officers in charge of the different departments involved in the construction. 'So here are new standing orders: prayers at dawn every day – full attendance; sacrifice on alternate days – full attendance; and an absolute dedication to duty in between. I expect weekly reports on progress and realistic projections of work yet to be accomplished. You can hand these to my new assistants.' He indicated Romulus and Remus who, since their heroism in capturing Roscius single-handed, had been elevated from soldier class to administrator class – positions which they found greatly to their liking. They smirked and nodded, indicating that they, like Burrus, were men of no nonsense and expected the architects, drain-layers, carpenters and stone-masons as well as the boffins from the Branodunum Military Research Camp to pull finger and jump to it.

Geoganthos, a sad-eyed Greek who had been drafted from the architects' college at the Battle Dome and whose job it was to arrange a pretty spectacle for the firing, raised his hand tentatively. 'May I respectfully request that we pray to Mercury for wings of speed, Jupiter that there be no rain, Phoebus that the sun shine on our labours, and Minerva for wisdom on how to proceed when supplies do not arrive?'

Burrus was not sure how to take this request. Like many of his kind he regarded Greeks, and especially artistic Greeks, as suspect. 'Too clever by half. Too clever for their own good,' was his opinion. 'You can leave all that to us,' he replied. 'We will cover all contingencies. If you have any complaints submit them in writing. Now if there are no more questions . . . ?' There weren't. 'Dismiss.'

And strange to say, after the harsh winter and all the interruptions of supplies and soggy half-cooked meals, suddenly things did begin to run more smoothly. The spring air was balmy, the sun shone with a hint of warmth and supplies began to arrive regularly and on schedule. The drain-layers were able to open secure trenches to drain away the surplus water. The heavy construction began in earnest.

The site chosen for the first ceremonial burning was located in a shallow open-ended valley just a mile and a half east of Castra Skusa. To the south were the gentle slopes of some hills. To the east, and reaching all the way to the sea, stretched the wide vale bordered by the moors to the north and the wolds to the south. The people who lived in the town of Derventio had been assured in person that they would be at no risk. Wide fire-breaks would keep the conflagration well away from the town as the fires swept past them and on to the sea. Later, when the stumps were removed, grass would be sown on the deforested hills and by high summer the first sheep should be nibbling. An idyllic pastoral landscape would be created with lakes and groves and statues of Pan.

A week after Burrus' pep talk, a detachment of the Horribles arrived marching up from Camp Lucius, singing their battle-songs. They were set to work cutting fire-breaks and dragging away the logs to make high platforms to serve as lookout posts. These were established along the southern edges of the moors so that the progress of the great fire could be followed and reported. They also undertook an extension of the sky-road linking Eburacum to Castra Skusa. This new road was specifically to accommodate the Emperor's flagship, the *Pandora*.

Many convoys passed over the small bridge under which was stashed Angus' Dragon. The drivers never looked down, but even if they had they would hardly have seen anything for the ferns had grown tall and the Dragon was hidden under the forest litter.

Builders and gardeners arrived from the Eburacum Battle Dome and began to construct two vast amphitheatres. Between them they built a small separate stand for the Emperor and his closest guests. The view would be magnificent. From the safety of the terraces, the guests would be able to witness the entire pageant, from drama to ignition.

Meanwhile, supplies of building materials and shaped stone arrived every day at the deserted sea port of Cliff Town and the heavy convoys moved steadily inland.

Visits from Marcus Augustus Ulysses and Marmellius Caesar became frequent. To them, the construction of the bonfire site was the top priority.

Gaius Daedalus requested and was granted a force of men to dig foundations for his twin cannon. The foundations needed to be deep, to the bed-rock if possible for Daedalus had modified the design of the cannon somewhat and had changed the specifications. The new cannon were bigger and heavier than the prototypes. They had greater thrust and were able to squirt larger volumes of liquid phlogiston and Cretan water to a greater altitude.

If Marcus Ulysses wanted a show to impress the Emperor – well, he Daedalus would give him a show to remember. He was determined to erase the memory of the fiasco in the marshes at Branodunum.

While the foundations were being dug, tall pressure towers were constructed close to the site. These towers, also modified by Daedalus, could generate a pressure wave every minute.

The construction work on the bunkers and the foundations was completed ahead of schedule. A small dedication ceremony was held when the gleaming cannon were winched up out of their straw-lined troughs and lowered into position. They were mounted on gimbals and could be given new alignments in a matter of seconds. When changes in inclination were synchronized with the pressure waves, it was possible (and intended) for the cannon to maintain an almost continuous drizzle of blazing chemicals over vast stretches of the forest.

One day, after prayers, the firing range was cleared of all workers. That morning there was to be a test firing. Vats of liquid, each with the same specific gravity as the two chemicals but completely inert, were made ready. Everyone gathered to watch as the pressure towers were connected. Daedalus was white-faced and jumpy. He was confident he had solved the technical problems, but there were always the gremlins to contend with. Unlike Burrus, Gaius Daedalus doubted the gods' knowledge of fluid dynamics. But he thanked his lucky stars that at least he had the opportunity for a test firing. Not like the last time . . . not like . . .

Burrus took him by the arm and led him to the Emperor's seat in the concrete observation bunker. 'Trust the gods,' rumbled Burrus. 'They won't let a pious man down.'

Daedalus thanked him weakly and gave the order to fire. He could barely bring himself to look. The first pressure wave arrived, the cannon roared, the twin plumes of dark liquid shot high into the sky, mingled and fell to earth with a heavy splatter. Moments later there came another wave and then another and another . . . It worked. It worked perfectly.

'Call it off. Call it off,' screamed Geoganthos. 'You'll soak the building materials. I've got paint and canvas stored under there.'

Majestically Gaius Daedalus gave the signal which brought the test to a halt and acknowledged the cheers of the soldiers. They had been impressed by the raw energy of the cannon. Suddenly Daedalus was popular. Everyone scented success.

'Now perhaps I can build my set,' said Geoganthos grumpily. 'Now that the mechanical bits and pieces are working.'

Geoganthos had designed more than a set. He had designed an entire entertainment. Being sceptical with regard to the gods and yet aware of the needs of patronage, he had chosen to create a multilevel scene celebrating the time when Prometheus, friend to mankind and mocker of the gods, stole fire from the heavens. Geoganthos liked building mountains, and so he had designed a mountain to resemble Olympus. For his cast he had been given dancers and acrobats as well as a group of condemned criminals who would play the gods. In the final act, Emperor Prometheus would press the control switch and the cannon would spout and the mountain, the convicts and everything else in the area would end in a deluge of fire. Geoganthos expected to be well rewarded, for there was flattery on many levels in his scene and he expected a man as literate as the Emperor to be appreciative.

Once the mountain was blazing and the cannon had done their job, both Geoganthos and Daedalus could relax. Then the Horribles would take over. After much debate in Eburacum, it had been agreed that they would take on the dangerous job of guiding the fire to the sea. They had placed incendiary devices strategically all the way to the shore and they had a plentiful supply of liquid phlogiston and Cretan water in reserve. They would keep the fire blazing.

'We're right on target,' said Romulus to Remus, gleefully. 'Get all this right and there could be promotion in this for you and me, my boy. Chief fire-raisers to his Emperorship.'

'Still. It's a funny time to have a fire,' said Remus. 'I mean, straight after winter, before everything's dried out. Be much better in summer.'

Romulus groaned in mock exasperation. 'Symbolism,' he said. 'You've got to appreciate the symbolism. That's what the world turns on. Not what's right, or proper or what actually is. But whatever the powers-that-be want it to be. Got it?'

'Got it.'

13   The Ordinary Ecstasy of a Tree

For a while Coll could not believe that Cormac was gone.

So attuned was he to the old man's strangeness – wandering in the night, talking to streams, coming and going without explanation – that Coll found himself setting out two plates and listening for the old man wheezing down the steps under the tree. He would practise songs alone in the tree and invent melodies, and then want to play them to Cormac, and that was when he missed him most.

At the same time, Coll was filled with a sense of terrible urgency. If he sat down he felt he ought to be standing. When he set the cithara aside at night in order to sleep he felt he ought to be practising. Finally, in desperation almost – and because he needed wise counsel – he shouldered the cithara, saddled the donkey and went in search of Dark Eagle.

Dark Eagle seemed agitated when Coll asked him why everything seemed so out of joint.

'I can see so far,' he said holding his finger and thumb about an inch apart, 'but no farther. That troubles me. I have seen bad times and good times. But never before have I been blind. I cannot help you. I can teach you. But you must apply my teaching. It is sad when we who are old must put such weight on the young. But for you to learn, you must enter my world properly. That too is dangerous. Everything is dangerous. Breathing is dangerous. So what is new? The warrior walks with danger, and because he walks in safety, others may follow. Come over to my world.'

'How do I—' Coll began. But before he could finish, Dark Eagle reached out and hooked his finger in the boar-tusk ornaments round Coll's neck and pulled. For a moment Coll felt sick. All his fears tumbled together, and then he found himself sitting on the stony ground while a cold wind blew.

Opposite him and laughing was Dark Eagle. 'You pig people think you are clever. Oh, but you can be led by the tusk. Now the eagle will make you fly.'

Again Dark Eagle reached out, but this time he put his hand over Coll's crown and Coll felt a great surge of energy flow into him from the man's hand and arm. For a moment there was pain. And then there was freedom and wind surging and lifting. A voice inside his head said, 'Hey. The eagle lends you his eyes as the pig lends you his strength and wisdom. Learn this.' When Coll opened his eyes he found himself staring down at the ground from a great height and the ground was moving. He could see two figures, himself and Dark Eagle squatting on the ground.

Coll stared through bright yellow eyes and saw the hop of a mouse in the thicket, the kick of a rabbit outside its burrow and the swirl of a fish in reeds where the river was shallow.

'Learn by these,' said the voice of Dark Eagle loud in his head, and Coll became a rabbit on the ground staring into the two sharp imperious yellow eyes above the cruel curving beak. They stared at him. The eyes watched and blinked. Then the beak opened and the bird cried a harsh call and it spread its wings and lifted.

Coll felt himself released. He sat amid the waste of stones. A cold wind blew.

Coll awoke. His fire was burning brightly. The stick he had dropped in the embers just before picking up the cithara to summon Dark Eagle had not yet caught fire – but he felt tired and hungry as though he had been away for hours.

That night he slept in the moon shadow of the burial mound. Though the night was cold he felt warm. At one point a wild pig came barrelling through the thickets. It stopped, grunted, stirred the leaves with its tusks and then charged on.

In the morning Coll stretched and stared up into the cold blue sky. High above a bird was circling. For a moment Coll remembered the staring yellow eyes and immediately he lost himself. He was with the bird and flying over the Roman road and looking down at the small burial mound where a donkey stamped and the remains of a fire were a black spot amid the green grass and a pig rolled in a green cloak. Coll laughed and was himself again.

'So that's how it's done,' he murmured. And from far away, as though at the end of a long tunnel, he heard the answering laughter of Dark Eagle.

During the next few weeks Coll revisited the burial mound many times, trudging through the autumn rain and wind and the early snow to sit with the long dead wanderer. Sometimes he ran with the warrior, while the warrior hopped, covering the ground as quickly as Coll. And he learned new songs. They made him feel comfortable and strange, and he came to know that the particles from which his body was made were stardust. He learned to sing so that the birds came and the fish, the animals too and even the spiders.

But still it was not enough. He said to Dark Eagle, 'Once, before he passed over, Cormac told me you could teach me to bend the trees and the language of the trees. Teach me that skill.'

Dark Eagle looked at him in surprise. 'You think you are strong enough for that?' He shook his head. 'No, you're not strong enough. You have passed too far down the road of the head. You have forgotten the road of the earth and the sun.'

'Teach me.'

'You must be prepared to give up all power.'

'But . . .'

'There you see. I said it would be hard. At the first hint of the price of knowledge you start to argue.'

'But . . .'

'Fight me.' The voice had come from elsewhere. From behind. Coll recognized it and turned round. He groaned. Facing him was the enraged and insolent figure of Alexander still bloody and cut.

'You again,' said Coll. 'I hoped I'd seen the last of you.'

'Fight me,' said Alexander in a loud harsh voice.

'Not now. I have things to do.'

'You will accomplish nothing until you fight me.'

Coll looked at Dark Eagle. 'I've been down this road before,' he said.

'And what did you learn?'

'To live. To accept my destiny. To push ahead even if I didn't know what was ahead. Not to be afraid.'

'So what do you think you have to learn this time?'

Coll sat for a while and then he shook his head. 'I won't fight him,' he said. 'If fighting him is the price I have to pay for knowledge, then the knowledge is rotten, and I want none of it. Sorry. I'll go my own way.'

'Hey. Hey. Hey,' called Dark Eagle. 'Not so fast. You might be getting the hang of things. Take a good look at Alexander. Get an eyeful of him. Say goodbye to Alexander. He's served you well in many guises.'

Coll turned to Alexander expecting to see him in some new malevolent guise. But what he saw was an image of himself as a child, as Viti, dressed in a Roman centurion's uniform several sizes too large and with a toy sword. The sad-faced child smiled wearily and waved. Then he became a pile of brown leaves that blew away in the wind.

Dark Eagle looked on and his eyes were bright with a fire that Coll had never seen before. 'So here we are. At ladder start. Eh? Now we climb? Eh? Knowledge is never rotten. Everything is what we make of it, eh? And if you want to join the world of the trees you must learn to separate what is real and put it in this pile, and what is not real and put it in that pile. Because the trees only deal in what is real. They know much more than us.' He laughed again, 'But us. Ha! Me, you and Cormac and the rest, we carry bits from every pile, all tumble-together. So here's the problem. When we learn we must unlearn. And we must never, ever try to cheat. Come on.'

Dark Eagle led Coll. He took him into the forest to where a dark tree grew above a grey river. 'You want to learn the language of the trees,' he said unslinging a rope from his back. 'Here you start. Here the pig can't help you. Here you must stay for a while.'

So saying Dark Eagle tied Coll's hands above his head. He climbed high in the tree and hoisted Coll up and tied off the rope. There he left him dangling.

Coll turned in the wind. He felt himself dry and harden. He wished he could drop from the tree down into the grey stream. But even as the thought was born in him, a mighty wind came.

It was as though he had been struck with the back of a shovel and he banged about in the tree until darkness fell.

When he came to himself, he was back by his fire in his own world. He could hardly move.

The next day he built a small tent of skins beside the burial mound and set up camp. In the evening he tried to visit Dark Eagle again, but immediately he entered the dream-world he found himself tied high in the branches of the same tree but with birds pecking at him. Later a black wind came howling and blew round the tree and he knew no more.

When Coll woke up this time he was blind. Only gradually did his sight return. First he saw images of grey on grey and only after some hours did his world regain colour. That night he lay within his small tent. It seemed as though he could feel where the birds had pecked holes in him. He lay awake thinking. He felt a great stillness.

Outside the wind moaned and the temperature dropped to freezing. But Coll was warm. He had mastered some part of Cormac's teaching.

Over the next days he returned to the tree whenever he entered the dream-world. Once he found himself tied to a stake under the river and for a terrible moment he heard Alexander's mocking laughter while the fishes ate his flesh. Once he was buried in the roots and the worms made their way through him.

The days slipped past. Coll lost count of the time. Sometimes he did not know what world he was in.

The same snowstorm which greeted the birth of Perol's babies, and stopped the construction at the bonfire site, engulfed Coll. The snow lay deep round the burial mound. It made the roof of his tent dip.

Coll sat in his tent and played the cithara. He wondered if he was learning anything. The images he saw in the dream-world were as solid as stone, but yet ... He felt at peace ... but nothing seemed to be happening. Was there something he was not seeing? He played on.

Outside he heard a noise and when he looked out he found

the trees heavy with birds and the snow pattered with thousands of animals. 'Go away,' he called laughing. 'Go home.' He struck a chord on the cithara and all the animals scampered away and the birds took to the air at once with a noisy clatter of wings which sent a shower of snow down on to Coll. It was then that Coll noticed that the tree he had been visiting in the dream-world was right outside his door. This seemed significant. How come he had never noticed it before? It was just a tree, an ordinary tree, an ash tree . . . he had seen millions like it. But it was as though he was seeing it for the first time.

For a week Coll was unable to enter the dream-world and did not know why. That was the week when the snows melted. He wandered in the forest gathering wood for his fire. He caught fish and spread them out to cook over the flames. He used the time to tidy the area round the old burial mound. Occasionally vehicles passed down the Roman road but Coll paid them no attention. They did not distract him: they belonged elsewhere. He was aware of time passing but it no longer mattered.

Finally, with a sense of relief, Coll found himself sitting down with Dark Eagle. A subtle change had taken place in their relationship. Dark Eagle was no longer the teacher, though he was still the guide.

'Are you climbing the ladder?' he asked.

'Very slowly, very gradually,' replied Coll. And then he told Dark Eagle about all his adventures and that the tree he had visited was actually there, outside his tent.

Dark Eagle nodded. 'And how does it look to you, this tree?'

'Good,' said Coll. 'There. Solid. Very real.'

'Well be ready. Soon you won't have two piles of knowledge to confuse you. Soon there will be only one pile – for there only is one pile. That is what is real. Be ready.'

Winter eased.

One morning at dawn, Coll sat outside the tent and stared at the tree. It seemed different.

Later, when he had entered the dream-world, he found himself inside the tree, living with its fibres, aware of its juices as they pummelled and pumped through him. He heard a great beating of drums which also seemed to pulse through him. How long he stayed there he did not know, nor did he care. Day and night, summer and winter became a flickering round. He joined with a surge which began deep in the earth, gained power as it rose, flowed up through the tree and on and out and up to the moon and the stars; later to return with greater energy, sweeping down into the darkness. Thus Coll came to know the ordinary every-day ecstasy of the tree.

Finally he stepped out of the tree and fell on his knees in its roots.

The tree had revealed itself to him. What he had learned in those moments could not be put into words. It had no reality but itself. The tree had offered itself to him with a simple uncom-plicated directness: because it could not help but do so, because that was its nature, that was its life. It had given Coll its life. Just as he had offered himself to the tree. Life to life. There was nothing difficult about it at all. It was easy, natural, the birth-right of every living creature.

Later that day Coll sat in front of the tree. Its buds had formed but were not yet open. He experimented, reaching out to the life of the tree, letting it flow through him and guide his playing of the cithara. Then he took charge of the melody and played in such a way that one of the buds gradually opened of its own accord. He had made that happen. It had been what he intended. That bud would now die ... but that did not matter. It had served its purpose, it had opened willingly.

That night Coll packed up his cithara and his small tent and set off back to his oak-tree home. How different the forest now felt. On every side he was aware of a massive life force which surged and lifted and filled the planet with its music. There was a kind of knowledge there, a rugged vitality which made the most of all circumstances whether in light or shade. There was history too which stretched back to the first murmurings of life. Billions of plant forms with moist cells which every day received the light and poured out their energy. Coll was now part of that world.

He stared up through the old oak tree, riven by numerous bolts of lightning in its long life. Its energy almost knocked him over, and that energy was now his. Calmly Coll began to play. He was not surprised when the branches moved and the tree reached down and touched him.

14   *Final Plans*

'Beautiful weather. Gorgeous spring. A man can be excused for feeling optimistic.' So said Emperor Prometheus.

'Totally agree,' said Marcus Augustus Ulysses. 'Never felt better or more . . .' he struck his belly with both hands, 'robust.' Across the bed from him Calpurnia smiled and stretched. She too was feeling content. He put his finger to his lips to indicate she should not make a sound. Then he mouthed conspicuously, 'Emperor Lucius,' and pulled a face. Calpurnia rolled over, cat-like, and stroked Marcus in a way intended to distract him.

'Well sorry to wake you so early . . .'

'Not a problem. Been up for hours.'

'. . . but affairs of state you understand.'

'Completely.'

'Hm.' The Emperor was obviously nonplussed. He was not used to a boisterous Ulysses. 'Well I just thought I'd check with you. All going well? Camp Lucius . . . ?'

'Full. We'll be able to ship the first consignment of workers whenever you give the word.'

'And the site for the bonfire . . . ?'

'Almost ready. A few more licks of paint for the Spectacular. A few more days for the beer to brew. Everything else is ready.'

'You *have* been working.'

'We pride ourselves on service to the State,' said Marcus grandly. Calpurnia nipped him. 'And we are looking forward to the bonfire and to your visit. We have many entertainments planned.'

'Good, good. Well that was the other thing I was calling about. I've decided to come a bit earlier. I'll open the bridge between Britannia and Gallia – that too is almost ready. Then I'll travel up to the north in time for the Reformed Lupercalia. I have a detailed timetable.'

'That's what we've been waiting for. Marmellius Caesar is in charge of your visit. Tell your aides to contact his staff. There'll be no problems I can promise you. And no trouble with a dragon either. Marmellius tracked the mechanical one. It's at the bottom of a swamp . . . so.'

There was a pause. Marcus wanted to get rid of the Emperor but the Emperor did not want to end the conversation while he had a feeling that he was not quite in charge.

'Glad to hear it.' he said. 'Oh, by the way, I enjoyed meeting that Gallica woman at a banquet a while ago. Very astute woman. Quite wicked I imagine.'

'She can be.'

'But a bit prickly too.'

'On occasions.'

'Has she mentioned me?'

'Not a word. Actually, we haven't seen one another for a long time. She's very involved with her family. Doesn't give much time to politics.'

'Well let me know if she does say anything. I like to know who my friends are.'

'Of course.'

Another pause.

'So. I'll let you get back to *affairs of state*,' said the Emperor with heavy emphasis. It had suddenly dawned on him that Marcus Ulysses might not be alone and that was the reason for his brevity. 'Do you have a woman with you?' he asked suddenly.

'Yes,' said Marcus. He heard the Emperor sigh and then laugh.

'Well, glad to know you're still up to it. Don't work too hard. All work and no play, Marcus . . . And I want you in top form to entertain me. So, in a few weeks' time, all right?'

'Don't you worry. When you've tasted our Britannic hospitality you won't want to get back to Roma in a hurry.' He laughed, and the Emperor laughed with him, drily.

'*Ciao.*'

Calpurnia rolled away and Ulysses lay back among the pillows and slipped his arm round her.

'Could you hear what he said?' he asked.

'Not a word. Just your replies. I can guess the rest.'

'He asked about you.'

186

Calpurnia sniffed. 'Your man there is a beast,' she said. 'I won't be coming for his bonfire. Urgent family business will call me away. I'm too old for all these games.'

'He'll be upset.'

'No he won't. He'll be piqued that someone isn't dancing attendance on him. But that is all. The man is completely out of touch with himself.'

'Oh he's not so bad,' began Ulysses, but Calpurnia hit him with a pillow.

'Don't be a fool, Marcus. He's the most dangerous man on the planet. He believes in nothing. He plays games with power. He makes you look like a teddy bear and you can be pretty wicked when you want to.'

Marcus was not sure whether this was a compliment.

'So what shall I tell him? He'll want to know why you're not there. He wants everyone there.'

'Tell him . . .' Calpurnia paused. 'Tell him I'm visiting Quintus Herculis in Hibernia who is after all a distant cousin by marriage. Tell him that.' Calpurnia stood up. 'If you want my advice, you'll give him his silly bonfire and then get him out of the country as quickly as possible along with those thugs . . . the Miserables or whatever their name is. Don't have any dealings with him, Marcus. I mean that.' She reached for her gown.

'Don't go.'

'I must. The brightness is gone from the morning.' She shivered and then she looked down at him tenderly. 'But I enjoyed last night with you, Marcus. It's been a long time.'

'Too long.'

She smiled. 'Now don't go getting chivalrous. You'll end up saying things you don't mean, and there's too much of that already. Just be careful, my love.' She kissed him and then slipped away before he could get an arm round her.

Marcus Ulysses lay in the cooling bed. The happiness of the love-making in the night had brought his walls crashing down. And now, the woman's words had touched him. How long since anyone had called him their 'love'? He felt lonely and desperate. If Calpurnia could have seen him she would have been horrified. If she had been with him he might have buried his splendid head between her splendid breasts and cried his heart out, telling of all the intrigue and the threat and the danger, and begging for her help. But she was gone. The chance was missed.

Moments later there came a discreet tap at the door. He looked up hopefully, but it was only Pontius, carrying his newly pressed dress uniform.

'Excuse me for interrupting, sir. But Marmellius Caesar is already waiting. He says you have an appointment ... something about a timetable. The Emperor's visit.'

Old Ulysses groaned. 'I forgot about Marmellius. All right, I'm coming.'

It so happened that later that day Angus was monitoring the radio waves, jumping from frequency to frequency. He had rigged an aerial at the top of the cliff above the caves. Reception was excellent.

First he listened to a couple of radio operators, one in a supply depot outside Eburacum and the other at Castra Skusa, discussing the construction at the bonfire site. It was an official call mainly concerned with supplies but from time to time titbits of gossip slipped out and Angus was able to form a good idea of what was happening.

'They're planning to burn part of the forest,' he said to Perol when the conversation ended. She had just tucked the babies down for their morning nap and was tired having been up several times in the night.

'Why?'

Angus shrugged. 'Search me. Something about a sheep farm. Going to be quite a party. The Emperor's coming up from Roma.' He consulted a map of the region he had drawn with the help of Sean and Drummer and pointed to a place not far from Castra Skusa. 'There, that's where they're having their bonfire. Hm. About seven miles from here.'

'They won't be coming near here, will they? We won't be discovered?'

'No. No danger of that. This is the wilderness.'

There they let the matter drop and Angus went back to rigging up an automatic pump to bring water from the stream. He did not tell Perol, but thereafter he spent quite a lot of time listening in to the radio calls, and one day he intercepted a detailed message from Roma to Eburacum giving departure and arrival times for the Emperor's visit. The information was not especially private for this was a state visit and no one could have anticipated its being used for sabotage, not in Britannia. But now Angus knew exactly when the Emperor would be travelling the sky-road and where.

And Angus, being Angus, began to plan.

15   Coll's Song

Coll, sitting alone in his oak-tree home, knew the apprehension of the forest: why the acorns were small, why the flowers were late, why the birds preferred to build their nests elsewhere. Why, despite a brilliant spring, there was a heaviness in the air and the sun seemed muted as though seen through smoke. In this small part of Britannia Nature told a prophetic tale and he listened, sensing the darkness to come.

But yet nothing was certain. He could not *see* the future as a series of definite images: he could only sense the darkness, waiting. To Coll, whose deepest languages were no longer the languages of words, those things which other men might call symbolic statements were simply facts. The darkness was a fact. And what made everything worse was the knowledge that it could all be avoided.

But *could* and *would* were a pole apart. On the one hand was a plunging darkness, unfathomable, the consequence of greed, cruelty and a love of death. And on the other ... well, on the other hand there were only abstractions: a new direction, a retraction, a change of policy, a rethinking, a sudden and desperate withdrawal from patterns of thought laid down by centuries and to which Coll was an heir. As Coll now saw things, such a change would be tantamount to a miracle, and Coll really did not believe in miracles. He could not feel a miracle in the offing. If a miracle were imminent, some indication would be on hand. So all he was left with was readiness. The words which had so troubled Cormac now came back to haunt the mind of Coll: 'The readiness is all.'

But was it enough? Coll knew that something would happen in the deep of the forest. Perhaps life would bolt. Perhaps universes kept apart as the earth evolved would collide. Perhaps chaos and death would seep out like a stain of ink that, having travelled up a thread, now mars an entire fabric. All were possible, and all would cause the darkness he saw spreading.

And what would survive? Coll knew that he would not – but he had known that for a long time. It was not survival that mattered but that the ending have meaning. Not to strive to the very end and push to a place beyond hope, would be to give way to the darkness. That was unthinkable – as unthinkable as jumping into a stream with stones in his pocket.

The trees would not survive. They would give up everything, as they always had for that was their nature. In their place would be . . .

The animals would not survive, though they ran in terror from a darkness not of their making.

The people would not survive – neither the innocent nor the stupid.

All that would survive would be . . .

. . . and it was at this point that Coll reached the end of his understanding. Try as he would, sing as he might, he could not conceive of a state beyond nothingness.

It was time to take action. Coll saddled up Aristotle, threw his green cloak round his shoulders, tucked his cithara into its black sack and closed his house. As the spring sun warmed the air, he set out to sing his warning. He prepared two songs, one for the people and one for the animals.

He travelled far and wide following the small tracks, singing whenever the urge took him, striking the old cithara with all the energy he could, making the instrument boom. His songs were heard by many who never saw him. The deer pricked up their ears and ran, the bears growled and lumbered away while the wolves paused, tongues out, one foot raised before they ran like arrows.

Coll found the small communities which the Roman soldiers had missed. He reached places where new communities of people – those whose homes had been burned – had gathered in glade and koad. Wherever he stopped he called everyone together, young and old. They all could read something in his manner and all of them could sense the unease in the air.

Coll's song told of departure: of filling carts with sacks of seed, of gathering provisions, of driving cattle and goats, of taking the cheese press and the mortar and pestle and the weaver's loom and the cobbler's last and the butchers' knives and the silver plate and the herbs for medicine . . . and of fleeing. The song was a warning. And such was the power of Coll's singing that wherever he sang, families began packing that very night and by dawn the carts were rumbling. Nor did they ask any questions. Coll could not tell them how far to flee, only to keep on moving.

He came upon Hetty and Danea and Marcus the teacher when they were hoeing their garden. They looked in surprise at the slim young man in a green cloak several sizes too large for him perched on an old donkey. Though they got the drift of his message, they ignored it. They were having too much fun. But Hetty gave him some berries she had gathered and Danea gave him apples that had been stored over the winter and Marcus, after slapping his pockets, gave him a cigar. They waved while the donkey ambled on.

Coll travelled to the sea and on his way passed through a grove by a stream. The ground was littered with bleached and pecked bones with tatters of uniform and rusting weapons. Two wicked-eyed children sat in a tree and watched him pass. They knew better than to taunt a being that the trees loved.

Once he was aware of Miranda, or thought he was . . . there was certainly a presence, but when he tried to locate it it vanished. Miranda, vast and terrifying as she now was, heard Coll's song and immediately she instructed Gwellan to take the children and flee. 'Time is spinning down. Find a place of safety.' Gwellan did not protest. She felt such deep fear of the thing that Miranda had now become that she wanted to run away and hide. Later, when Lem and Sulla came looking for her, she sent them away, back to their own dimension. They had played their part in her evolution and now they must be patient.

Coll halted in Cliff Town. He passed unseen by the soldiers unloading red wine from Italia and barrels of olives from Greece. He remembered the inn where he had healed the cat, and made his way there. But the inn had been looted and burned. So Coll played in the empty streets and the thin scrawny cats and the lean dogs loped away, up into the hills. Even the rats and wood-lice began to run for shelter.

Coll entered Derventio in the evening, but before he could strike up on the cithara, a patrol apprehended him. He was thrown into prison. There he heard the news that the Emperor was on his way and would soon be in Britannia. Coll played to the convicts and jailers, and then used the tricks that Cormac had taught him to escape, leaving the jail doors wide.

Finally, after wandering the narrow lanes of the deep forest, Coll came close to the place where the Dragon Warriors lived in Drummer's caves. Time was already running out. He sang to the wind and trees and hoped that this would be enough. Nobody heard, except the goats and the chickens. In the morning when Gargamelle set out to milk the goats and gather eggs, she found the creatures had escaped.

At the end of his journey Coll returned to the tree-house. He climbed down from the donkey wearily and was just about to enter the oak-tree home when he heard someone calling.

'Singer. Coll the Singer. Come and talk to me. Come and rest. Come and bathe.'

Coll could hardly believe his ears. It was the spirit of the stream calling and when he looked carefully, he could see her. She hovered like spray at the place where the spring gushed from the hillside, and she waved to him. When she shook her hair the water droplets sparkled.

Coll walked slowly and sat down on one of the flat stones by the spring.

'You're weary, man.'

Coll nodded.

'I had a way of healing Cormac when he was weary. Come in. Don't bother about the dust and the sweat. Just throw off your cloak and come in.'

The idea was appealing. Coll dabbled his fingers in the stream and the water made him tingle. Moments later he was crouching down in the stream with the water pouring over his shoulders, teasing out the pain and the tiredness. He drank and the water flowed through him like wine. The spirit of the stream crouched beside him. She kept changing. Once she looked like Miranda, once like Salli. Briefly she took the form of a man, one of Coll's tutors whom he had idolized when he was a trainee officer at the Eburacum Military Academy, and for a few flickering moments she was like Diana. Then she settled to be a brown-skinned woman with wild green eyes.

'Be yourself,' said Coll.

'I am myself. Do you like me?' He nodded. 'Then sing to me.'

'Why did you never let me see you before?'

'You were a bit young. Not ready for me then. You're old now. I like old men. You're hard too, like stone. I like stone. You're a singer. I love singers. Sing to me.'

And Coll did. He sang of the passing of Cormac, while the shadows by the stream lengthened. It was a slow and thoughtful song about the passing of ages: about what is lost, what is saved, what is found. And at the end of it he cried and the spirit of the stream cried with him. Then he sang his song of departure and the stream listened with a faraway look in her eye.

'Will you go?' he asked. 'For what is to come is dangerous to man and beast and flower and spirit.'

She shook her head and laughed. 'No. I'll stay. So long as there is water in the creek, I'll stay. And besides, if what you say is even half true, this land is going to need all the magic it can muster when the darkness comes.'

Coll climbed from the stream. All the tiredness was washed from him. He felt young and strong and primed – the way he used to feel after battle practice, but without the anger.

'Can I came to you again. Before I depart?' he asked.

'Come to me any time,' said the river. 'I'm here. I'm yours.'

True to his nature – and with an eye to his security – Emperor Prometheus changed his plans. He decided to leave for Britannia two days earlier than scheduled. This decision sent shock waves ricocheting through every stage of his journey. Chefs kicked their assistants and the assistants kicked the pot boys. Officers ordered extra drill and cleaning duty. Marine mechanics responsible for the Channel Bridge linking Dubris with the coast of Gallia worked through the night, climbing about beneath the bridge testing the flexible organic linkages. In Eburacum old Ulysses roared while Gnaeus Marmellius Caesar reworked schedules. The road-monitors worked overtime handling the quantities of supplies required to entertain the Emperor, for he did not travel light.

Months earlier, when the visit was first mooted, Lucius' personal security staff had spread out infiltrating the management and staff of any organization that might have a hand in the procession. Now at the eleventh hour, this secret force was joined by more obvious agents who inspected every facility and studied all arrangements, making it known that any mistakes would be dealt with 'in the old-fashioned manner'. Meanwhile in Roma, the full entourage was gathered. Accompanying the Emperor were his medical corps, his hairdressers, his masseurs, his mistresses and catamites, his armourers, his astrologers (led by Lazarus the Dark Seer now in his dotage), his chefs, his private communication officers, his musicians and tumblers as well as his personal bodyguard of several hundred hand-picked soldiers. Not to mention the distinguished guests such as Gaius Germanicus, Trismagister Neptuna and Publius Pacificus all of whom had been invited to attend along with their retinue.

Thus, on a fine morning just five days before the celebration of the Reformed Lupercalia in Britannia, the vehicles which made up the Imperial cavalcade lifted one by one from the palace in Roma and negotiated their way on to the sky-road which would carry them north by west. They made a magnificent, stately sight, each craft newly painted with the Imperial colours, decked with flags, their beacons flashing and their horns calling. Bands played lively music. Bulls were slaughtered and the smoke of sweet incense rose.

Aboard the *Pandora*, actors, wigged and padded to resemble the Emperor, waved from different windows to the cheering crowds as the ship gathered speed over the city. The day was declared a national holiday.

Meanwhile, the Emperor was down below in a conference on the second floor. He was attending a secret planning meeting with only his very closest advisers, Trismagister, Germanicus and Publius. He was in fine form, speaking quickly, making his points with boundless energy, tapping the table for emphasis.

'I called this briefing because I want you lads to be aware of what is in the offing. This isn't just a pleasure cruise. It is the prelude to a confrontation between me and those smart-arsed bastards who run Britannia. It is about land and power, and don't believe the propaganda which says that I reverence Britannia. To be frank, Britannia pisses me off with its green woods and pansified natives. Not to mention that stuck-up cow Calpurnia or that loony Herculis in Hibernia or that boring old fart Ulysses. Have I made myself plain?'

Trismagister Neptuna nodded his black head sagely. 'As ever succinct and lucid, Lucius.'

'Good. So here is what I intend. First, you've all heard me say many times that I intend to establish a sheep farm in Britannia.' They nodded. 'Well what you may not have grasped is that I really do intend to burn down every tree in the country. And in order to do that I need to get control of all the land. At present I've got old Marcus Ulysses doing my monkey business and eating out of my hand, but the others are jumpy. It will probably come to war, and I shall manufacture some pretext for invasion. I'll expect your help there, Trismagister.'

'Of course.'

'Now thanks to the brilliance of old Publius here, an entire legion of the Dread are already in Britannia.' Gaius Germanicus and Trismagister Neptuna raised their eyebrows in surprise. This was news to them. It spoke of the political naivety of the Britannic leaders. 'Oh yes,' continued the Emperor, 'those boys are living the high life, helping to build things, making themselves useful, increasing the population. Of course the Gallica woman and Marmalade Caesar want them out. But if I play my cards right, I think I can get them permission to stay. Here's the gamble.' They all leaned closer. 'You see, I intend to use the Dread force to invade Hibernia and unseat the Herculis. I've already dropped hints about this. And to make it sweet and seem legitimate, I'll offer all the big families spoils if they supply mercenaries.'

Gaius Germanicus indicated he had a question. 'But surely, Prometheus, if you attack Quintus Herculis in Hibernia, they will unify. I mean, he's one of theirs, isn't he? They won't stand by and—'

'They will. You underestimate the power of greed, Germanicus. Britannia is little more than a confederacy of avarice. In any case, I have clear evidence that the Herculis clan do not have title to their land. By the gods, I'll make this a holy war to redress a historic injustice. Do you think they'll want to be seen supporting illegitimacy? What is more, the Britannic leaders are already divided. Manaviensis would sell his daughter into a brothel if he thought he could make a profit from it. Old Ulysses is half mad on account of his son. The Gallica woman thinks she can solve any problem simply by wiggling her bum. The only one with any wit is Marmellius and he has a weakness.'

'What is that?'

'He has a noble nature. You may have to give him a few lessons, Publius, on how the world really operates.'

Publius Pacificus smiled a rare smile.

'So gentlemen, on balance I think we will win. I find it instructive to compare them to hungry rats in a bucket. Throw them a piece of meat and they start attacking one another. I will offer them Hibernia, and then, when the battle is over, I'll round them up and chop off their heads. No more resistance. The burning can go ahead.'

'With all due respect,' said Gaius Germanicus, 'I think you may be underestimating popular resistance.'

'Not when people hear the truth. In any case, we won't touch the cities and we'll increase the meat ration. We'll simply call

Ulysses and the rest traitors. We'll blacken them. Look how they harboured that little rat Roscius all these years while he was publishing his vile little notes about liberty, trying to undermine our state – beautiful prose style though, have to admit that. Look how they prospered while our people felt the griping pains of starvation.' The Emperor's eyes twinkled. 'I could write the script myself. But I take your point that we must control the means of communication. Create our own truth. Right, Trismagister?'

'Right.'

'So. I hope I can rely on all of you.' He glanced round and they nodded.

'Of course.'

'Without question.'

'To the bitter end.'

'Good. I knew I could trust you. And the only reason I tell you these things is because I want you to be on your guard. I want you to watch, listen and look. See what dirt you can sniff out. And I want you to be ready, for when the time comes to strike I want you to be as deadly as a knife between the sheets. OK? For the rest. Be merry. Eat, drink and have your way. Let's have a jolly bonfire. But watch me closely for signs. Any more questions? No? Dismiss.'

Gaius Germanicus and Publius Pacificus made their farewells and departed to their own flagships slightly dazed, but Trismagister lingered.

'You have something on your mind?' asked the Emperor.

'A question,' rumbled Trismagister. 'I have followed you closer than most. I was on hand when you became Emperor. I claim a certain privilege.'

'A privilege I happily acknowledge. Fire away with your question, black man.'

'I have always been interested to observe men's limits. What are your limits, Prometheus? After you have hunted Britannia and Hibernia and reduced their land to ash – what then? Will you not come hunting the rest of us?'

The Emperor regarded Trismagister for a long time. Then he came round the table and placed his hands on either side of the man's head and kissed him on the forehead. 'Oh Trismagister, only you would dare to ask me this, and that is why you are the only man I love. You are asking me what I dream, are you not? Sit down with me, for the question you ask is the question I ask myself every day in a hundred different ways. And I have never yet found an answer. What are my limits?'

They sat together on the same couch.

'I'm hungry, Trismagister, and thirsty and cold, but my curiosity is boundless. I'm like a child that is given a beautiful toy and who sits down and pulls it to bits and who cries when its beauty is gone. I think I am mad, Trismagister, I really do ... because other men have their limits – but I don't. I don't know what I'll do when I've burnt Britannia. I may burn the Western Empire. I may burn the rest of the world. I may try to pull the moon down and extinguish it in the sea. I'd like to boil the sea and all the crawling things that live in it. I'd like to pluck the birds from the sky and pull out their feathers. But why? Why do I want to do all this? Because I want proof of meaning. Do the gods give proof of meaning? Very well, let them come down and protect their precious creation. Only when Zeus reaches out with his thunderbolt and strikes me dead for my impiety will I rejoice. But it won't happen, will it? There are no gods, Trismagister. I know that. You know that. There are only convenient fictions. And so I will burn and pillage and rape and bull and swan about until some man arises who is yet more impious than me, and him I will revere – though he will have to kill me first.'

He paused and looked at Trismagister, his face wistful. 'All a bit sad, isn't it, really? But there's no alternative. Everything is a lie and a sham, and I must expose it, otherwise I am a lie and a sham.' He sighed and picked up a grape. 'So what about you, Trismagister, my red warrior, terror of the hearth, eater of babies? Could you dare me, Trismagister? I think you would like to, wouldn't you? But I think you still have scruples and they will trip you up like petticoats round your ankles. And while you are pausing, I will move first, for I walk naked.' He laughed and his face looked boyish and roguish. 'I've just had a wonderful thought, Trismagister. I imagined that you and I were the last two men alive and we were living on a heap of ash which was all that was left of the world after we'd burnt it and shat in it. And we had one knife between us. Do you know what we'd do, Trismagister? We'd fight for that one knife so that we could be the one to stab. And then, "when the deed was done" as they say, the last adventure would be to kill ourself. Hallelujah. The End.' He pressed the grape between finger and thumb. 'Have I answered your question?'

'I think you have. I shall observe your progress. I hope that I am there at the end – perhaps then I shall discover my limits ... or you will.'

The Emperor bowed. 'To the last meeting then.' He clapped his hands and immediately servants entered bearing food and wine. 'But now enough of words. I'm a busy man. I have an Empire to run. So if you'll excuse me . . .'

The cavalcade climbed over the Apennines and dropped down into the valley of the River Padus. There it moved quickly and soon began the winding journey up through the Alps. It was a clear day and the winter snow clung to the mountain slopes as though painted on. The view across the peaks was magnificent. For many of those travelling it was the first time they had been high in the mountains and they were in awe of the rugged gleaming summits and the sheer stony valleys which fell away beneath them.

Emperor Lucius looked out though his window and sighed. 'But what does it mean?' he murmured to himself.

Gradually they dropped down from the Alps. They skirted a bow-shaped lake at the end of which was a small town and there they set down for the night. A party had been organized in the Emperor's honour but he declined to attend. He sent Publius in his stead, with gifts, and the explanation that he was preoccupied with affairs of state. 'Does he never relax?' asked the disappointed burghers.

'Rarely,' replied Publius, speaking the absolute truth.

The next morning, they departed shortly after dawn. The journey was now a straight run across Gallia. They were scheduled to reach the bridge to Britannia early in the afternoon and the road-monitors maintained the vehicles at a steady pace so that the moment of their arrival could be timed to the second.

Thus it was that some hours later, the *Pandora*, with all flags flying, gradually shifted across energy lines until it was guided on to the sky-road leading directly to the bridge. A curtain of ribbons and balloons enclosed the bridge opening and the *Pandora* came to a halt just feet in front of them.

Emperor Prometheus appeared on the bridge of the *Pandora*. His amplified voice boomed out over the waves and the construction town. 'In the name of the Empire, and in memory of all the brave souls who gave their lives to achieve this engineering wonder, I Emperor Lucius Prometheus Petronius declare this bridge open. May it provide safe passage for generations to come.' So saying he gave a signal and the giant ship edged forwards. Its horns blared as the prow began to break the ribbons and release the balloons.

While bands played and people cheered, the giant ship slowly entered the bridge tunnel. The nervous engineers looked on while the kelp-bound stanchions took the weight. Power hummed as the road-monitors urged the vehicle forwards. Moving faster, it vanished inside the tube and its shape could be seen, gliding smoothly, within the translucent laminate. Soon it was far out over the sea and the second vehicle, the flagship of Trismagister, entered the bridge.

There were no problems, and the engineers clapped one another on the back and cheered as the Emperor's ship emerged at the Dubris end. With scarcely a pause, the *Pandora* again crossed energy lines as it was conducted to a temporary landing-site. Here it settled.

Marcus Augustus Ulysses was waiting. He was dressed in full uniform with plumed helmet and polished breastplate, his stomach flat and braced, while his cloak rippled in the breeze.

One by one the other flagships emerged from the tunnel, nosed their way to the docking arena and landed. Finally, when everything was ready, trumpets peeled out a welcome. A door high in the *Pandora* opened and a hydraulic balcony lowered into place. An automatic stairway unfolded to reveal a purple carpet. Then the Emperor himself appeared, splendid in crimson and gold robes, a golden laurel wreath in his dark hair. He acknowledged the cheering. Moments later the stairway began to turn and he was lowered down to the reception platform.

The trumpets fell silent and the echoes of their clamour faded into the distance as he reached the small stage. In silence he stepped down on to Britannia. Then there came solemn drum-beats from one of the old battle-drums that dated from the time of the first conquest. The Emperor raised his arms and Marcus Ulysses and all those with him bowed low.

'Arise, Britannia,' said the Emperor.

'Britannia welcomes you,' breathed a thousand voices in reply. Choirs burst into song while Marcus Ulysses clasped the Emperor's arm in formal greeting.

'Any problems?' whispered the Emperor.

'Everything under control,' whispered old Ulysses in reply.

That evening there was a banquet.

It was the first of several as gradually the Emperor worked his way up the country, visiting places of historical interest, until on the third day, the eve of the Reformed Lupercalia, the cavalcade reached Eburacum.

Privately the Ulysses was interested to see how well the Emperor would stand up to the punishing round of entertainment. But the Emperor seemed unaffected by the carousing and it was always old Ulysses who made his excuses first and tottered to his bed.

It was there, when he was already in bed, that the Emperor came to visit him on the eve of the Reformed Lupercalia.

'Excuse my butting in like this, Lord Ulysses, but we haven't had a moment together since I arrived. I just wanted to say how appreciative I am of all the trouble you have taken and how pleasing I have found the revels.'

'The pleasure has been mine,' said Marcus Ulysses, stifling a yawn.

'So tomorrow's the big day?'

'Everything is ready.'

'Good. Good. I am looking forward to it. This begins a new chapter in the history of Britannia. We must be mindful of destiny.'

Old Ulysses nodded. Vaguely he wondered if the Emperor was practising a speech for the morrow.

'But there was one thing I wanted to ask you. Will Quintus

Herculis Quinctius be present? Has he responded to our invitation?

'He has not responded. I take it he will not be present. Don't worry. He'll be no loss. He'd probably just get into a fight anyway . . .'

'And that beautiful, intelligent lady, the Gallica . . . ? I haven't seen her yet.'

'She sends her apologies. Unavoidable family business.'

'I see. Where?'

'In . . . er . . . in Hibernia, actually.'

There was a long pause.

'Well, Quintus' gain is my loss. He must have something, some charm that I lack.'

'Oh, I'm sure there's nothing like that. It really is fam—'

'Good night, Marcus Augustus. See you in the morning.'

The Emperor rolled into his bed and pulled up the silk sheets.

He was genuinely surprised. He really thought the Gallica trollop had more sense. Surely she must have known that he would find out. What game was she playing? Hm. She'd keep.

He lay back and used the words he had learned while serving in the Western Mountains to induce a deep sleep. Moments later his big body relaxed and the bed supports creaked under him.

But for once the charm did not work quite as intended.

The Emperor dreamed he was swimming naked in darkness through black water. Then in the darkness he heard a growling. It seemed close. It seemed all about him. His feet touched bottom – a soft slimy ooze – and he clambered out of the water calling for light. But there were no lights until suddenly, in front of him, two eyes blinked on and stared down at him. The growling came again, louder than before, and this time he felt hot breath which singed the hair on his chest. He heard the clash of razor-sharp teeth and he turned and began to run, and running . . .

. . . he fell out of bed.

'Damn the stuffed mussels,' he muttered, crawling to his feet. 'I knew they were off.'

17 *The Festival of Fire*

The Emperor was up before dawn. The bad dream had broken the rhythm of his sleep and he felt jaded.

A massage later he felt somewhat better, but the unrest lingered. What was wrong with him? He remembered the stuffed mussels . . . but no one else seemed affected. Old Marcus Ulysses was already up and about and he'd eaten as much as anyone.

Outside the sky was a clear egg-shell blue with a light breeze blowing from the west. Perfect conditions. Everything seemed so right. So why. . . .

Alone at his toilet, the Emperor took stock of himself. If anything had caused him distress it was the dream. The darkness had seemed so complete, so absolute, like the darkness that night in the pyramid when . . . He shuddered.

For a moment Lucius Prometheus contemplated postponing the bonfire for a day, or a week – but that might have been construed as weakness. No. The dream would pass. He'd had nightmares before, quite often when he thought about it, and they always faded away. 'Onward, upward,' he murmured and rang the bell for his dressers.

Festivities were scheduled to begin at midday. During the morning the guests were ferried the half-hour ride from Eburacum to the bonfire site. While they awaited the Emperor, they were entertained by equestrian acts which took place on the vast cleared plain in front of the mountain.

The Emperor dallied, fussing about his toilet, but finally declared himself ready and he and Marcus ascended into the *Pandora* which then lifted and glided smoothly up on to the sky-road.

Marcus Ulysses was aware that the Emperor was moody and did his best to entertain him and jog him into better spirits.

'There,' he said pointing out from the window. 'There's the Battle Dome. We'll be coming back here for the reception after the burning. Then tomorrow we'll have the graduation games. Some excellent talent this year I'm told. Bold fighters. More women graduating this year too. Interesting change in affairs, eh? Different from when you and I were young.'

The Emperor merely grunted.

'Normally, of course, there are plenty of bonfires at this time of the year,' continued the Ulysses, desperately keeping up his end of the conversation, 'this being their Beltane festival and all that. They always used to have a bonfire down here, in one of the glades near the Battle Dome. They used to jump through the fire and dance about. 'Course there won't be a fire this year.'

'Why not?' asked the Emperor.

'No savages,' grinned Ulysses. 'All rounded up. All in Camp Lucius.'

The *Pandora* hummed along just above the level of the forest canopy. The warm weather had brought the trees on quickly and the leaves were a bright green. Neither man spoke for several minutes, lost in their own thoughts. Then the *Pandora* rocked as it shifted from the Eburacum–Derventio road-monitor to the Castra Skusa monitor.

'If you look up there,' said Marcus, 'you can just see the Moors. That's where the Caligula camp was. Nice park now. We can see it if you—'

'Did you ever find the Dragon?'

'Ha. That! Deep in a swamp, as I told you. Not worth the salvage. I've a better machine now. You're welcome to try it. That one was an old beast. Spent more time in the workshops than on the field if truth be known. Good riddance to it.' Marcus was trying to make light of the situation.

'Not quite the story I heard,' said the Emperor slowly.

Moments later the *Pandora* glided round the slope of a hill, dropped down a gradient and passed over a small bridge above a steep ravine. Then it accelerated as it reached a long straight stretch.

'Your lads helped fix all this up,' said Marcus airily. 'They constructed the Bonfire Switchway too. Damn fine builders, if you don't mind my saying. Damned fine.'

The Emperor offered no comment.

At the Bonfire Switchway they slowed as the new road-monitor took charge of them. 'Straight on leads to Castra Skusa,' said Marcus. 'That's where we've parked the chemicals. This is the new bit. There, look ahead. You can see the top of the mountain that that Greek chappie, Geoganthos, made. Remember, you met him last night at the reception. Clever little bugger by all accounts.'

The *Pandora* began to slow down. It cruised in a wide semicircle and settled gently at the turn-about junction just behind the stand reserved for the Emperor.

All the guests in the stands came to their feet and began clapping as the Emperor emerged from the *Pandora*. He was followed closely by Marcus Ulysses who guided him up a shallow flight of steps and into the stand. Here were comfortable couches placed beside heaters. Soldiers with fans wafted the warm air. Technicians, cooks and wine stewards hovered ready.

Standing alone at the edge of the front parapet was a neatly designed control desk above which were a cluster of microphones. Beyond, the view was uninterrupted. They could see a vast cleared area of tilled soil. To left and right, behind protective walls of concrete, stood the twin gleaming cannon pointing into the sky. Beyond them, in the precise centre of their view, rose the artificial mountain and beyond that the wild forest.

'Impressive,' grunted the Emperor.

The Emperor advanced to the cluster of microphones. He wiped his lips and instantly a steward was there to offer him iced wine with cinnamon. But the Emperor refused. He cleared his throat.

Old Ulysses took his place behind him and watched. He was perplexed by the Emperor's behaviour. He had seen him in many moods: violent, sarcastic, lascivious, gentle, caring, but never sombre. He did not know what had gone wrong. He just hoped that all would go according to plan. He had made it known that if there were any cock-ups, he would personally skin the person responsible alive. But he felt confident too. The technology was proven, the pumps worked, the mountain was primed, the wood behind it was dry, the wind was right, the actors were in place. 'Oh what the hell,' he muttered and signalled to one of the stewards to bring him a drink, a big one, no spice.

The Emperor again wiped his lips as though uncertain what

to say. Finally he began, speaking slowly. His voice boomed.

'Honoured guests invited here from many parts of our Empire; honoured civic leaders who have given your time and energy to make this occasion possible; honoured Citizens, carpenters, electricians, painters, gardeners and even you, honoured criminals who will play your part in today's festivities.' At this many of the audience laughed and one of the criminals, overcome with the situation, waved and bowed. 'Honoured Romans. Honoured Soldiers. Honoured members of this Great Empire. Welcome. Welcome.'

The Emperor began to clap his hands in front of him and everyone responded, standing up and clapping. After a minute or so, the Emperor raised his hands and gradually the assembly became quiet. 'Today is an important day in the history of Britannia, may I say in the history of the entire Empire. For today we will take the first steps in appeasing the almighty gods who have shown their displeasure by visiting our State with a pestilence which has ravaged our livestock. We have seen starvation in Gallia, Italia, Hispania, Germania and the eastern provinces. Britannia alone, favoured by the gods, stands clean and wholesome. Who can say why pestilence strikes? No man, nor woman either. We can only pray for wise guidance while we seek to discover and root out those evils that pollute our State. We are not gods, we are men and women, mortals only, limited in our wisdom. Yet, every one of us must pay a price, if we are to overcome evil and restore our lands to grace. So, while this is a sombre occasion, it is also a time for joy. For affirmation. For hope.

'It is to the eternal honour of this province, of Britannia, that she has shown herself prepared to sacrifice a part of her fair land that all may prosper. I am sure that sacrifice will not go unrewarded by the ever-diligent gods.

'I wish now, with great pleasure and before you all, to thank the wise leaders of Britannia who have made this project possible. I mean Gnaeus Marmellius Caesar, honourable leader of an honourable family, and Sextus Valerius Manaviensis Maximus whose wisdom and generosity is legendary.' Lucius Prometheus pointed to the two men named and indicated they should stand up, which they did and received the applause of the audience.

They sat down again and the applause died away. 'I can only regret that Calpurnia Gallica and Quintus Herculis have failed to attend this gathering and therefore cannot be part of our celebration.' A murmur of voices and a craning of heads greeted these words and then silence. 'But last and foremost in this assembly, I wish to thank my deputy in Britannia, Marcus Augustus Ulysses, whose generosity in donating this land for our sheep farm, whose sense of duty at a time of crisis and personal tragedy and whose tolerance of our moods and whims all deserve our heartfelt admiration.' People started to clap but he stifled the applause with a gesture. 'We all wish to be remembered for what we achieve. Well, Africa alone testifies to the Ulysses' genius, but on this occasion, as a singular honour, I invite Marcus Ulysses to begin the entertainment and to complete it by igniting the fire. Marcus Augustus Ulysses!'

Held back until now, the crowds began to cheer and clap as old Ulysses stepped forwards. He was in a bit of a daze. On the one hand he thought the Emperor had gone over the top – everyone knew that Manaviensis Maximus was the least generous of men – and yet he had spoken with conviction and fervour and he certainly knew how to move a crowd. He bowed in gratitude and then settled himself behind the control desk. He had not been briefed on the controls and was glad when he saw Geoganthos and Gaius Daedalus standing by. But the controls were simple. To the left of the board was a small switch marked Entertainment which was blinking on and off. In the centre was a raised pressure pad about the size of his fist. It was coloured red and bore the single word FIRE.

Geoganthos leant forwards and murmured, 'Everything is automatic. Just press the small button.'

This Marcus did and immediately there was a sound of drumming. Everyone settled down in anticipation. Moments later a horse, bearing the handsome actor who was to play Prometheus, galloped into the arena in front of the distant mountain and reared.

Coll had slept in the woods near the artificial mountain. All morning he had heard the coming and going of the different craft, the shouted orders, the panic when one of the actor's costumes had gone missing. Round him were wild pigs which browsed the soil at the foot of the trees.

Crouched down in the dappled shade among the tree-roots, Coll heard the *Pandora* arrive, and then the Emperor's speech.

Gently he fingered the tuned cithara, waiting his moment.

A grey mist moved through the forest. Within it were small vortices of energy which coiled and gleamed and faded. Spokes of light darted down from above, from the blue sky, and were returned with a rush.

Where the mist passed, a sound of ringing filled the air, like millions of tiny cymbals vibrating together.

Such was Miranda.

Meanwhile, far away in Camp Lucius, Gwydion, crouching close to the perimeter fence, stood up and glanced round. The heat was in him and his eyes were the colour of green flint. The small snake tattooed on his forehead seemed to writhe as his forehead creased. Throughout the compound, men and women were in position, looking at him from the corner of their eyes as they whittled sticks or crouched on the ground tossing pebbles. Gwydion breathed deeply, fanning the flames of his battle-ardour, praying to his name-god for strength. He gave a brief nod and in a far corner of the compound two women started fighting, kicking up a hell of a din, hurling abuse.

Moments later two guards arrived at a run. Since the departure of the Horribles, the local guards were hard pressed to contain the many small fights and disturbances which broke out daily among the inmates.

As soon as the guards were occupied, Gwydion rammed a length of pipe under the bottom wire of the fence. With a shout that could be heard for miles, he heaved upwards. The first wire gave way with a loud twang. Then quickly the second and third. Finally the fence lifted and toppled. Already men and women were through the wire and running zig-zag up towards the chalet and the small neat houses where the guards lived. A guard just about to come on duty, fastening his buttons, was felled at the knees and his keys taken.

Gwydion let the pipe drop. Fences all round Camp Lucius

had been breached, and everywhere angry men and women were leaping through the wire, carrying whatever they could find for weapons. Already smoke was rising from the chalet and flames flickered beneath it.

'Away, mam. This way,' called Gwydion to Bella. She hurried out of the hut clutching a cloth bundle. He pointed down the hill to where a small copse bordered the road. 'Wait for me in the trees there. We'll strike across country when night falls.'

'Where are you going?'

'The heat is on me. I'm burning up. I've got to fight. I'll find you in a few hours.'

Angus got the time wrong.

He'd told Perol he wanted to get some more of the black ivy that he used for the electrics and that the best supply was a day's hike away. 'You be careful. Don't go taking risks,' had been her last words. Then he'd set out, taking the mobile radio, hoping to reach the bridge where the Dragon was hidden well before the Emperor came past in his flagship.

His plan was simple but sure. Since he couldn't be certain that the Dragon would still drive, even though he had visited it many times over the winter and kept its systems alive, he'd given up the idea of using it. All he intended to do was fuse the road-monitor when the flagship was passing in the hope of making it crash.

But the *Pandora* cruised over the ravine even as Angus scrambled down through the bracken.

He reached the Dragon, opened up its side door and sat inside cursing. 'Just my bloody luck. Best chance I could ever have had to do some damage and I cock it up.'

Gradually he calmed down. More by instinct than for any purpose, he climbed up into the control seat and switched the systems on. The control lights flickered and came on. Some circuits had died, some responded when he gave them the familiar tap with his knuckle, most blazed merrily. 'Bloody incredible machine. After all the abuse and wear and tear, it's still game.' He checked the fly-wheel. It was turning at just under fifty per cent. 'You'd get us back to Eburacum, you would, if I drove you down the road.'

Thoughts of the Roman road brought Angus back to the present. He tuned the radio and was able to catch part of the Emperor's speech. *Fat old slug*, he thought. He mimicked the Emperor, 'Thanks to Gnaeus Marmellius Caesar for being such an arse-licker. Thanks to Sextus Valerius Manaviensis for being a cheat and a swindler . . .'

But it was the flattery of Marcus Augustus Ulysses which really offended Angus for he had a small pocket of contempt reserved for that man. 'Right. You've asked for it. I'll bring one of you bastards down if it's the last thing I do,' he muttered.

Making sure he had the key that Sean had made tied round his neck, he collected a few tools and then scrambled out of the Dragon and up the side of the ravine. It was easy for him to climb out on to the cross-beams of the bridge and work his way along until he was directly under the nearest road-monitor compartment. Then he climbed up one of the stanchions until he came to a ledge. Now came the only tricky bit. But he'd done it before when he'd powered up the Dragon and was confident. He reached up over the ledge and felt about until he located the welded door handle of the compartment. Holding it firmly, he pulled himself up and over the ledge. Overhead a vehicle cruised past. But Angus was safe. He could not be seen from the road, though if he stood up he could just see down the road in the direction of Castra Skusa.

Angus turned the key in the road-monitor compartment but did not open the door. He knew what was inside. Now all he had to do was wait. As soon as he saw the Emperor's convoy on its way back for the reception at the Battle Dome, he'd open the door, cut one of the connections and short-circuit the bridge section of the road. With luck, there'd be a bit of a pile-up. Then he'd climb down into the ravine and set off home.

Angus settled himself comfortably, his feet dangling down over the edge. He tuned the small radio and found the waveband which was reporting events at the bonfire site. There seemed to be some confusion. Something was happening. He heard an explosion and then moments later he felt the bridge shake and a sound like thunder rolled over him.

When he looked up he saw a light like a radiant sunset over

the hills to the north. Except that it was still early afternoon and the sun would not set for another few hours.

He spun the dial frantically and picked up a signal. It was from the *Pandora* itself. The ship was on the move. It was coming his way. The Emperor was aboard.

What it all meant Angus did not know. But he was ready.

18   The Fire

The horse reared.

The actor playing Prometheus, an excellent horseman, made it walk a few paces on its rear legs, before encouraging it into a trot. High stepping it ran in a circle while Prometheus climbed on to its back. He stood for an entire circuit with his arms spread and then jumped to the ground with a double somersault. The audience applauded. They loved a horse show.

Using extravagant mime, Prometheus pointed at the mountain, and then at himself shivering with cold and then at the mountain again. He limbered up, pumping his pectoral muscles and strutting about, and completed the clowning with an effeminate routine with his back to the audience and his short tunic hitched up. Many people glanced across to see how the Emperor was taking this bit of cheek, but he was smiling.

Finally the actor signalled to the musicians and they obliged with a drum-roll. Prometheus performed a single cartwheel and sprinted directly at the mountain.

He drew a gasp of astonishment when he ran directly up the mountain and posed standing at right angles to the slope. This was a trick they had never seen before and it brought a round of applause which the actor acknowledged. Then he began to climb properly, moving from handhold to handhold. Once he pretended to slip, just managing to save himself.

Up above, the gods were having a high old time, reeling about, drinking and pretending to copulate with one another. They had been given clear directions what to do by Geoganthos, but he had not told them their fate, hinting rather that if they performed well they might receive an Imperial pardon. They performed with gusto, therefore.

Prometheus climbed over the balcony rail and arrived in Olympus. There he was immediately seduced by a Venus with vast breasts while Vulcan's back was turned pumping a bellows.

He was wined and dined by Jupiter and Bacchus and at the climax of the party he stole a burning torch of fire and launched himself off the mountain top.

He rode down to earth on an invisible wire waving the blazing fennel wand. This was a cue for applause, led by the Emperor who seemed to have completely recovered his good spirits.

No sooner had Prometheus landed than hundreds of nymphs and dryads and satyrs came running round from behind the mountain. They carried torches which they ignited from Prometheus' fennel wand and then joined Prometheus in a dance of celebration. They carried the fire towards the stand where the Emperor and Marcus Ulysses were seated.

'Get ready,' said the Emperor nudging the old Ulysses. 'It'll be your big moment soon.'

The actors gathered at the foot of the Imperial stand and sang a last song in praise of the Emperor, bringer of light and bringer of fire. At its conclusion, the Emperor signalled to two of his attendants who carried a heavy chest to the edge of the balcony. They opened it and began throwing gold coins down to the dryads and nymphs and fauns who scrambled about collecting them.

The actor who had played Prometheus was invited up to the Imperial stand to meet the Emperor in person and receive a special gold crown. It had just been placed on his head and everyone was on their feet cheering, when there came a sound from the clearing in front of the mountain.

It was a strange sound, a growling sound, partly like a drum, partly like strings being plucked, ominous amid the revelry, and everyone who heard it stopped and looked.

Emerging from behind the mountain came a strange procession. In front rode a small green-cloaked figure on an old donkey. He was seen to be strumming an instrument, but the sound it produced, the sound that had gained everyone's attention, was far louder than the size of the instrument or the distance would seem to allow. He was accompanied by a pack of pigs, who ran like hounds, but whose every movement suggested an energy far greater than that of any dog. They reached a place in front of the mountain and stopped.

Marcus Ulysses looked across at Geoganthos enquiringly, and

that man bowed and spread his hands expressively as if to say, 'Nothing to do with me. I didn't arrange this.'

'Shall I get the guard to clear them out of the way? We don't want any distraction,' said old Ulysses to the Emperor. But the Emperor stilled him with a hand on his arm. He had a faraway look – the sound that had come from the instrument was the sound he had heard in his dream. 'No, let us listen,' he said. 'We may learn something. We are in no hurry.'

The crowds in the terraces, unaware that anything untoward was happening, settled back, helped themselves to more drinks, assuming that this was some extra piece of entertainment not announced on the programme. It was certainly different.

The figure in the green cloak, a man by his movements, climbed down from the donkey and slapped it on its rump. It ambled away unprotesting and began to nose the ground looking for grass. Then the man raised the dark old cithara and his fingers danced over the strings producing a rich melody which shifted through pitches. The melody set many people's teeth on edge, some covered their ears, but they found that the sound reached them just the same. The pigs lifted their heads and grunted as though singing.

Old Ulysses watched with a look of disbelief. If this was some new entertainment that had been slipped in without his knowledge he'd have whoever was responsible strung up. 'Look, why don't we . . .' he began, but then lost his train of thought as the music intensified. He stared at the open space where the figure played. Suddenly everything seemed clearer and yet more unreal.

The man stopped playing. He stood holding the cithara at his side. The pigs became quiet. 'I come with a warning,' he said, and his voice was louder than any amplifier could have made it. It rolled round the silent stands where the people sat, glasses raised but unsipped. 'A warning of great danger that affects you, me, these creatures' – he indicated the pigs – 'everything you see about you, the whole family.' He paused and his head moved under his hood. He seemed to be looking round the assembly. 'I have been given leave to appeal to you – no, not by the Emperor whose power is nothing except what you give him, but by other powers that have begun to stir. Mine is the last voice you will hear, and my last words are words of hope, if you can but hear. Abandon this burning. It is madness. It is an insult to all life. I beg you. Now. Pull back the soldiers. Turn the cannon away. Hold still, breathe, doubt. Now while there is still time. Watch.'

He raised the cithara and began to stroke the strings.

One of the trees at the edge of the clearing moved. Its branches stretched. The leaves still just emerging suddenly sprouted and opened. They showed a vivid green which gradually darkened. Many of the people watching looked away for they heard, or thought they heard, the crying of the tree.

The music intensified. The pigs began to scamper about with a kind of glee. Squirrels came bounding from the forest. Foxes and wolves and bears and other animals came running from the woods and stood in the plain. Snakes appeared in the furrows. The ground began to shift and heave as the worms and ants and spiders and grubs came working to the surface, driven by a music that they could not resist.

The music intensified more. The small green figure was now pounding the cithara, crouched over it, beating it like a woman beating washing, driving the notes into the air with all the power at his command. Lines of force appeared in the air as Nature was coerced into new patterns of being. Rising from the ground came leaves, wriggling up. Stalks grew. Flowers opened with a sound that could be heard and pollen puffed in the air.

Where there had been bare tilled earth was now a riot of colour and scent. The flowers grew up round the musician, almost to his waist. Soldiers on duty at the perimeter, wearing traditional uniform, felt the movement of the grass under their sandals. They felt the flowers grip their legs and grow between their toes and over their feet.

And still the music intensified until it seemed to fill every particle of space. Nowhere was there silence, neither in breathing in nor in breathing out. The music was everywhere. It consumed everything and entered everything, every cell and lattice.

The flowers lived through their spring.

They were full in the summer and began to droop as autumn came.

Then winter brought silence.

The music stopped. And if anything the silence was worse, as everyday reality rushed back to fill the void. Many people had fainted. Many people had scratched their faces and arms in an ecstasy that had squeezed them and battered them and left them gasping.

At the height of the music many had visions, moments from childhood which combined cruelty with discovery.

Marcus Ulysses was one. As a boy he had once pulled the legs off a daddy-longlegs and been impressed by the way the creature continued to try to run and fly. He had never forgotten that.

Marmellius too remembered a time when, after exercising long and hard, he threw himself down in the grass by a stream and was amazed when a fat old trout nosed its way to the surface and took a fly only inches from his nose. He thought the trout had spoken to him. He knew that in a way, it had. But he never told anyone.

Manaviensis, sitting beside him, remembered how he had once kept flowers pressed in a book and had been beaten by his tutor and ridiculed by his father when it was found out.

Publius Pacificus recalled how frightened and fascinated he had been when one night a snake had entered his tent. It had reared before him, no more than two feet from his face, and he had seen its black tongue lick out. The snake had studied him before lowering and easing its way over the floor and out. He'd never forgotten.

Trismagister remembered eating a rose.

Gaius Daedalus had once sat for hours studying the inside of a sea shell, wondering about mathematical progressions . . .

And so it went on. Only the Emperor looked around unmoved. He wondered what all the fuss was about. Sure the music was loud, and yes, it was a clever trick to get the flowers to come up on cue and he would reward whoever had devised it – it must have taken hours wiring up all those flowers and training the animals – but finally what was it all about? He was hearing a rather poor singer with a terrible sense of rhythm. And what was all this talk about calling everything off?

But then the Emperor saw something else. Rising from the

forest behind the tree he saw tendrils of mist which began to flow together to make a shape which might have been a woman or might have been a pair of staring eyes or the blunt shape of a beast, a reptile. He could not be certain, but he shuddered with disgust. Something was brewing, something deeply strange. Something wholly unforeseen. He didn't know what it was – another trick perhaps?

If the mist had taken the shape of an angry Jupiter reaching down to transfix him with a thunderbolt, he would have understood and would have rejoiced, for that would have been the answer to his prayers. He would have provoked whatever powers there were to notice him and reveal themselves. But this thing that was emerging had none of the grandeur of mythology to his eyes, none of the attributes of the great legendary figures, except stark and unforgiving power. And so he did not understand.

The cithara was broken. It was the last frenzied strokes that had done it. Coll had given his all. For a few moments he had managed to coerce Nature to perform in a way unnatural. The price of course would be death, for he had trespassed too far outside the normal realms and had used up all the energy he had borrowed from Dark Eagle, from the spirit of the stream, from Cormac and from all the animals and insects and plants and trees that had lent him their life. They lay dead about him. All the energy was gone. He was a husk, spent. In his last few moments he threw back his hood.

His hair was trimmed. The beard was gone. He was recognizable to those who knew him. He wiped the white saliva from his mouth, aware of his dark companion who moved closer.

Old Ulysses came to his feet, uncertainly. He seemed to have aged ten years and tottered forwards and held the balcony rail. His jaw worked but for several moments no sound emerged. Others in the stands who remembered Viti stared and pointed. They murmured his name in wonder.

But it was old Ulysses who finally found his voice. 'Viti,' he called, and opened his arms wide.

But at that moment, the Emperor leaned across behind him, and brought his fist down on the switch marked FIRE.

*

Everything was automatic.

The signal flashed from the Emperor's platform to the tall pressure towers a mile and a half behind the stands where the pumps began to work. It flashed to the teams of soldiers waiting beside the cannon in the concrete bunkers. Some of the men sprang into action. Others remained dazed by what they had seen in the clearing. A few threw down their helmets and ran out of the concrete bunkers and made for the trees. They were not chased for many of the guards were themselves in a state of shock.

For a moment there it had seemed as though everything was coming to an end. That they'd be on their way home soon. That the whole adventure had been a strange and sorry dream. But no. The warning bell clanged. The pressure mounted. The sumps were full. The firing was on. It would occur in a few minutes.

On the Emperor's platform Gaius Daedalus came out of his dream of spiralling shells with a jolt. He came to his senses and saw what was happening. His face was white and he looked sick. It had finally dawned on him what was about to be released. He turned to Marcus Ulysses. 'There's still time to stop it, sir,' he said.

'Stop it. Stop what?' said the old man vaguely.

'The burning, sir.'

'Burning?' Old Ulysses turned round and saw where the Emperor's hand still rested on the FIRE control. He stared without comprehension. Then his brow furrowed. 'That's my son out there,' he said. 'That's my—'

The last word was lost as with a violent roar twin columns of liquid were fired into the air. Even those who knew what to expect were astonished at the power as the cannon were forced back into their groundings. Those of the guests who had expected something like a firework display screamed as the sky darkened and the sun was masked by the particles of dark liquid.

The two streams met with a mighty detonation which shook the ground and the sky above became incandescent. Fire blossomed like a giant rose. It seemed to turn in the air, moving in slow motion. But it did not fall.

A second pulsed jet was hurled into the air and its detonation lifted the first fireball higher and made it spread.

The Emperor stared. Beyond the mountain the mist was rising quickly, it was streaked with orange and purple, some great horror was gathering there, reaching out with long hands, joining the fire, shaping it – was he the only one who could see it? He sprang to his feet and pushed past Geoganthos who stood open-mouthed. He barged down the shallow steps and ran as fast as he could towards the *Pandora*.

The pilot and crew aboard the flagship had been watching the proceedings through the tinted glass windows. They saw him coming. They were trained for emergency – for a quick get-away in case of an assassination attempt – and within seconds, the mobile stairway was lifting the Emperor up towards the small door. Already the ship was starting to move.

Another roar and twin salvos streaked up into the sky, driving the flames higher and wider. The lower chemicals were the last to burn, protecting the ground from a sudden scorching. But the balance would not hold for long. As the Emperor's ship accelerated up on to the sky-road, another pulse of liquid was driven straight into the heart of the fireball. The fire now hung suspended above the mountain, above the stands filled with people, above the forest. It curled and roared in the air. Then the wind began to blow.

Daedalus banged down on the control switch, hammering it with his fist. Two bangs were all that was needed to call the test off – but he was far too late. In any case, the men at the pumps had worked overtime. They did not want to be the ones at fault if the fire didn't jet high enough, and so the final surge they sent down the pipes was the greatest of all, completely emptying the pressure towers.

That final salvo ignited before it reached the blanket of fire. It rippled and spread across the entire sky, enclosing the hills. Beneath it everything was black or white. Fire fell as rain. But before the rain came a heat-wave so intense that everything it touched was fused.

There was little pain. The heat-wave passed leaving statues of ash in its wake. Little gods with goblets in their hands, soldiers with their hands over their eyes, women pointing, an old man, stiff and still, the ash of his hands fused to the ash of the balcony rail.

Coll looked up in his last few moments. To him, the ripple of the fire in the sky was like the rippling of water in a stream. It was all like a dream finally. Everything. Everything that had happened. A dream that belonged to someone else; from another time; and far away: a song really ... He hoped that Cormac was pleased.

But no sooner had this thought formed than his dark companion, standing close, reached out and touched him.

The shock-wave of heat spread out. As it spread it cooled to simple fire. And even when it was no longer fire it travelled on as a hot wind.

The heat reached Castra Skusa and there an explosion occurred which left the ground looking like the crater of Mount Etna.

Not far away an ancient oak tree that had survived many a lightning strike suddenly blazed and the fire reached down through the roots and into the caverns beneath.

The heat flowed over the fire-break and the houses of Derventio began to burn. The grass and heather at the foot of the Moors scorched and smouldered.

At the margins the green growth of spring conquered the fire. Smoke billowed and vegetation blackened but the fire stopped.

At its centre, at the place where it started, the mist curled to a ball, and vanished.

Moments later the screaming began.

Angus wasted no time. He didn't want to miss this opportunity. He pulled the door of the road-monitor open and the warning light flashed on. *Well just too bad!* he thought. *They'll have more than a fucking fuse to think about when I've finished.*

He glanced down the road and was appalled to see a black cloud of smoke rising over the horizon. Its underbelly was a deep flickering red. 'What the hell have they been doing over there? I thought they were just going to burn a few trees, not set fire to the whole bloody forest.' He heard a roaring in the air, a deep-throated sound which told of flames leaping twenty or thirty yards high and trees exploding into fire. Then above that noise he heard the whine of the road-monitor as it took the strain. Some vehicle was coming, and fast.

Angus looked down the road and saw the *Pandora* come round the distant bend. It began to accelerate down the straight towards him. 'Tally ho, you bastard,' shouted Angus and he took the cable in his pliers and squeezed. The road-monitor was already building up potential ready to take the mass of the speeding *Pandora*. The cable severed. There was a blue flash and Angus' arm jolted back, numbed at the funny-bone. 'Ya! Sod off,' shouted Angus.

Using one arm only he slithered off the ledge and felt with his feet for the stanchion below. He gripped it with his legs and began to work his way down. Above him sparks crackled as the severed cable jumped about.

Angus had just reached the cross-piece when he felt the bridge begin to shake. The ship had reached it and the road-monitor having lost most of its power was using remote battery back-up to lower the flagship to the road. But there had been a lot of traffic lately and the batteries were not fully charged.

Angus scampered along the shaking cross-piece and reached the wall of the ravine just as the giant ship began to crash. He threw himself down among the rocks and heard the supports of the bridge buckle and tear. But they did not break. Nor did the concrete platform above begin to fall apart. It cracked but its reinforced slabs held together and took the weight of the ship. With his face pressed into the rock of the ravine wall, Angus praised the solidity of Roman technology. What it lacked in flair it more than compensated for in rugged strength.

The *Pandora* skidded down the concrete surface of the road with a shrieking of metal. It snapped the road-monitor lights in the centre of the road and sent them cartwheeling down into the ravine. Showers of sparks cascaded over Angus as the *Pandora* slid to a halt above him. Its entire undercarriage was torn out revealing its drive transformers and racks of batteries. Water and oil and acid slopped from the ship and poured over the edge of the road and down into the ravine.

For a few moments Angus' wolf-skin was on fire. He slapped at the flames wildly and beat them out. But Angus was on fire in more ways than one. At this moment he and Gwydion could have been twins. All Angus could think about was destruction. He leaped down the sides of the ravine careless of his life and limbs and reached the Dragon. He climbed inside, slammed the door, and rammed home its bolts. He settled himself at the controls, strapping the harness tight.

'One last fight, old Dragon, then you can have your rest. Come on. Don't let me down.' The systems were already warm with the drive cylinders up to pressure. Angus engaged the main tractor drive. He heard the relays hammer home and then the Dragon lurched as the tractor blades found purchase on the rock. It heaved forward, tearing the bracken from the ravine wall and sloughing off the tree branches, forest litter and the road-monitor lighting pole that had fallen across it. With a grinding of metal on stone, the Dragon churned out from under the bridge.

Once clear of the foundations Angus turned the Dragon until it was facing up against the ravine wall. He remembered the climb out of the Caverna – when was it, a century ago? – well this was similar. He extended the head up the slope like a lizard and set the giant rear drive claws deep into the rock. He fed just enough power to test the strength of the footing. Nothing slipped. The Dragon rocked with suppressed power. Angus slammed it into maximum drive, keeping the centre of gravity low, driving with one leg then the other, like a frog climbing a bank.

The wall of the ravine was steeper than the Caverna but not as deep. Rocks jutted out from the side and dented the plating, but none stopped the Dragon. It surged up.

Like something reborn after a long sleep, the Dragon emerged from the ravine. It limbered its way up into the road and advanced on the crumpled *Pandora*.

The sky above was black with smoke and a rim of fire marked the distant hills.

The luck which had accompanied Lucius Prometheus Petronius all his life did not desert him now. As the *Pandora* lost power and began to sink down on to the road, he threw himself amid the cushions and quilts in his stateroom. He heard a mighty banging as the ship hit the the light poles. Then it lurched throwing him over against a wall, tangled with quilts and pillows. One of the couches flipped completely over and pinned him against the wall. It was this that saved him for moments later part of the ceiling caved in when the ship ploughed into the bridge. The tearing and grinding of the *Pandora* skidding along the bridge deafened him and briefly he passed out.

When he came to, the ship was still and the only sound was the noise of water.

He crawled out from under the couch, calling for his attendants but nothing moved and no one came. The Emperor crawled through the debris, himself somewhat like one of the reptiles he so despised and feared, and reached one of the windows. The security catches still worked and he managed to open the window and leant for a moment, breathing deeply.

He was looking down the bridge when he saw movement.

Rising up against the rail of the bridge came the scaly head of a dragon. He stared in horror as the beast reared and climbed jerkily on to the bridge and began to advance.

Dear gods, what had he unleashed? Was the whole world turning to reptiles? Where had it come from? Was Britannia the land of the dragons? Ulysses had said it was dead, and now here it was, walking, coming for him, sniffing him out.

The Emperor backed away from the window. He heard a loud clanging as the Dragon reached the *Pandora* and began to tear at it. He felt the ship lurch and realized what the Dragon was trying to do. It was going to tip the whole ship off the bridge. He had to get out.

The Emperor scrambled down through the ship until he came to the place where the undercarriage had been torn away. The ship was lurching as the Dragon heaved at it, but he could see the road and a hole in the ship's side big enough to climb through. He could also see one of the scaly iron feet of the Dragon.

With luck ... The Emperor climbed down on to the road, tearing his clothes and opening a wound on his arm as he squeezed through the hole but otherwise unscathed. He edged past the giant scaly leg which was lifting and advancing as the Dragon pushed the *Pandora* to the edge.

But the leg stopped in mid-stride. The Emperor froze and slowly turned and looked up. Staring down at him, only a few feet away, was the head of the beast.

Angus couldn't believe his eyes. He'd assumed that no one had survived the crash. But suddenly he saw movement, and when he focused down he found himself staring at the chubby bedraggled form of the Emperor. He looked pathetic. His robes of state were bloodstained and torn. He had lost part of his toga and his bare back was revealed. Without the clothes of office he was just a man, as vulnerable as any other.

Angus began to reverse the Dragon. This gave the Emperor his chance. He ran down the bridge and when he came to its end, he hopped off the road and began to clamber round the hillside.

It took precious minutes for Angus to disengage the Dragon from the *Pandora* and slew it round. But then he went after the Emperor.

Angus had to be careful. If the Emperor had stayed on the road he would have caught him easily. But the sloping hillside was different. If the Dragon was vulnerable it was here, for if the centre of gravity moved too high it could roll and once rolling nothing could stop it. So Angus drove the beast with caution, easing it down the rocks and through the scrub. Occasionally he lost sight of the Emperor only to catch him again as he scrambled over a boulder.

The Emperor was making for the woods at the bottom of the valley. But before he reached them there was an open patch of scrub and here the Dragon could move quickly. Angus took a chance. He withdrew the tractor mechanism which was safe but slow and used the big drive feet. The Dragon began to lope, heaving over the ground. It would soon overtake the Emperor who was limping and obviously coming to the end of his endurance.

It was almost on him when he came to the first of the trees and dodged behind it.

Now began a game of cat and mouse. Angus could drive the Dragon between the trees and could tear down many of them, but there were oak and beech too, and these he could not uproot.

Once he almost had the Emperor when he tripped and fell and Angus opened the Dragon's jaws and snapped at him. But the Emperor rolled away at the last moment and the Dragon's jaws closed on nothing more substantial than rotting leaves.

Angus was aware that he was losing power rapidly. He was down to twenty per cent. He needed to do something bold. From his elevated position in the Dragon he could see a clearing ahead. The Emperor was lumbering towards it all unaware.

This was Angus' chance. When he came to the edge of the clearing he stopped the Dragon and gathered its rear drive feet together. The Emperor ahead was reeling and staggering as he crossed the clearing. He was just reaching the trees at the far end when the Dragon pounced. Angus gave it everything and the giant beast leaped, head and neck extended, front pincer claws advanced.

The Emperor was wild with panic. His vision was blurred. His breathing hurt. His legs would hardly support him. With a last effort he forced himself to plunge between two oak trees. And he tripped and rolled. His last act was to squirm round.

He saw the Dragon leap, its razor jaws wide. It was coming right at him. Like his dream in the pyramid. And surely then, if dreams could predict, then the universe must have some meaning . . .

The jaws came to a sudden juddering halt just inches from his belly. They snapped with a clashing of knives. The Emperor smelled its oily breath. He felt the wind of the jaws, but they did not touch him. He didn't take his eyes off them, expecting them to open again any moment. Slowly he scrambled backwards. But the jaws did not open. With a jerk the fierce-eyed head lowered until it rested, chin down, on the ground. The Dragon was stuck, wedged firmly by its own weight and momentum between the two oak trees. It began to shake.

The Emperor heard shouting from inside the Dragon as cautiously he staggered to his feet. He began to wander away. He was in a state of shock. He could smell smoke in the air, but he didn't think about it. If he thought of anything it was that all his questions had been answered.

Angus was trapped. He kicked at the lugs which held the side door closed and they would not budge. The sides were buckled. Where the Dragon was wedged between two trees the scales had been ripped off, but he could not escape there because of the tree-trunks. He was aware of the shaking which was getting worse. He guessed at the trouble. It was the worst thing possible for a creature such as the Dragon. The impact had knocked the fly-wheel a fraction off-balance. It would now be grating on its bearings. Heat was building up. It could only get progressively worse, and quickly. A fly-wheel even at twenty per cent of its capacity is still a fearful thing unleashed. He had to get out.

He climbed up to the control cabin and tried to undo the hatch locks. These had not been used for some time and were rusty. The shaking grew worse. Angus had never seen a fly-wheel break loose from its housing but he'd heard the stories. It would destroy everything it touched. He didn't know how long he had. Not long – a few minutes at most. Already there was a smell of burning oil. Angus coughed and began looking round for something to hit the lugs with. Nothing. He put his hand to his throat, breathing was already getting difficult. The key. Sean's key. It wasn't very big but if he gripped it in his fist . . .

Angus held the key and banged its end against the stiff lugs.

Two came easily but then the shaking suddenly got worse. He was sweating and having trouble standing still to aim. One good blow and the third lug opened. One to go. Angus heard a chafing sound below him and a sudden rattling and banging as a linkage broke and began flailing about. Smoke filled the small cabin. One final blow and the last lug shifted. He heaved up and the door opened a fraction on its rusty hinges. One more heave and it tore open.

Angus pulled himself through the hatch. Smoke billowed with him and the entire beast began to rock and jerk back and forth. There was a branch just below him and Angus jumped. He was winded but he was able to swing down and roll away. He scampered on all fours until he came to a fallen trunk and threw himself down behind it.

The Dragon was now shaking wildly, like a creature having a fit. Smoke belched from the escape hatch and then with a whoosh came the flame. One of the front scissor legs detached and was flung away. The plates of armour began to tear loose and were sent wheeling. The noise was appalling, like a thousand hammers beating on anvils. The neck section flopped about like a snake and the head came off and tumbled into the bushes. Angus could see the fly-wheel chamber through the broken sides. It was red hot, and then it tore open, peeling back. The wheel bounded free. It bounced round the inside of the Dragon, tearing it to bits. Fragments of hot metal showered from it – bolts, chain linkages, heavy screws, washers, ball bearings, magnets from the relays. Finally the wheel tore completely through the side of the Dragon. It bounded to the ground, rolled in a tight circle crushing a tree, and spent its last energy churning up the soil. Finally it lay still in a bed of smouldering leaves.

The Dragon was dead, its parts scattered, its oil and rubber burning and bubbling.

Angus sat on the log staring at it, while overhead the sky darkened.

It was there that Garlyck found him some ten minutes later.

'Angus. Away. You're needed at the caves. Perol and the children . . .'

'The Emperor . . .' began Angus gesturing weakly.

'Stuff the Emperor. Can't you see what's happening. Can't you hear it?'

Angus looked at him vacantly. And then he frowned. The madness left him. Faintly, as though coming from a great distance he could hear a sound.

It seemed like a great screaming.

Miranda could be known by many names.

The Greeks might have called her Moira. Others might call her Kali. And some would see her as no more or less than the simple working out of a natural law: as ye sow, so . . .

She was the keeper of the thread – the creator, the preserver and the destroyer. These were the aspects by which she was known to humankind.

But Miranda was more. Her dimension of existence was the deepest of all, and touched all realms. Miranda could move freely. If she settled in part of the world for a while, the trees and grass absorbed something of her spirit, and those places became sacred.

On balance she was more the protector than the destroyer, but if she showed her destructive face then no mountain or valley was safe.

She was self-aware, even as she drifted like mist through the forest, with a knowledge that came from a time before time. Miranda conversed with stars. She had come into being at that same white moment when the universe blossomed from nothing. She was, in the deepest way possible, part of the natural order of things: an intangible essence, drifting in space, waiting to serve the coming of life, and which could, for a time, be content as a spirit of water.

She had a sense of timing too. She knew she must wait for Coll to finish singing, to see the outcome of his song. That was the way of things. There was always a bargain struck, a moment of grace given.

As Miranda drifted through the trees she remembered everything of her brief time as a human.

Beautiful Viti, whose beauty lay in his troubled self-doubting anguished spirit. Viti whom the animals loved instinctively, and who, like her, had had to claw his way through pain and strangeness to discover himself. She heard him now, as Coll, with a spirit as keen as a blade, the greatest of the Romans did they but know it, speaking his fierce message and showing his last greatest song. Would they see? Would they listen? Time would tell and time was slipping away as Miranda coiled round the trees and rose through the branches, moving steadily towards the place of burning.

Magnificent angry Angus, there was a man! Angus who would never let an injustice pass, and who struggled with ideas always a hair's breadth beyond his ability to grasp. How she had loved him, pure and simple: for his passion, for his wrong-headedness, for his generosity. He was out there now, she knew, somewhere, struggling to discover a code of living, finding a pattern of decency and fairness, learning to love and be loved. With Angus the world would be safe, for Angus could learn. She remembered their first love-making on a sunny bank protected by trees. Those days! Never was sex sweeter or her coming more fulsome and abandoned. Not even with Gwydion. She had been happier then than in the whole of her life as a human.

And Gwydion, the golden man, the restless warrior, who would fight and die and be reborn to fight again until fighting ended . . . and that might be never. Gwydion who could never settle for fear that the sky might fall.

Eve Duff who sensed the strangeness in her daughter but kept that knowledge to herself. And Bella . . . and . . . so many! Time was running out.

Miranda moved quickly. She rose above the trees as a coil of mist. There she saw Coll surrounded by flowers pouring out his spirit, tearing melodies from the old cithara which stopped Nature in its tracks, offering love that was fierce and blind and without compromise . . . like justice.

Like Coll, Miranda had many languages for experience. Though she was aware of the inflammable mountain and the stacked dried timber and the chemicals waiting in the sumps of the cannon, she did not see the burning as really the matter at issue here. Fires come, fires go. Life lives on. No, it was the mind which lay behind the fire that was the enemy – and she did not mean poor Emperor Lucius Prometheus Petronius either, who even at this moment was looking at her and seeing his fears etched in the sky – it was what he represented that counted, that was the enemy. Deadly power that enslaves. Whenever two or three are gathered together, there will be a struggle for supremacy. The deadly legacy that comes where there is power but no love.

The song ended. Miranda let the mind of the assembly open to her. She saw every dreamer and every dream, thousands of them. All were memories of connection, of meeting, of learning. The daddy-longlegs struggling on the table, the staring snake, the pressed flower – so many many more. The song had been heard – and there was hope.

Perhaps Coll had turned the tide at the eleventh hour. It had never happened before but that did not mean ... Miranda's interest became keen. She span in the air above the doomed forest and energy sparkled as light was born and vanished within her. Perhaps they'd pull down the paper mountain, pack up the stands, drink the wine, eat the food and then go home. Perhaps there would be no confrontation and she could slip back to her own time and place ...

She contemplated sad, mad, old Ulysses, crying inside his head for love of his son, though no tears showed on his face. Standing with his arms wide open. There if ever was a man who had learned things the hard way. But now something had opened in him. There was hope ... Perhaps.

Moments later Miranda saw the cannon fire their twin jets. She saw the explosion in the sky and the hope died within her. Her aspect began to change. The preserver became the destroyer. Her face was terrible to behold, and that was the face that the Emperor saw.

She watched the fire spread in the sky. She let herself flow beneath the fire and absorbed some of its energy. Beneath her people were running. Some ran to the forest. Some ran to the hills. Some stood where they were, staring upwards at the rippling ceiling of fire.

Time ticked on. Miranda, having now absorbed enough energy, withdrew into herself. Immediately the blazing sky fell downwards. She saw people cremated to statues, the earth

232

turned black and then glowed a cherry red, trees vanished, in an instant turned to vapour.

Miranda began to contract, compressing her essence. She became smaller than a ladybird, smaller than the head of a pin, smaller than a molecule of DNA, smaller than an atom, an electron. Finally she came to the place where all laws break down, where time ceases to have any meaning, the place of final unity where dimensions meet and slide over one another and form new realities. She reached the place where symbolic forms take shape, the start of all creation, the place of mind. There she fashioned a black egg in the palm of her hand. It absorbed all light and gave nothing back. This would be the symbol. She carried the egg back to the world and chose a place in the very heart of the fire. There she breathed lightly on the egg and the egg began to grow.

As it grew it began to devour. First it ate the space about it, then the stones, the glowing embers, the seeds, the air and all living things. And as they were consumed, all things began to scream.

Trees can scream. Even stones can scream. For there are many types of screaming.

This was not so much a scream of pain, as a scream of warning. It told of the advance of something that would destroy everything in its path, something that was mindless and hence susceptible to no appeal of reason. It would eat grass, devour people, consume buildings, gobble down a forest, sup streams, bite ... Even the dogs of war know some humanity, but this had none. The new and voracious dimension knew no limits. And it never spat anything out.

The black egg grew quickly and as it grew the screaming intensified.

Within minutes of Miranda's placing it amid the glowing ash it was the size of a rugby ball and shortly thereafter a boulder. Miranda considered it, rather as an artist might consider a statue. She smoothed away an anomaly which deformed the surface, and then settled herself, like a halo of cloud above it, to watch over it and wait. She would rise with it and expand as it grew.

The surface of the blackness looked smooth, but nothing was ever reflected from it. It looked as though solid, but it crept outwards, absorbing everything.

Occasionally lights seemed to move within it, whirling round, and striations appeared on its surface like thin red hairs. But these were whipped away instantly.

The blackness grew larger. It was now the size of a house. It grew like a black bubble in the heart of the fire and soon it was higher than the flames. It expanded more quickly now, engulfing the twisted structure which was all that remained of the mountain and the puddles of molten metal which was all that remained of the cannon. It reached the statues of Coll and the donkey Aristotle and they vanished inside. Minutes later, the ash from which old man Ulysses was now formed collapsed into a heap before the advancing black wall.

The surface of the blackness teemed, like water boiling behind black glass. But there was no heat, just a ravenous energy which advanced at about the speed of a man walking, and a wall of screaming which ran before.

While Angus and Garlyck ran, they never lost the sound of the screaming.

If they dropped down into a valley the sound became muted among the trees, only to be waiting, louder than ever, when they emerged at the top of a hill. The smoke of the burning hung like thunderclouds over them.

Angus was not in good shape but he would not stop. The screaming was like no sound he had ever heard – worse than the din of the workshops where he learned his trade or the frenzied timpani of the Dragon as it tore itself to pieces – and it seemed to get inside his head and nowhere could he escape from it. It whipped him on.

Garlyck too was white and drained. He had heard this screaming before, or something like it, at the Caligula.

At last they came to the path which led to the twin oak trees and the narrow cleft between the cliffs. They were home, at Drummer's caves. The sky was dark with smoke.

Perol was waiting. With her were the small band of Dragon Warriors, standing silent like refugees abandoned at the road-side, their few pathetic belongings piled in bundles.

Perol had known what the screaming meant as soon as she heard it: it was everything she had fought against all her life. Immediately she sent Garlyck to track down Angus. She took charge of the small camp and ordered the people to pack and be ready to depart. Everyone had a job to do, even those whose wits had been weakened in the Caligula, even the little children. Together she and Gargamelle made hammocks of cloth which they could lace up in which to carry the babies. Then they waited, while the smoke rose in the sky and the screaming got louder.

Angus threw himself down outside the cave gasping.

'I was giving you ten minutes more, then we were leaving,' said Perol. 'I was beginning to think I'd lost you.'

Angus managed to grin. 'No such luck, sweetheart. I'm here for the duration.'

'Everyone's packed.'

'Good. Where were you going to go?'

'I hadn't got that far,' said Perol. 'Away from that.' She pointed at the smoke drifting over the hills. 'And the noise. I just knew we had to go. That's all.'

The people gathered round silently.

'Well I've had an idea,' said Angus, standing up. He was recovering and even as he spoke he slung one of the small hammocks round his neck. 'It's a place I visited once, on the way to Stand Alone Stan. It's a long way from here and it'll take some finding. But we'll be safe there.' He looked round. 'What worries me is the little ones. The going is hard. They'll have to keep up.'

'They'll manage,' said Garlyck. 'You lead at the front. I'll be at the back. The sooner we—'

He never finished for at that moment, through the sound of the screaming, they heard another sound, one they had never expected to hear again. It was a drumming.

They looked from one to another, an unbelievable hope rising in them.

Seconds later the figure of Drummer came charging down between the twin oaks at the end of the valley. Even at this distance they could see that he was thinner and seemed to have lost some of his hair. He ran towards them with his long loping stride and then stopped and waited.

Everyone waved and called but Drummer didn't move. 'What the hell's he doing?' asked Angus.

'He's waiting to see if he's welcome,' said Garlyck.

''Course he's welcome,' said Perol and so saying she put her fingers to her lips and whistled. The sound woke up one of the babies which started to cry. Finally it was Gargamelle who hurried down the slope and ran to Drummer and took him by the hand and led him.

Drummer approached slowly. 'Hey. Big trouble, eh An-goos?' He shook his head as though trying to clear it of the sound. 'Drummer can't think any more.' Then without more words he picked up two of the smallest children and hoisted them on to his shoulders. 'This place not safe now. We gotta move.'

Angus picked up one of the bundles. 'Everyone ready?' he called.

Wallace Duff had been standing to one side with Deric the Lame. He now raised his hand. 'Angus. We've been talking, Deric and me. We've decided not to come. We've had enough of running and we'll only hold you up. We're grateful for all you've done, aren't we, Deric?' Deric nodded. 'So you go on, and good luck to all of you.'

'I've no time to argue with you,' said Angus.

'And no need for arguments either. We've made our decision. You get going, now. We'll just sit here.' So saying old Wallace Duff sat down in front of the upended round of a log and Deric joined him on the other side. The top of the log was carved with lines to resemble a draughts board. Deric produced some draughts he had carved. 'Right,' he said. 'Whose start?'

Angus might have had more to say, but suddenly one of the children cried out in fear and pointed up at the distant hill. Rising slowly behind it was a huge black dome. Even as they watched, its front lip advanced over the hill and gradually moved down towards them.

Angus led the small group out of the valley.

Behind them the screaming grew louder.

The Emperor heard the death of the Dragon. He was lying behind a tree no more than two hundred yards from where Angus sat. The Emperor could not have moved even if prodded with a spear. His exhaustion was complete. His mind seemed to have moved outside his body and he contemplated his aches and the cut on his arm, which had pulled open again and was bleeding, with a curious detachment. Such detachment was not new to him, it was the way he had lived his life, always one step ahead of his feelings, always ready to change tack, always the one at the front leaving others bobbing in his wake.

Despite the screaming and the pain, he fell asleep.

When he awoke some hours later, the sky was dark with evening and he was hungry. He could smell smoke and hear a screaming as though people were being boiled alive. He tried to stand, but his body had stiffened up. Eventually he managed to roll over and then crawl to his feet by holding on to the tree-trunk. Once up, the moving was easier. He could no longer run, but he managed to wander away from the screaming. He had no idea where he was or where he was going. But to be moving seemed better than sitting. At least it gave an illusion of progress.

Eventually, he came upon a path which wandered through the forest and seemed to be leading somewhere. As night fell he could no longer see his way but by looking up he could just make out a path of starlight between the trees. The smoke seemed to have cleared and the air was fresher – if it weren't for the damned noise . . .

He did not know how long he blundered along, bumping into bushes and catching the rags of his purple toga on brambles, but eventually, to his astonishment, he saw a light in front of him. The path widened and there was a lighted window. He smelled food and he heard voices. A woman was speaking.

'And I still say it is an act of rebellion,' said Hetty, 'and it is unconscious. Trees don't think. Berries don't ponder. But they can still rebel.'

'And I still say that rebellion is a conscious act that requires mind and purpose and an appreciation of circumstance,' said Marcus heatedly. 'Anything else is merely an avalanche or worse . . . a miracle.'

'Mythologically speaking . . .' began Hetty.

They were arguing about the screaming which had grown gradually louder during the day and which they could not explain.

'You two,' said Danea and she banged her spoon down on the table. 'Stop bickering about the causes of things and be practical. What are we going to do? Are we going to leave here? Are we going to try to weather it out? Shall I start knitting us some earmuffs? What?'

At that moment the Emperor stumbled against the door and they all jumped to their feet. 'It'll be the horse again,' said Danea. 'It's getting frantic with fear. Either we turn it loose or we leave.'

She crossed to the door and opened it firmly and the Emperor fell in.

'Save me,' he said. 'For pity's sake.'

Half an hour later he sat at the table having consumed half a smoked trout, some potatoes cooked in their jackets, a raw carrot, an onion and several spoonsful of crab-apple jelly. Now he sat back and held a glass full of berry juice which Marcus had been trying to ferment.

Hetty, Marcus and Danea looked at him.

'Don't I know you?' said Hetty finally, peering over her glasses. 'Haven't we met somewhere before? Your face is familiar.'

'First time in Britannia, ma'am,' replied the Emperor, guardedly, trying to affect a voice like a common soldier. 'Just arrived from Roma. Got lost on duty. In the woods. The centurion will be wild.'

Danea nodded, digesting this piece of information. 'Yes. He will,' she said. 'Especially when he sees how badly you've messed up your nice purple toga. Isn't that the Imperial crest—'

'I can explain that,' said the Emperor hurriedly.

They looked at him and waited.

'Er ... You see ... Well er ...' For almost the first time in his life the Emperor's mind was bereft of any ideas.

'I know where I've seen you before,' said Hetty suddenly. She produced a coin from her pocket and flipped it on to the table. It was recently minted. It span and settled, face-up. All four of them stared at the coin.

'I'm an Emperor look-alike,' said the Emperor lamely. 'On special duty.'

The three nodded slowly.

'Well, well,' said Hetty, peering at him as though at an interesting specimen. 'I said there were strange things happening in the forest. But I didn't expect them to be this strange. An Imperial look-alike at loose in the wild wood. Well, well.'

'And whom do I have the pleasure of ... ?' asked Lucius, trying to sound urbane.

Marcus cleared his throat. He indicated Hetty. 'Well this here is the Gorgon,' he said. 'But don't worry, she's having a few days off at present so you're perfectly safe.' He gestured to Danea. 'And this splendid specimen of womanhood is Aphrodite – she just popped over from Greece for a bit of naughty on the side. And me? I'm Dionysus. I made the wine you are drinking. Cheers.'

'Pleased to meet you,' said Lucius, and he drank.

'So, Mr Imperial Look-alike,' said Hetty. 'If you've just arrived from Roma you can give us some news, you can tell us what's happening in the big wide world. We heard the Emperor was coming to Britannia. And please, feel free to talk in the first person singular. It will be much easier on all of us.'

And talk the Emperor did. He had no option. They grilled him. If he tried to lie they tripped him up. He told of the fate of Roscius with hemlock, and they seemed to approve. He talked about his plans for Aegyptus and for burning Britannia and how it had all got out of hand. He digressed on how much he liked sheep-meat and how afraid he was of reptiles and that he'd been chased through the wood by a dragon which finally blew up.

'And do you expect us to believe all that?' said Danea. 'I'd sooner believe that the Emperor of Roma is a complete lunatic than all that rubbish.'

'But it's the truth,' wailed Lucius.

'Ah yes. The Truth,' said Marcus heavily. 'Listen to that.' He pointed to the wall. They heard the screaming coming from outside. It was closer now and suddenly much louder. 'Now that is the truth. Unmistakable.'

They had talked the night away.

Outside the sky was pale with dawn.

The screaming was louder, much closer.

'I'm going to see what's happening,' announced Hetty. 'I may be gone some time. You two make up your own minds what you want to do. I'll stay in the woods whatever happens. You know me, I always wished I could have been there when Troy fell. Well this is the next best thing. They'll be writing stories about this, you mark my words. In any case, after what I've heard tonight—' she glanced at the Imperial Look-alike, 'I've no desire to rejoin the world of men.'

Then she was gone.

'So what do you think?' asked Danea addressing Marcus. 'What are your plans?'

'Well, I still rather like this world, even though it does stink occasionally.' He glanced at the Emperor. 'I'll take my chance out there. And I'd take it kindly if . . . that is, I'd be honoured if . . . what I'm trying to say is . . .' he took a deep breath, 'that I like the cigars you make and wonder if you would come with me.'

'Well that's all right then,' said Danea. 'I packed the cart yesterday. If you give me a kiss, it's a bargain.'

For the first time, they kissed. Both were amateurs with a lot to learn and catch up on.

'Er, excuse me,' said the Imperial Look-alike. 'Er, me? What about me?'

'What about you?'

'Can I come with you?'

'Oh no,' said Danea. 'Two is company enough. Here's a cold potato, a piece of fish wrapped up in paper and a dried-up old apple. It's all we have. It's more than you came into the world with, and it's more than you can take with you when you go. Now make your own way. Out there. Like the rest of us.' She pointed to the door. Marcus held it open. The Emperor took the food that was offered and walked through the doorway, and as he did so Marcus gave him a mighty kick up the backside which sent him sprawling.

'And that's for the Emperor of Roma. Give him our regards the next time you see him.'

Minutes later Danea and Marcus were up on the cart and heading down the lane away from the screaming as fast as the horse could canter.

Lucius Prometheus wandered under the trees. The screaming seemed to be all about him and it destroyed his sense of direction. Once he tried to run away from the noise but instead it got louder until it was like bells ringing and he was the clapper being biffed about.

He tripped and fell and found himself staring at Hetty who was sitting with her back to a tree writing in a small notebook. She glanced at him and then continued writing.

'Don't disturb me, I'm busy,' she called. 'I find I can't think unless I write things down. Must be getting old.' She continued writing frantically, added a small drawing and then closed her notebook and poked her pencil into her hair. 'Now, Mr Imperial Look-alike, what can I do for you? I'm surprised to see you here. I'd have thought you'd have run away long ago. That would be the sensible thing to do. I wouldn't mind betting that you and I are the only two animals near here. The rest have all run off. The trees would run too if they could. So what can I do for you?'

'What is it? This noise. This screaming.'

Hetty heard him. And then she laughed. 'Typical. Bloody typical. You pee in the wine bucket and then you wonder why the wine tastes sour. Well to answer your question, you'll have to come with me.' So saying she scrambled to her feet and began to walk in the direction of the screaming. Lucius put his hands up over his ears and followed. Ahead there was something moving. He wasn't sure what. A tree toppled and fell away from them. There was darkness ahead. It was like walking into the night.

Lucius stopped but Hetty walked on.

The Emperor could see clearly. It was in front of him, a wall of blackness which seemed to boil as the leaves and branches touched it and vanished. It was moving towards them.

And what was the damned fool woman doing now? She was taking all her clothes off. Now she was sitting down on the forest floor. She had her notebook out again and was scribbling.

The Emperor watched in horror as the blackness consumed her feet and still she wrote. It consumed her thighs, her hips, her waist and only then did she drop the pencil and book and lie back. She stretched her arms as the blackness rolled over her head and the last that the Emperor saw was her hand twist and a thumb lift. It could have been a signal.

He jumped back. The black wall had almost caught him that time.

He scampered away and still the darkness advanced. He began to run, but found he had run in a circle. Again the black wall reared. The screaming battered and slapped him.

He ran again. In front of him was the small house in the wood where he had spent the night with Dionysus and Aphrodite and Medusa. What a joke!

He ran inside and shut the door.

He sat at the table.

He drew his knees up to his chest.

He covered his ears.

He closed his eyes.

He heard the screaming come close.

He waited....

Nothing happened. A moment of hope. He opened his eyes ...

... and the darkness closed.

Panic in the cobbled streets of old Eburacum.

At first Citizens gathered on the walls to look out at the strange black dome that was growing in the forest. No one knew what it was and so speculation replaced hard news. Some reckoned it was a new kind of Battle Dome being erected by the Horribles for their own kind of sports. Others that it was only a black rainbow – a mixture of smoke and rain on a sunny day. And there were jokes too, about the Trismagister Neptuna washing his underwear and the water taking fright. But then they heard the screaming, and that stopped the smiles.

It was noticed that the dome was growing steadily, creeping down from the north. The fire had been bad enough with the flames visible and the wood-smoke drifting through the streets. But the fire had stopped at the outlying state farms, well short of the city. The screaming black wall showed no sign of stopping. As night was falling in Eburacum, the wall of darkness was looming close.

Those who could escape, already had. The road to the north was gone. Stories leaked through to the city of a vehicle that had tried to escape but had driven into the darkness and vanished. Front-line troops from the Imperial Guard went out. But their bullets meant nothing. They withdrew into Eburacum in confusion, even as the great wall of darkness loomed over the city walls.

There was no one to give orders, and so order broke down. In some places there was looting, in others an habitual orderliness – a man washing out his work clothes, a woman cooking the evening meal, children playing in the garden.

Escape to the south was still possible and some Citizens packed a few belongings and set out, running down the road, or trundling wheelbarrows. No soldiers stopped them for by now the soldiers had already gone.

At six in the evening the darkness touched the city. It swept over the walls and on, consuming the Military Academy and a short time later the Imperial Palace. The river, the houses, the pleasure gardens, the neat parks, the polytech where Miranda had studied and the statue which old man Ulysses had erected in memory of his arch rival Julius Caesar XIX, all vanished. In their place was a dome of blackness. By dawn Eburacum was completely gone.

At about the same time the darkness reached what remained of Roscius' Camp VI and moved on. Later it climbed to the site of the Caligula Memorial Park and rolled on over.

'One last game,' said Deric the Lame.
'I don't think there's time,' said Wallace.

Several people, refugees mainly, gathered on the headland at Cliff Town. They had heard the screaming approach in the night and, following an ancient instinct, they climbed high to avoid danger.

At dawn they were horrified to see the great dome of blackness which towered over them like a wave about to break. Its crest was lost amid the clouds. It covered the land to the north and south and was moving. Only to the east was escape possible . . .

Soon small fishing-boats were putting out to sea. People rowed desperately as the sheer wall of darkness tore through the valley. It rolled on over the sea. It absorbed the cliffs and the headland and a lonely Roman freighter that had arrived in the night to unload its cargo of anchovies, olives, pomegranates and wine.

25 Fox

They had been running for an hour, heading east by south.

Drummer was in the lead, tapping out a steady rhythm, guiding them through a maze of paths under the trees. He did not enter the wild tangle of forest. Even so, the going was hard and they had to make frequent short stops. Angus' directions had been simple and to the point. Since he couldn't remember the name of the small community he simply said, 'Just get us to the Wolds safely. Somewhere on the way to Stand Alone Stan. I'll figure out the rest from there.'

The afternoon slipped past and evening came.

'We'll have to make a proper stop,' said Perol. 'The children are beside themselves. Gargamelle's got a blister as big as an egg. And I can't feed the babies on the run.'

'OK. OK,' said Angus. 'We camp here for a while.'

They were in a clearing by a tinkling stream. For a while the screaming seemed muted.

The bigger children threw themselves down on the grass by the stream and soon started to play. The little ones lolled heavy as logs in the women's arms or hung piggy-backed over the men's shoulders, asleep. Strangely, the people who coped best in the whole journey were Peter the Scribe, who was built as though he was made from wire, and two of the men who had lost their wits at the Caligula. They carried more bundles than anyone else and still seemed quite fresh.

Angus cast them an admiring glance. 'Never thought I'd see the day when I'd be glad of their company. But give them their due, eh?'

Drummer seemed tired. He sat apart from the rest, squatting on his haunches, staring at nothing, his chest heaving.

Garlyck, Perol and Angus conferred in whispers.

'We've got to keep moving,' said Angus.

'Everyone needs a rest, even you,' said Perol. 'Ten minutes. All right?'

'All right. But Drummer looks knackered out. I'm worried about him.'

'How much further?' asked Garlyck.

Angus shrugged. 'Can't be that far. We've got to be close to the Wolds by now. Then it'll be a bit of a climb. And then . . . And then we'll see. I'm going to have a word with the big fella.'

'You OK?' asked Angus, sitting down beside Drummer. The big creature looked at him sadly. 'You tell An-goos, eh?'

'Drummer dying,' he said simply. 'Drummer dies with the forest, eh An-goos?' He shook his head as though to clear it. A tear formed in the corner of Drummer's eye and he brushed it away. 'The great drumming is gone. Now all Drummer hears is . . .' His big ugly face creased with concentration. When he spoke again it was very slowly, and with an effort. 'Once Drummer knew every path and every tree. Drummer remembers in here.' He pointed to his head, and then uncertainly he struck his chest near his heart. 'And in here. Long ago, there was only the music, An-goos. Only the drumming . . . on every side, long ago. Before all . . . before all . . .'

'Before all what?' asked Angus.

Drummer shook his head. He could not find the words. Finally he threw back his head and howled, his lips drawn back.

'Time to go,' said Perol softly.

Angus put his arm round Drummer and tried to lift him. But he might as well have tried to lift an oak tree. 'Come on, Drummer,' he said. 'We're not finished yet. One last run through the forest. I need you to show me the way. We can't be far from the Wolds. Then we'll be safe. Bet that blackness can't run up hills like we can, eh? Then this screaming'll stop, you see. It's making all of us feel sick. Then you can drum in the woods like in the old days. You can teach me to drum. We'll go out in the woods together. We'll chase the wolves. Come on.'

Drummer nodded wearily. He climbed to his feet. He stretched, hoisted his wooden drum high and beat on it for a few seconds. It was a call. Everyone stood up. The little children rubbed the sleep from their eyes and climbed up on to shoulders.

'Now everyone keep close,' said Angus. 'It's getting dark.

Listen to the drumming. Don't lose contact. You, Garlyck . . .
At the back. OK? Let's go.'

Drummer led them up the path by the stream and on through
the darkening woods.

Behind them there was a crashing of falling trees. Some time
later the grove where they had sat was gone.

After an hour the path began to rise. It joined with a wide track
that was easy to follow and rutted with the wheel marks of a
cart. The trees thinned out. They made good progress. For a
while the sound of the screaming faded.

Then, suddenly, just as the light was failing, the forest ended.
They found themselves facing a hillside which rose steeply and
was covered with pale grass.

'The Wolds,' said Angus with excitement. 'Now we start to
climb.'

They were not at exactly the place where Angus and Miranda
and Coll had met the boy Lenod, but not too far from it, judging
by the slope and the style of the land.

Here the wheel marks ended and they found an abandoned
cart. The horse had been turned loose and was nowhere to be
seen. 'Looks like others had the same idea,' said Garlyck.

'Maybe,' said Angus.

It was now dark. Drummer suddenly sat down at the foot of
the slope with his head in his hands. 'I don't know where I am,
An-goos,' he said. 'Help me.'

Angus was at a loss. On an impulse, he placed the drum in
front of Drummer. 'Here, beat this. Get your bearings.'

Drummer struck the drum but its sound was muted. 'Harder
for fuck's sake,' said Angus. 'Give it a right bloody belt.' Drummer struck harder, then he paused and listened.

'No wolves now.' He beat the drum again, even harder. Still
there was no answering call. 'The wolves are all gone.'

'Come on,' said Angus. He was suddenly stern. 'Don't bloody
sit there feeling sorry for yourself. Come on.' So saying he picked
up Drummer's drum and began to climb up the hillside beating it.

Drummer stirred and followed.

*

The night was black and the moon, just a day old, would not rise for some hours. They could not see one another and the climbing was painfully slow and blind. Angus organized them into relays. He would lead, followed by Drummer who was now almost useless for any carrying and seemed to be getting weaker. After crawling twenty or thirty yards, Angus would leave Drummer sitting in the grass, tapping on his drum to guide the others. Then Angus would climb back down and lead them up one by one until everyone was at the new base camp. Then they would repeat the process.

Once they lost precious time when Gargamelle fell and rolled. The grass was slippery and she could not stop herself or find anything to hold on to. Angus left Garlyck in charge. 'And keep that bloody drum beating so I can find you again,' he said. He climbed back down and located Gargamelle by her wheezing. A small bush had stopped her fall and she clung on to it. 'Eee. I'm finished, Angus lad. I can't climb another step. You just go back and leave me here. I'll be all right.'

'Like hell. Perol'd never forgive me. She needs you. And so do the kids. Who's going to tell them dirty stories if you don't, eh? Come on. Give us your hand. Put your arm round my shoulders. Pretend you're back in your dancing days and give us a squeeze. There, that's it. Now up we go. Steady does it. One two, one two.'

And so they made it back to the others.

By the time a thin new moon appeared four hours later they had climbed little more than three hundred yards, but they had reached a small plateau with a few trees. It gave them some protection and a brief sense of security. No one could move any further. Angus' legs had turned to jelly. Garlyck lay flat on his back with a child asleep over one arm. Perol was already asleep, the two babies tucked close. Drummer lay curled round his drum. Everyone else lay still, keeping close for warmth, some higher, some lower. The curve of the hill protected them from the shrillness of the screaming. But at that moment, nothing could have kept them awake.

Angus looked down the hill. He could see nothing. The moonlight was too dim. Everything was black and he might just as well have had his head in a sack.

*

Perol was shaking him. 'Wake up, Angus. Wake up.'

Angus blinked in the grey light of dawn. His head seemed to be on fire from the noise. 'Look,' shouted Perol in his ear, and she dragged him into a sitting position.

At first he couldn't make out what he was looking at. In front of him and rising as high as he could see was what looked like a great bubble of black mud. Its edge was no more than ten yards below him. The black surface rose like a screen. There was movement within it. Small patterns, like bubbles rising in beer or the scampering of tiny mouse feet in a dark glass. If he reached out he could . . .

Perol slapped his hand down and he came fully awake. The edge of the blackness was creeping steadily upwards.

'It's got one of the children,' screamed Perol, 'and Betsy's gone too. She was below me.'

Angus was on his feet. He kicked Garlyck who was still unconscious and then Drummer. He dragged Perol up. Both babies were in their hammocks round her shoulders and she tried to protect their ears from the noise.

Hand in hand, helping one another, they started to climb and in a few moments they came to a path which cut across the side of the hill. Angus recognized it. The path led to the village called Fox. That was it. The name he'd forgotten. If only he'd known . . . it'd been there all the time.

Garlyck came puffing up. He set a child down on its feet and plunged back down the hill. Peter the Scribe came next dragging Ruth and Estelle, each of whom was dragging one of the others. Gargamelle arrived under her own steam. Ada dragging bundles. June with a child on her back. Below them the woman called Edna stood up and tried to climb but she slipped back and fell. She fell into the blackness and vanished without a trace.

Only Drummer was left.

Angus looked at Perol. 'I can't . . .' he began and then he climbed back down to where the giant figure lay still. Angus shook him, grabbing him by his coarse hair. But the eyes didn't open.

Suddenly Garlyck was by him. 'He's dead,' he shouted. '*Dead. Leave him.*'

Angus stepped back. 'Dead . . . ?' He took the cord which held the drum and pulled it free. That made the difference. The drum had been restraining the body like a wedge. Drummer now slumped and rolled and slowly sank into the black tide.

They hurried along the path. In his heart Angus felt it was all hopeless now. He'd done his best, but still something in him would not let him stop. He would not give way.

The path climbed and after a few minutes joined a lane which led downwards into a valley.

There, at the bottom where the lane flattened, was a stream and a ford where the water ran noisily over shingle. It was all as Angus remembered, even the gate which now stood open. A few people were standing there staring away, down the stream.

Angus led the way. He splashed through the stream and came inside the gate.

People moved aside to make room for the small party, but otherwise paid them no attention. They were staring at the great wall of blackness which was pushing up the valley towards them. It completely enclosed the narrow space and rose sheer to the sky. The stream tumbled into it merrily and vanished. The bushes twitched and were absorbed. The stones fell away and were gone.

Here was the end of running.

There was nothing now to do but stand and watch. If the blackness had reached this far then all the other valleys would be closed. Soon the screaming would end.

Angus turned to the darkness.

Perol stood beside him, wide-eyed, her arms crossed in front of her protecting the babies' ears. Garlyck was behind, white hair stiff, face expressionless. Then the others: Gargamelle, still panting; Eric the Scribe, squinting; Ada, June and Estelle down on the ground; the children and the injured. Further back stood a wild-eyed woman surrounded by her own brood of children. Near her a handsome woman stood relaxed, arm in arm with a big man puffing on a home-made cigar. Then people from the town of Fox; a few others. Not many.

No one spoke.

*

252

The blackness edged closer. It crept across the ford. It came to the gate. It was inches away from Angus' nose.

It . . .

It stopped.

Slowly the screaming died away to echoes. The silence was hollow.

Nothing moved as gradually the black surface hardened to a polished smoothness reflecting back their faces.

'Now that was close,' said Angus quietly. 'Too bloody close.'

Post scriptum

It was enough.

The power of Miranda's breath was exhausted and the black egg ceased to grow. Miranda the Destroyer changed aspects and became Miranda the Healer, Miranda the Preserver.

Immediately, clouds began to form round the hard black dome and soon rain was sluicing down its sides and forming puddles, which ran together to form ponds and occasionally lakes.

At the same time, the dome wrinkled as a slow contraction began. It might take many thousands of years before the dome was an egg again. And by the time it was gone, Britannia might no longer be an island. It might be a chain of islands in the mid-Atlantic. It might be under the sea. In the meantime, the black dome would stand as a reminder, for those who cared to remember, of a time when the earth brushed against disaster. And each time a contraction occurred, a shock-wave was sent bounding round the world and a brief screaming was heard.

Miranda neither knew nor cared how long the change in the dome might take. All her concerns were for the present, to nurture and guide. Miranda would stay until the land was healed. Only then would she return to her own resting place.

That is unless she was called on to breathe again. And the next time it would be harder.

A final vision persists.

Beside the shiny black wall two figures move. The woman carries a bundle and the man is pulling a cart. They find a place on a hill and there Bella builds her last inn. It offers wonderful views of the black dome, but it is a strange place. No birds sing and the air has a certain gravity. There is the stillness of a graveyard. And never the sound of drumming.

Nevertheless, the inn prospers as the tourist trade picks up.

Visitors from Germania and the far eastern provinces come to look and ponder. Some sensitives claim they can smell the black dome when the wind blows from the east and others that they can just hear the screaming if they press their ears to the liquor-ice-black, adamantine-hard surface.

Gwydion, now middle-aged with a bit of a paunch, but still golden, still torced and powerful with the sign of the snake between his eyes, Gwydion is in great demand for his stories.

After the meal and when the dishes are gone, he sits with his elbows on the table and a jug of beer to hand. Any who wish can listen. He usually begins all his stories the same way.

'Lest we forget,' he says, 'that this is a land fit for heroes . . .'

THE END